Radio Message from Attu:

THREE SHINZAN SQUADRONS STANDING BY HERE STOP IF WEATHER CONDITIONS FAVORABLE FIRST ATTACK POSSIBLE IN FORTY-EIGHT HOURS......

Captain Hidaka read it with relief and exultation. At last the war was being brought to the enemy's own country!

It was 1942. The Japanese had taken Attu, farthermost island in the Aleutians, and turned it into an airfield. Hidden deep inside Alaska, the Japanese captain and his men were transmitting weather bulletins to Attu—reports that were vital to the bombing mission.

If American scouts could not find Hidaka's transmitter and smash it, Japanese bombs would soon rain down on American cities.

And there were only forty-eight hours left!

DUEL IN THE SNOW

by
HANS MEISSNER

Translated from the German by
ERICA POMERANS

PYRAMID BOOKS • NEW YORK

DUEL IN THE SNOW
A PYRAMID BOOK
Published by arrangement with William Morrow and Co., Inc.

Published in the United States in 1972.
Translation copyright © 1970 by Peter Davies Ltd.
Published in Great Britain in 1970.
German-language edition copyright © 1964 by Sigbert Mohn
Verlag, Gütersloh.

Pyramid edition published April 1974

ISBN 0-515-03351-0

Library of Congress Catalog Card Number: 70-142392

Printed in the United States of America

1

There was no school on Attu Island on 18 June 1942, although it was a Thursday and the summer holidays had not yet begun. The island children, all native Aleutians, had stayed nervously at home. The others, who had set out for school, quickly turned back when they heard the strange noise. There was a general air of panic.

Hector McGilroy was the only white man on the island. He acted as teacher, weather-station officer and radio operator all in one. He and his wife lived in the schoolhouse on a hill overlooking the flat pebbly beach of the bay. Next to the schoolhouse stood a modest radio mast made of perforated steel and wire. The transmitter was in a little room next door.

Betty McGilroy was the first to hear the odd whirring in the air when she went out to feed the hens before breakfast. It sounded like the flapping of enormous birds' wings but she could not see anything because the sky, the land and the sea were shrouded in thick mist. When her husband came outside a little later, it sounded to him like an aircraft coasting over the island with its engine cut out.

"They're lost in this foul weather," he said to his wife. "There isn't anywhere for them to land. They'll crash any moment."

They both listened hard for sounds from the clouds but the expected disaster never happened. The whirring noise disappeared but the teacher's uneasiness remained. While his wife hurried inside to put the kettle on for coffee, he stayed behind in the drizzle. They were used to this kind of weather; it rained almost every day on Attu, and the wind never stopped. The thin, razor-sharp blades of eel-grass rose and fell in the wind like the swell of a green sea. Attu was the outermost of the Aleutian Islands and there was not a single tree or flower on it. As far back as the inhabitants could remember, nothing of note had ever happened there.

McGilroy went up to the flagpole at the end of the playground, took the flag out of its white box and attached it to the halyard. Each time he raised the "Stars and Stripes" he was doing so in the most remote possession the United States held: no other island was so far out in the Pacific. As the flag beat noisily against the pole in the wind and rain, he felt almost like a soldier on sentry-duty, for war had broken out once more, this time against the Japanese.

Then the strange roar began again. This time it came from the sea, and grew steadily louder. It seemed to McGilroy that he could hear the noise of a hundred horses stampeding, the clanking of heavy chains, the hollow thud of large objects falling, and waves pounding the sides of ships. Betty McGilroy threw a shawl over her shoulders and ran across the playground. Her husband was leaning intently over the balustrade and hardly noticed as she joined him and caught his arm. When she saw what he was looking at, she gasped. From behind the thick pall of mist, which had now receded to the water's edge, a vast fleet of monsters edged forward in close formation. They smashed their way through the breakers and onto the shingle, a flaming red sun against a white background emblazoned on every steely-grey side.

"The Japs," McGilroy cried out. "It's the Japs."

At that moment the hatches of the strange vehicles fell open and hordes of small figures in mud-coloured uniforms began pouring out.

McGilroy ran into the house to perform his last duty. He stumbled over a chair that lay in his way, picked himself up and went into the radio room through the door from the kitchen. To save time, his

6

transmitter was always tuned in on the wavelength of the meteorological office in Dutch Harbor. He forced himself to remain calm as he sat down at the controls. Though ice-cold shivers were running down his back, he managed to operate the set with his normal meticulous care.

"The Japs are landing on Attu," he shouted into the microphone. "There are hundreds of them ... hundreds!"

As he repeated the message, a violent explosion shook the hut and shattered all the windows. He was blown from his chair by the blast, while glass splinters cascaded down on him. He heard his wife scream and as he crawled out through the open doorway towards her he was just in time to see the radio mast totter and collapse. He could hear words of command yelled above the metallic rumble of the tanks. Then the Japs burst into the house. They kicked open all the doors, shouted at each other, overturned furniture and smashed the transmitter. Betty and Hector McGilroy found themselves looking down the muzzles of rifles, held in the hands of men whose slit-eyes stared searingly and with deadly hatred at them. The section commander pushed his way to the front of his men. His reddish-brown skin was drawn tightly across the sharp, high cheekbones. His English was clipped and abrupt.

"How many Americans on Attu now?"

McGilroy swallowed hard, then forced himself to reply.

"There are one hundred and sixty-five people on the island."

"I do not mean natives," the Japanese barked. "How many real Americans?"

"Just the two of us. I am the teacher ..."

The Japanese came up closer. His piercing eyes, almost devoid of lashes, were now only a hand's breadth away from McGilroy's face.

7

"Did you radio that we have landed?"

The teacher nodded and was immediately struck in the chest. He would have fallen over backwards if the soldiers behind had not held him up.

The two prisoners were led away down the school path to the shore. The mist had lifted, as it often does in the Aleutians after sunrise, to reveal a powerful Japanese battle fleet tossing in the swell in front of the island. It must have had a complement of at least a thousand guns, although McGilroy could not distinguish exactly how many troop-carriers, cruisers, destroyers and aircraft-carriers there were. It looked as if the landing on Attu was only the beginning of a huge onslaught aimed at America's back door.

McGilroy and his wife were put on board one of the ships and taken to Japan. They were never heard of again.

2

Nobody had expected the Japanese to invade the Aleutians. Even though the archipelago was three thousand miles from the nearest American city, the United States' sense of security had been badly shaken. Over a thousand miles of wasteland separated the United States from its Alaskan possession in the Far North and no strategist could suggest a way of countering the enemy's advance. Some men and freight could, of course, be transported by air, but moving an entire army with all its heavy equipment to Alaska presented an insuperable problem. The Far North lay defenceless before the surprise attack.

General Hamilton, Commander-in-Chief, Alaska, had scarcely three thousand men under his command. They had no modern equipment, no long-range aircraft and no naval units. The staff officers, who had long regarded their duties as consisting solely of training reservists for action elsewhere, had never expected the war to come so close. Now they were sitting around a conference table at Fort Richardson, near Anchorage, facing their commanding officer. A map of Alaska covered the wall to one side; opposite hung a map of the Aleutian Islands.

"I can't believe for a moment that they're making for the mainland," Colonel Henley, the Chief-of-Staff, said. "There's the whole breadth of Canada between Alaska and the United States. They've got mountains, swamps and forests barring their way to any inhabited territory, and it's all under several feet of snow anyway between October and May. It would be madness to try and carry out large troop movements under such conditions. And in the spring it'd be even worse. The rivers would be swollen and impassable, and the troops would get bogged down in the swamps. So what use is Alaska to the Japs? There's no industry here and the whole population is less than an average New York suburb. What point could there possibly be in their landing here? It's my view that they have no conceivable reason for coming, and that they won't."

General Hamilton turned to Lieutenant-Colonel Hagerty. "What does the Air Force think?"

"The Air Force can't do anything. First they took away our best planes, and then they took away our second best. We haven't a single effective unit left. All we can do is a bit of transport work, and try and teach the youngsters a little rudimentary flying in the few old crates we've got."

The general seemed weary. "That doesn't answer my question. What I want to know is what the Japanese Air Force could do from here, supposing they got a foothold on the Alaskan coast."

Hagerty leaned back and folded his arms across his chest.

"I've been thinking about that, too. And the answer is negative, negative from the Japs' point of view, I mean. Given good weather, their new four-engined Shinzans might get through to some worthwhile targets in the States and back again. Seattle and Portland are a little under fifteen hundred miles away as the crow flies, making a total flying distance of just under three thousand. To do it, however, the Shinzans would have to be loaded right up with fuel, with extra tanks all over the place, in the fuselage, in the tail and the wings. And in that case, gentlemen, they wouldn't have room to carry a single solitary bomb."

"So whatever happened, you think it wouldn't be worth their while?"

"Look, to begin with, they'd have to transport their bomb loads to Alaska. The Shinzans need a long runway. The nearest suitable one is four thousand miles away, in Japan, at Haneda airfield near Tokyo."

"What about Attu?" added Captain William, a guerilla veteran and one of the general's trusted advisers.

"You couldn't even play football there," Hagerty answered. "It's all mountain peaks and deep gorges and the weather is the worst in the world."

The captain nodded. "But they must have had some reason for landing there."

Hamilton now turned politely towards an elderly officer, who in civilian life had been a distinguished historian at the University of Oregon, and had spent several years at the Universities of Kyoto and Sapporo.

"You know the kind of people they are," the general said to him. "What would you say was their reason for invading Attu?"

Webster did not need long to consider. "In my opinion, military considerations were secondary. What the Japanese value above all is honour. They took Attu merely for the glory of occupying a piece of American soil: a marvellous boost to Japanese prestige. That, in my opinion, was their only purpose, sir."

3

During the summer the Japanese landed on Attu, the island became the springboard for one of the most audacious exploits behind the enemy lines ever planned by the Japanese. Colonel Hanto Nagai, the Chief Personnel Officer, had the job of selecting a leader for this operation. He did not find it an easy task. The officer had to be the right age, neither too young nor too old. The most suitable age range was thought to be between twenty-six and thirty-three. He needed guerilla experience and though he had to possess considerable courage, it would have to be tempered with caution. They wanted an officer for whom men would go gladly through hell and high water, and he himself would have to be a latter-day Samurai, prepared to make, if necessary, the supreme sacrifice in order to accomplish his mission.

Had these been the only qualifications required, Colonel Nagai would have been able to come up with any number of names. But the man selected would also have to speak perfect English, be trained as a parachutist, and be able to live off the land in a northern wilderness, behind enemy lines and without expectation of any supply drops. He would have to have some knowledge of meteorology, signals and elementary medicine; be a first-class skier and mountaineer, and have a high degree of resistance to extreme cold. As if all this was not enough, a whole series of personal qualities, all enumerated in the paper on the colonel's desk, were asked for. In the end, only three names appeared on the short-list, although the candidates' personal files showed that none of them completely fitted the bill. Lieutenant Ikeda had not been trained as a radio operator, Captain Hidaka had no parachute drops to his credit, and Captain Nogi had not been through a medical course. If one of these three men were selected, however, a crash course could be arranged to fill the gaps in his training.

All three came from families of proved loyalty to the Emperor. Ikeda and Hidaka were descended from Samurai and Captain Nogi was the great-nephew of a national hero of the Russo-Japanese War.

Captain Hidaka had not originally wanted a military career. As a small child, he had loved roaming in the bush, and after his two-year stint of military service he had gone to university to read geography and geodesy, and had stated his preference for a career with the National Land Survey in Korea or Manchuria. He was a fine athlete and had won a great many sports events, even gaining a place in the Japanese athletics team. He had won a silver medal for Japan in the decathlon at the last Olympic Games, and what had particularly impressed the colonel was that Hidaka had applied for a place in the officer cadet college instead of training for the next Games, at which he was confidently tipped for a gold. He had passed out of the cadet college with the highest honours and been posted to the staff of the Kwantung Army in Manchuria for special duties.

It was this that decided the colonel. Here was a man who was prepared to turn his back on a world so enthusiastic about sport that it worshipped its Olympic stars as demigods, and take up the life of a soldier. Such a man, he argued, would surely have the qualities of self-denial and singleness of purpose which the job demanded.

The colonel put Captain Hidaka's personal file under his arm and went off to see the Chief of the General Staff.

4

A man stood in front of his cabin by the shore of Lake Nunalto, completely oblivious of the Armageddon unleashed by the great powers. His name was Allan McCluire; he was tall, rangy, and about thirty years old. He appeared a little shorter than he really was, because like most woodsmen he kept his eyes on the ground.

He worked for the Wild Life Preservation Department and his present job was to capture alive a number of beavers, which were to be used to start a beaver colony on Afognak Island. The forests there consisted mainly of ash trees mixed with alders, an ideal habitat for beavers. The rainfall was high on the island, and a multitude of small streams emptied into the ocean. When the spring thaws came, the streams washed away the soil supporting the roots of the trees and it was for this reason that his chief had suggested that beavers be mobilized to dam the streams and turn them into a harmless chain of small lakes. What the beaver colonists needed now was a master-builder who knew his job.

McCluire sat down on a bench by the log cabin and set to work again. The cord attached to the trap had been wedged tight, and the gate would not drop properly. The large, very dark beaver, whom Allan believed to be the best builder along the whole of the river, had escaped again. The animal seemed to be able to make complex statistical calculations when building, and sense, even before the water level began to rise, what the eventual water pressure would be. As soon as he set to work, the other beavers followed his example. And when they had finished, they followed him to the next building-site. So this beaver foreman had to go to

14

Afognak as well; the new colony would be incomplete without the benefit of his experience.

Allan greased the hemp cord and to reduce the friction still further nailed tinplate over the two corners round which it had to run. The trap had also to be camouflaged more thoroughly than before. The beaver, once bitten, would be twice shy now.

He carried the trap into the shed where the beavers he had caught already were caged. When they heard him coming, they cowered as far back in their cages as they could, but he spoke to them softly and calmly. It was the tone of voice that mattered. They understood and realized that there was no threat of danger from him. He took an armful of fresh alder twigs and pushed them between the bars of the cages. The beavers pulled the twigs in at once and began to gnaw at them. Their big yellow incisors went at an incredible pace and the twigs rotated in their paws as if turning on a lathe.

The days were long at this time of year, the air heavy with summer heat. The lake shimmered like a velvety cloth stretched taut for miles. Black forest framed it on all sides, climbing up the slopes and, in places, reaching as far as the foot of the sheer cliffs, their crevices still white with last year's snow. Five peaks, clad in eternal snow, pointed towards the sky like the fingers of some giant's frozen hand. Nobody had ever climbed them.

This was uninhabited country, a wilderness as far as the eye could see, acknowledging no master. Only two men lived by the lake, Allan McCluire and his Indian assistant Harry Chiefson. The nearest settlement—in fact nothing but a small landing-stage on the mighty Yukon—was called Raffles and consisted of six or seven log cabins and huts. The few trappers who lived in the remote surrounding area brought their skins in to

15

Raffles and at Peter O'Hara's store bought everything they needed back in the wilds.

Allan felt no need to visit Raffles; he regarded the place as an outpost of the outside world he mistrusted. When there was bad news, the only way it could reach Lake Nunalto was by way of Raffles, and there was nothing Allan feared more than finding a message recalling him to Anchorage or Fairbanks, where he would have to live among crowds of people again.

Wilfrid Frazer, the head of the Alaskan Wild Life Service, had hinted a number of times that all Allan McCluire needed in order to be in line for promotion to Chief Wildlife Officer was to put in a stint at head office. But Allan was not ambitious. His unfettered life in the great forests had made him so independent that he wanted neither to obey orders nor to give them. City life would have restricted him like a straitjacket. He would sooner have left the Service and made his living as a freelance trapper.

Each time Harry came back from Raffles, Allan feared for his freedom. And as the boat drew closer this time, he had to pull himself together sharply so as not to show how heavily his forebodings weighed on him.

"We've got to hurry up with the beavers," Harry called before he had beached the canoe. "Frazer is asking when he can send the flying-boat to pick them up."

Allan was relieved. "Nothing else from him? No letters or anything?"

"No, but we're to get a move on and let him know."

Harry Chiefson was small and stocky; his round skull seemed to be joined straight on to his shoulders, and his squat body was enormously and deceptively strong. His coarse, matted hair, trimmed by himself some months ago, now hung over his forehead and neck in a great black fringe.

Allan helped him to carry the supplies into the house

16

and told him about his piece of bad luck with the trap. "I've fixed the damn thing now and it works like a charm. Let's hope the big fellow hasn't moved out of the area."

"We've got to get him this week, boss."

"I know, but if the weather changes I can't help it, whatever Frazer says, can I?"

They brewed coffee and sat down at the table. The Indian seemed unhappy about something, but words were not needed between them all the time; they got on well in silence, too. It was not until they had finished their third cup that Harry suddenly raised his head. "It wasn't because of Frazer that I said we had to catch him this week. It was because of me."

Suddenly Allan saw the look of despair in his friend's eyes. "Come on now, Harry, tell me, what's the matter?"

The Indian swallowed once or twice before answering.

"In Raffles, when I got to Peter's store, there was a funny sort of atmosphere. There were four or five people standing around, swearing and cursing. O'Hara said they were afraid the Japs might come. And he had a letter for me too. I've got to go and be a soldier."

He looked in the pockets of his anorak which was on the bench beside him and handed Allan his call-up papers.

"I've got to go on the 'plane they're sending to Raffles on Monday."

5

There had been many changes on Attu. The native Aleuts had long since been deported to Japan and the island was now swarming with little Japanese soldiers, who were digging themselves in everywhere. Like mice, they penetrated every cranny whether in the soil or the rocks and, like moles, they had created a system of trenches and tunnels covering the entire island, into which they could vanish in a matter of seconds. Attu had been turned into a fortress.

Marquis Saito, a colonel on the Imperial General Staff, was still expecting an enemy counter-attack. But it never came. The United States was doing nothing to prevent the Rising Sun shining over this part of its territory and the Japanese were baffled.

"We have humbled them and now they have left the way open to the mainland," the colonel said exultantly to his officers. "Our advance will be resumed shortly."

A radio signal announcing the arrival of another convoy seemd to confirm Saito's forecast, although at first all they could see was a naval launch emerging from the mist. To everyone's astonishment it brought Admiral Takado Yamada, the conqueror of Burma, whose name was a byword for glory to every Japanese. Takado Yamada was tiny and plump, somewhat stooped, and the gold fringes on his admiral's epaulettes were tarnished. But he radiated a steely strength which became apparent as soon as one came into contact with him.

The admiral waded ashore without ceremony and gave a perfunctory salute. The sensational news of the arrival of the conqueror of Burma had spread like wildfire through the island, although the reasons for his coming were still unclear. Now the admiral sat down at

18

the teacher's desk in McGilroy's school and his expression conveyed the importance and secrecy of the orders he had brought. Only staff officers had been admitted.

"Shokun, you are mistaken, the convoy is not bringing you reinforcements. In any case, you do not need them: the enemy is occupied elsewhere. I am bringing in a large amount of building equipment, bulldozers and railway tracks, as well as two shiploads of cement and three thousand tons of TNT. I also have some engineers on board but most of the work will be done by the men already here."

He paused briefly to allow his audience to take in the news.

"We are going to build an airfield on this island big enough for squadrons of long-range aircraft. The hangars will be hollowed out of the mountains. The plan is of vital importance to our strategy and must be completed before the enemy is in a position to disturb us. Everybody concerned will have to make exceptional efforts to get the job done."

After a moment's stunned silence, the colonel said, "It means levelling quartz and granite mountains—and every time it rains here the streams turn into raging torrents."

Yamada shrugged impatiently. "I am quite familiar with the topographical conditions on the island. I think I may say I know Attu like the back of my hand. Our plans have been worked out to the last detail."

In spite of his personal disappointment, Colonel Saito felt proud of the vision of the Japanese High Command. "We shall accomplish the task, sir; I shall use every available man to make sure of that."

The admiral stood up. "That will be my responsibility, Shokun; I shall be in command of the operation myself."

6

It was the height of summer in Alaska; there was no wind and the heat was oppressive. The trees were so dry they crackled and everywhere the grass was like tinder. It was a dangerous time of year. The tiniest spark could set off a devastating forest fire and destroy all wildlife except the birds.

General Hamilton knew how ignorant most of his young recruits in Fort Richardson were of the dangers that threatened in the forest. He was particularly concerned about broken glass because hardly any of the recruits knew how hazardous it was. If, by mischance, a piece of broken bottle were caught by the sun at the right angle, it would act as a magnifying glass and disaster would ensue. He was determined that not one piece of broken glass should remain on the ground, and he therefore supervised the glass hunt himself. Standing in his jeep, he was driven up and down the column of his men, and watched closely over their efforts.

He had himself driven back again to the left flank, where a few men were dragging their almost empty sacks along the ground. He ordered them back to comb through their sector again.

"I know it's a hot day," Hamilton said, "but it'll be a damn sight hotter if the whole camp goes up in flames."

At the end of the line the general saw a small, stocky man who was really putting his back into the search and whose sack was almost full.

"You don't think this is all a lot of nonsense, do you?"

Harry Chiefson looked up and clumsily came to attention.

" 'Course not. Ought to have been done a long time ago."

"Sir," Hamilton prompted.

"What?"

"A soldier says 'sir' when he addresses his superior officer," Hamilton explained gently.

"Oh, yes. I'm sorry."

"I take it you're from Alaska. Where exactly?"

"I was on Nunalto last . . . That's three days by boat from Raffles, sir."

"Are you a trapper by trade, or what?"

"I work with Allan McCluire." Harry could not conceive of anyone in Alaska not knowing his boss.

"And who might he be?"

"He is a gamewarden, but he could go much further if he wanted to. Only he doesn't."

"Tell me about him."

Harry Chiefson told the general about Allan. He expressed all the admiration he felt for his boss and showed no awe at all of the silver stars on Hamilton's shoulders. The general listened with growing astonishment. He himself was an enthusiastic hunter and had often dreamt of just such a life in his youth.

He interrupted Harry. "Just a minute, they seem to be looking for me."

Followed by a cloud of dust, a jeep raced across the field and pulled up to a screeching stop just beside Hamilton. Colonel Henley leapt out. "At last, sir. I've been looking for you for half an hour."

"Why, what's all the excitement?"

"Yesterday our boys brought back a whole lot of aerial photographs from Attu. Sedgewick has just finished analysing them. It appears the Japs are building a full-scale airfield there. They're working day and night, they've blown huge chunks out of the rocks, and the place is crawling with bulldozers and trucks. They've put in ack-ack batteries all over the place and they

21

gave our boys quite a pasting. One of our 'planes is missing."

"That's bad, Henley. But the other bit of news is even worse. I'll have to fly to Washington at once. Will you see to it that I can get away as soon as possible and prepare all the reports for me? I'll read them on the 'plane."

Before his jeep roared off, the general turned to Harry Chiefson again. "Thanks for the talk."

"You're welcome," Harry replied and called a belated "sir" to the general's retreating figure.

7

Captain Enzo Hidaka was with the Kwantung Army in Manchuria. He had been ordered by his divisional commander to make contact with the Oshones, a tribe of nomad huntsmen who roamed the *taiga* and it had been Hidaka's job to discover whether they were in touch with Chiang Kai-Shek.

On his return to base, he was summoned to General Matsunami. "Hidaka-san, you have made us anxious. We have been waiting for you for weeks."

The general led Hidaka to a bare room at the back of the base's Confucian temple, offered him the only chair, and sat down himself on a camp bed.

"May I report on the result of my mission, Taisho-dono?"

"There will be time enough for that later. You are being posted elsewhere and must leave for Tokyo at once. First of all, you will be trained as a parachutist. As soon as possible after that, you'll be parachuted into enemy territory with ten or twelve men of your own choice. Once you have been dropped, it will be difficult to give you any further support. The purpose of your mission will be to send reliable weather reports ... to Attu."

"To Attu?" Hidaka asked, more astonished than ever.

Matsunami stubbed out his cigarette. "Yes. Hidaka-san, you and your men will be setting off from there. It seems very doubtful whether you'll ever get back. I was to tell you that expressly. You will be given a few days' leave to put your personal affairs in order."

"I do not need any leave, Taisho-dono. I am not married and my father will understand."

"Of course, Hidaka-san, I have heard of your illus-

23

trious father. He will be proud of you. But let us return to the subject of your mission. Your transmissions will betray you; the enemy will be able to pinpoint your position by taking radio bearings on you. He will do everything to track down your patrol and to destroy it. It will be your task to prevent this for as long as possible, mainly by changing your position rapidly and frequently. Cunning will be your most effective weapon."

Hidaka nodded. "Taisho-dono, you said that I could pick my own men."

"Yes, but two radio operators and two meteorologists will have to be among them. And, of course, you will have to have a second-in-command, who would be able to take your place in case of need. Apart from that, I would not advise you to pick anyone too intelligent. But it is your responsibility to select each man wisely, Hidaka-san."

"I shall choose with great care, Taisho-dono."

Matsunami looked up at him. "You will be given every opportunity to do so. Colonel Nagai will let you look at any personal files you require."

Hidaka asked if he could take Noboru, an Oshone he had brought with him from the *taiga*. He would be invaluable for tracking and other duties in the forest.

"Why not, if he passes the medical and can manage a parachute reasonably well? The main thing is that the man should be absolutely loyal to you."

"He belongs to a primitive people, Taisho-dono, who regard us Japanese almost as celestial beings. But it is on earth that he will be most useful to me."

"It is a good idea to take him. Now you must look for the others. Men proved in single combat would be best, I think."

"I will find them, Taisho-dono."

Matsunami nodded. He was satisfied with Captain Hidaka. The Chief of Army Personnel had done well to select him. Enzo Hidaka was not tall, but he was tough and powerful. His strong muscles bulged beneath his uniform, yet his movements were light and almost elegant. His face was not as flat and round as that of most Japanese. He was a natural officer; his lively intelligence was not apparent at first sight, but when he spoke, there was a gleam in his eye which could not fail to impress. However, when he himself was listening, or in repose, his eyes would be half-closed, and he would seem abstracted.

The general instructed the captain to give him a written report by next morning, though he knew very well that Hidaka had earned his rest.

"I am afraid I cannot let you sleep, Hidaka-san. You must fly to Harbin by the courier 'plane at 0800 hours tomorrow and straight on from there to Tokyo."

Then, quite out of character, he added, "I wish you luck."

Hidaka bowed and saluted.

8

Allan's face was glistening with sweat. The box-trap was heavy and its sharp corners cut into his shoulders painfully. The beaver was restive, throwing himself against the sides of the box and trying to gnaw through the tin lining of his prison. Allan felt sorry for him, if only because the animal had given him so much trouble. It had taken him weeks to catch him in spite of all his efforts. The beaver had finally taken refuge in a deserted burrow, overgrown with reeds, which Allan had carefully dug up. He had placed the trap in the driest part of the run, and then buried it again so skilfully that sharper eyes than the beaver's would not have noticed his intrusion. His patience and perseverance were at last rewarded, and he caught the master-builder.

Now he was talking to his prisoner, hoping to soothe him with his tone of voice. He explained to him that he and his companions would soon be given their freedom on an island called Afognak, and, undisturbed by trappers, would be able to live out their lives in peace.

Perhaps the beaver had come to realize that he could not gnaw through the box's tinplate lining, or Allan's voice really did have a calming effect; in any case he stopped thrashing about, and Allan was able to quicken his pace. He soon reached the lake, placed the box carefully in the bottom of the boat, sat down in the stern and picked up his paddle. The lake was as smooth as glass, and he could see far into its depths. Down in the submarine twilight lay sunken tree-trunks, the remains of rafts used many years ago on the lake, their branches now festooned with weed, through which fish glided silently back and forth.

Allan was in no hurry. There was no one waiting for

him in his cabin now: Harry Chiefson had left over a week ago. It was impossible to imagine Harry being forced to march in step. To be a small cog in a large machine, to move in time with others at a word of command, would be difficult enough for any woodsman, but especially for an Indian. Allan missed his companion more than he cared to admit, although he was well used to living in solitude for months on end.

The canoe rounded a point. Allan stopped paddling and allowed the boat to drift on without a sound. A moose-cow, with her calf beside her, was standing in the shallows. Her forelegs spread wide apart, she lowered her heavy head to the water. When she raised it again, dripping, there was a bunch of reeds in her mouth. The calf stumbled awkwardly up to her and took some of them. Allan waited patiently until the two animals had splashed their way towards the bank and disappeared into a clump of alders.

He had nearly made his way across the bay when the reason for Harry's call-up papers suddenly struck him. It was the fault of the Alaskan Scouts. Harry had been eager to help them in their search for the missing climbers on Mount McKinley, and again when they were rescuing a bush-pilot who had had to make a forced landing up on the Barren Grounds. The Scouts were volunteers who made up rescue parties, and Harry's Indian tracking skill was a great asset to them. Harry had been made an honorary member, and Allan supposed that when the Scouts had been taken over by the Army, Harry had been called up as well. Evidently Allan had been overlooked when his age-group was due to be called up because he had been without a fixed address for so long. You just had to make sure you kept your name off any of their damned lists, Allan concluded.

He lifted his paddle into the boat and let the canoe glide to the bank. The noise of the metal bottom scrap-

27

ing the shingle made the beaver nervous, and he threw himself about so violently in his prison that the box fell onto its side with a crash. Allan picked it up again, jumped ashore, and carried his prize to the shed where the other beavers were caged. Suddenly, he froze in his tracks.

The wire netting in the shed had been forcibly ripped away and the beavers had gone. Everything, the wood of the cages as well as the tin linings, was smeared with blood. Only a carcajou* could have gnawed through the metal, only a carcajou could have been responsible for such slaughter. No other animal inspires such fear and hatred in the forests of the north.

Allan McCluire stood stock still in front of the pillaged boxes and stared at them. It was his fault for not remembering this ruthless predator, which rarely ventured anywhere near human habitations. As he stood there helpless, he burned with increasing shame and guilt.

The beaver in the box-trap awakened him from his trance. The animal had smelled his fellows' blood and picked up the scent of their killer. He was struggling in terror to free himself with all the strength of an animal fighting for its life.

Allan seized the box with its terrified occupant and carried it quickly back to the boat.

Although the journey to the beaver-lake took nearly four hours, it took him half that time now. When he arrived, panting with the exertion, he opened the trap. The animal shot out, plunged into the lake, and dived out of sight.

When Allan turned back for a last glance, the beaver had surfaced again and was swimming around in a circle. Watching him, Allan had the feeling for a moment that he was saluting his liberator.

Back at his cabin, he threw himself on his bed and began to plan his revenge.

* A wolverine.

9

For the first time in many weeks work had come to a standstill on Attu. The pneumatic drills were silent, the excavators stood idle, and there were no explosions to rend the unwonted silence. Four thousand Japanese soldiers stood leaning on their tools, or with arms limp, their backs still bent from their labours, looking at the runway where a two-engined Hondo stood ready. The work was by no means finished but enough had been completed for a Hondo, which needs no more than seven hundred yards of runway, to take off. Captain Enzo Hidaka stood in front of the aircraft's wide-open door, his eleven men drawn up beside him, with Lieutenant Yoshi Tojimoto at the other end. Although the men all carried heavy packs as well as their parachutes, they stood rigidly to attention facing the admiral.

The staff officers were deeply moved, despite their impassive faces. With their left hands on their antique ceremonial swords, their eyes front and their heels together, they were honouring the departing patrol in the traditional manner.

"Comrades-in-arms," the admiral said, "before the sun has set, you will have parachuted into enemy territory and you will be entirely alone. Your mission is of enormous importance to Japan and we shall be thinking of you when the cities of America go up in flames. No Japanese soldier has ever penetrated so deeply into enemy country: you will be the first. No one will be able to help you: you will be on your own. Now go, my friends, and the blessings of His Imperial Majesty go with you."

As the first notes of the national anthem were struck, all officers and men on the field smartly about-turned to the west, to face in the direction of the Emperor, the

29

son of the sun and the living embodiment of the Japanese nation. The conquerors of Attu remained motionless, bowed from the waist, their upper bodies almost parallel to the ground, and eyes lowered, as long as the band played the anthem. This ancient Japanese tradition gave them a feeling of closeness to their ruler and his divine ancestors whose origins were lost in the mists of antiquity and legend.

The strains of the anthem died away; the four thousand men stood to attention again and about-turned to face the admiral once more.

"Hidaka-taiji, I hand you your command."

Hidaka ordered his men into the 'plane. The idling engines burst into a roar. The captain was the last aboard, and stood for a moment in the open doorway to give a final salute.

Yamada tore off his cocked hat and hoarsely yelled out the war cry:

"*Tenno heika . . . banzai . . . banzai . . . banzai!*"

Four thousand voices roared with him and four thousand forage-caps flew into the air.

"*Banzai . . . banzai . . . banzai!*"

The Hondo taxied forward, the wind from the propellers blowing into the faces of the officers. All eyes were on the aircraft as it became airborne at the end of the runway, climbed quickly and flew straight into the north-east.

The grey, rugged terrain of Attu sank further away and finally disappeared from view altogether, to be replaced by a vast expanse of dark blue water spotted with white horses as far as the eye could see. Inside the aircraft the throb of the engines made conversation impossible. In the centre of the compartment, the men's packs were piled high, although as they would have to carry every ounce of their load on their backs across mountains and rivers, through forests and deep snow, they had brought only the bare essentials.

Their destination was the foothills of the Brooks Range, nearly four hundred miles from the south coast of Alaska, in a region which even the Americans had not yet mapped. The choice of these foothills had been a good one since they would protect the patrol from the full force of the icy northerly gales, and would also provide places of sufficient altitude for transmissions to Attu to be beamed without interference.

The transmitter itself was not very powerful because its weight had had to be strictly limited in view of the difficult terrain over which it would have to be carried under all kinds of adverse conditions. It was, of course, the most valuable single item of equipment they had, and would have to be operated as long as there was anyone left to do so. Its power was generated by a large cranking-handle—the patrol could not afford the extra weight of a generator but there would always be a man to spare to crank up the transmitter.

At Hidaka's insistence, the idea of taking a second transmitter along had been dropped, and they had taken with them instead a large quantity of every conceivable spare part. Sergeant Kurakami, one of the best radio mechanics in the Japanese army, would carry out any repairs that might be needed. If anything happened to him, Corporal Lonti was to take over.

Hidaka looked at his men, so tightly packed together that they could scarcely move. Their pockets were full to bursting, and haversacks containing food and cooking utensils were slung across their chests. On his belt each man carried either an axe or a short field-spade, a broad-bladed knife, field-glasses and a first-aid kit. In addition, each had half a dozen hand grenades tucked inside his quilted jacket.

Above each man dangled the strap normally used for carrying small packs, looking for all the world like a hangman's noose suspended over each head. Very appropriate, Hidaka thought to himself, for surely most of

31

us will die; our souls, however, will be consigned to heaven in the Yasukuni shrine, and the Tenno himself will come and pray to Japan, the earth-mother, to receive us into the circle of immortal warriors. It will be for us to prove that we are worthy of this honour.

The captain was certain that each of his men felt as he did. He had known Yoshi Tojimoto since they had been at school and they were, indeed, distantly related. Hidaka's father, a landowner near Toyahara, had paid for Yoshi's studies. Yoshi had taken a passionate interest in botany while still at school, and later, when he had been called up, Hidaka had sent for him to come to Sakhalin. Yoshi had often joined him on surveying trips up-country, and had made himself useful by finding all sorts of edible plants and mosses. A patrol which included a man like Yoshi could live off the land for much longer and, therefore, cover much greater distances. Yoshi's name had, of course, sprung to mind immediately Hidaka had started picking his men. He was tough and determined; you could rely on him.

Next to him sat Sergeant Kurakami, the man in charge of the transmitter, who had already proved his sterling qualities. Then there was Tsunashima, also with the rank of sergeant, the patrol's meteorological officer. Hidaka had met him while both were in training for the Olympic Games. Tsunashima's athletic prowess, as well as his technical skill, had determined his selection. Corporal Watanabe was his number two and his potential replacement. Watanabe had acted as radio operator for the last Japanese Himalayan expedition and was naturally a very competent mountaineer. So was Sergeant Suda, who had led a daring sortie behind enemy lines in China and returned with valuable intelligence. If necessary, he could take the place of Lieutenant Tojimoto, or even Hidaka himself; he was a born leader of men.

Inaki and Inoué were only lance-corporals but they

belonged to the Household Company of the Imperial Guard, which acted as the Tenno's bodyguard. Hidaka knew that they would defend any post to which they might be sent to their last gasp—and with their bare hands, if need be.

Sinobu he had chosen because of his rugged and extrovert personality. The man had spent his entire life in the forests, and at one time or another had dispatched half a dozen black bears, single-handed, with his axe. Unfortunately, he also had a record as a cattle thief. The last time he had been arrested, however, he had escaped from custody and had holed out through the winter up-country in some of the most impenetrable ravines of the area. Only the war, in which he wanted to take part at all costs, had brought him out of hiding. He had calculated that the honour of belonging to Hidaka's unit would be useful after the war, but there was nothing calculated in his readiness at a moment's notice to do anything at all for his captain.

The Oshone would make up for what Sinobu lacked in the points of woodcraft. He could tell when a stranger's foot had bent a blade of grass, he could catch fish with his bare hands, he could see further with his own eyes than most people could with field-glasses, and he never tired. His only shortcoming was that he felt himself bound in loyalty to the captain alone. The chain of command meant nothing to him.

Hidaka unfastened his harness, clambered over the pile of luggage into the cockpit, and, crouched in behind the pilot and the co-pilot, watched the coast of Alaska come into view on the grey horizon.

The Hondo swung slightly southwards and Hidaka saw from his map that they were over the middle of Norton Sound. Slowly the bay disappeared behind them and they flew now over the mainland of the North American continent. The ground below appeared totally flat, a marshy tundra interlaced with rivers and lakes, everything green and grey in the height of summer.

Gradually the terrain became drier and more rugged, and bare mountain peaks began to appear. A wide plain covered with evergreen forests came suddenly into view, a great pale-blue river, which meandered round innumerable flat islands, flowing down the centre. Hidaka knew that this was the Yukon, the mightiest river in north-western America. At the turn of the century it had been the route for the prospectors of the Alaskan gold-rush, who had followed its course up to Klondike and Tanana. Now barely a handful was left of the tens of thousands who had sought their fortunes there half a century ago. No paddle-wheels churned up the waters of the Yukon today: it was as desolate as it had ever been. The pilot banked away from the river's course and turned north.

"About half an hour to go," he shouted above the noise of the engines.

A jagged line, just visible on the horizon, was the first indication of a vastly elongated mountain range. The Honda flew straight towards it at full throttle. In the distance the mountain tops gleamed white. These were the unconquered Brooks Mountains, as desolate as the mountains of the moon, beside which the European Alps pale almost into insignificance. Mysterious and impenetrable, the range runs for five hundred miles from east to west through the middle of Alaska, dividing the endless tundra of the north from the equally endless forests of the south. Up till now only a few prospectors and one or two trappers had ever wandered through this vast territory. No Eskimo had ever been as far. Hidaka had even heard vague rumours of a neolithic tribe of caribou-hunters who were supposed to roam this desolate country, completely isolated from the outside world and as shy as wild deer.

"About ten minutes now," the pilot shouted.

The aircraft roared over thickly wooded hilltops, so closely packed that they resembled the fleecy backs of huddled sheep. The backs arched and became green mountain peaks, streams rushing through the valleys between them. Hidaka's map had the legend "Schwatka Mountains" printed across the area and it showed clearly how they branched off from the central Brooks Range in a herring-bone pattern.

The pilot indicated with circular movements of his arm that he was going to look around for a suitable dropping zone. Hidaka slipped back into the compartment and took a firm hold of one of the hanging straps, aware immediately that all eyes were upon him. This was the big moment.

The red light at the end of the compartment came on, once, and again, and then a third time. Hidaka tensed involuntarily.

The engine was now making a sharp, humming noise. The eleven men stared fixedly at their captain. Slowly, he raised his hand.

The loading-hatch in the stern of the aircraft began to open. Immediately, an icy blast hit them.

"Prepare to jump!"

The trap was now a yawning void, and the freezing gale stung their faces.

A bell jangled harshly.

"Go!"

10

Torrents of rain blotted out the airfield at Elmendorf, and the trees along the perimeter bowed before the wind. The runway was a vast pool of water.

The Dakota bringing General Hamilton back from Washington skimmed over the forest, looking as if it might brush the treetops at any moment. The wheels touched, threw up a wave of spray and hissed along the concrete.

The general jumped lightly down without waiting for the steps.

"God-awful weather, sir," Henley said, as he saluted.

"I've had plenty of time to realize that."

The general, paler than usual, climbed into the jeep and slammed the door with such force that the noise reverberated over the airstrip. The jeep moved off along the tarred road, past piles of rubble and parked tractors.

"Well, Hendrik, the top brass don't propose doing anything about it. That is, they think sending a couple of miserable little destroyers to the Aleutians will be enough to stop the Japs building their damn airfield on Attu."

The colonel gazed straight ahead through the windscreen.

"So we'll just have to sit and wait for the Japs to drop their bombs all round us, sir."

The general had caught a cold; he sneezed violently.

"That's about it. They told me that everything at all seaworthy or airworthy is needed somewhere else."

Henley laughed to stop himself swearing. "Yes, I know. They'll fight to the last man for some God-forsaken Pacific island, but they'll leave their own back door wide open."

"That's your higher strategy for you," said Hamilton sarcastically. "The more Japs there are at work on Attu, the better for the overall picture. Our strategists were absolutely delighted when I gave them the list of the stuff the Japs are shipping to Attu. Wonderful, they said, great; that's so many ships that can't be used anywhere else."

The rain had now given way to hail which beat a tattoo on the roof of the jeep. Henley had to change down to third; he could hardly see the road.

"What if the Japs finish their airfield before we are ready for them? Have the great thinkers considered that possibility?"

"They have," Hamilton said, amid repeated sneezes. "They assured me that it could not possibly arise. Attu would be re-taken first."

"That's all very well, sir, but what if they're mistaken? What help can we count on then?"

"If the worst came to the worst, we wouldn't need to do much about it ourselves. Our great ally would make sure that the Jap bombers come to grief, every last one of them."

The general enjoyed his chief-of-staff's astonishment. "Might one ask, sir, who this great ally might be?"

Hamilton laughed out loud.

"Look for yourself. You can see it out there ... it's the weather, this stinking Alaskan weather. I had a bellyful of it today. Fog and drizzle to start out with, and gales, snow and loss of radio contact for the rest."

At the crossroads just before Anchorage, a despatch rider in muddy uniform stood at the side of the road, holding up a stop sign. The general opened the window and leaned out. "Are you looking for me, by any chance?"

"Yes, sir. Colonel Pollock would be grateful if you would come to Fort Richardson at once, sir."

"Right. Thank you." The general closed the window again.

"Dammit, I've got a temperature over a hundred. Still, I'd better go, Hendrik. Kindly see to it that I am buried with full military honours."

The colonel grinned.

When the C.-in-C., Alaska, charged into his office, coughing loudly, his handkerchief held demonstratively to his nose, his senior staff officers were already assembled.

"Right, what's up?"

"Pollock's got on to something, sir; continuous radio messages . . ." Lt. Col. Hagerty began.

Colonel Pollock was Chief of Intelligence and his responsibilities included radio direction-finding.

"Show me." The general snatched the piece of paper Pollock was holding delicately between thumb and index finger like some conclusive courtroom exhibit. All Hamilton saw was groups of letters which seemed to be gibberish.

"Something like this has been monitored three days running, sir, regular as clockwork at 1815 hours. It's always the same number of letters, transmitted at terrific speed. The cryptographers have turned it inside out and upside down and they can't come up with an answer."

The general saw no reason for excitement. "It's probably signals from shipping in the Pacific. The captains have to notify their positions daily."

"Yes, sir, we know. But if this little lot comes from a ship, the ship is sailing right through the mountains of Alaska."

The colonel pointed to a small note in the top left-hand corner.

"We have taken d.f. bearings on the transmitter. The result is a bit approximate but the messages come from somewhere round 66° 48′ North by 156° West."

They turned to the map which covered almost the entire wall behind Hamilton's desk.

"It would be round about here, sir, between the Lockwood Hills and the Schwatka Mountains. Practically unmapped territory. There's absolutely no one up there, not even natives. It is really *terra incognita*, as the old maps say, a great white blank in the heart of Alaska."

There was a few moments' silence. Hamilton gazed over the heads of his officers, apparently lost in contemplation of the "Stars and Stripes" draped over the portrait of President Roosevelt.

"Well, it's my opinion that there's someone up there now, someone made of flesh and blood whom we knew nothing about before and still know nothing about. And the reason we don't is that they're making damn sure we don't. It follows that, whoever they are, they're up to no good. That means they're probably Japs. Every child knows how keen the Nips are on espionage."

Captain William disagreed.

"We thought of that, sir. Our very first thought was that it's the Japs. But we dismissed it again at once. What would they be doing up there? It's completely uninhabited; it's hundreds of miles from anything of the slightest strategic importance, and there's nothing there worth spying on. We can think of no good reason why the enemy should be sending out coded messages from a God-forsaken region like that."

The general slapped the table with his hand.

"But it's *happening*, William, and it's up to us to find out why."

He swung his chair round to take another look at the map.

"The only thing we know is that there's an enemy transmitter hidden away up there somewhere, getting ready to make trouble."

Colonel Henley got the impression that his commanding officer had some inkling of a solution to the problem, but did not want to say so until he had more evidence to support his theory.

The general turned to Henley.

"I came across an Indian the other day . . . during Operation Glasshunt. You were there too. He seems to have worked for the Wild Life people, under a game-warden called McCluire, or something like that. I've no idea of the redskin's name, but you ought to be able to find him. Send him to me immediately!"

11

The daily transmission had already become routine; just one week in the field had seen to that. The meteorological officer took his readings about half an hour before transmission time and Kurakami put them into Japanese naval code. By that time, the transmitter would be assembled and ready for use. As it was always tuned in to Attu, the whole operation went off smoothly and quickly.

They had arranged with the Attu radio station to beam their reports at 1815 hours daily. It was a comfort to the isolated patrol in deepest Alaska to know that once a day their comrades on the far-away island were standing by to receive them. Up to now, everything had gone according to plan; the signal was loud and clear and Yamada was satisfied. Hidaka had ordered his two meteorologists and his two radio operators to work on alternate days, so that if anything happened to one pair the other would still be available.

The form the transmission took was invariable: it consisted of five different readings, always in the same order: wind strength, wind direction, cloud height, temperature and humidity. All that had to be done was to put these data into code and for the time being three letters sufficed for each reading.

Kurakami did not take long. He pushed the cipherbook back into its watertight wallet and replaced it in his haversack. Because the two bearers had gone down to the camp today, Hidaka cranked the transmitter up himself. A small light went on when there was enough power for the transmission. Kurakami had already put on his headphones, his eyes were half shut and he manipulated the controls with great delicacy. The captain looked at his watch and began the countdown.

41

"1814 . . . fifty seconds to go . . . forty . . . thirty . . . twenty . . . ten . . . five . . . three . . . go!"

Kurakami leaned forward and closed his eyes tightly. His fingers left the tuning knobs and now operated the key too fast for the eye to follow. He waited a moment for acknowledgment from Attu, nodded and then switched off.

"Well done, Kurakami," Hidaka said, "only six and a half seconds. But try and speed up even more; so much depends on it."

Kurakami knew that only too well. The shorter the transmission time, the less chance the enemy had of pinpointing them.

Quickly they stowed the transmitter away in an aluminium box lined with foam rubber. Kurakami put the box in a rubber bag, which, in turn, was put into a waterproof pack with inflatable sides. When blown up, the whole thing floated and would come to no harm if dropped in the river. The pack weighed about sixty pounds. Kurakami strapped it on and the meteorological officer carried the large crank. Hidaka rolled up the camouflage net, put it under his arm, and brought up the rear.

Before they went down the exposed slope at the double, Hidaka looked searchingly in all directions. Although they had never seen the slightest sign of human life, he thought it vital to get his men into the habit of using extreme caution at all times. He had given strict orders to his patrol never to break cover without first listening intently for the sound of aircraft engines. An air-reconnaissance would be the Americans' first step against them.

In fact, the Japanese camp was completely invisible until one actually stepped into it. It was in a hollow surrounded by boulders and pine trees, and overhanging branches concealed it completely from the air.

A trench had been dug for the fire and Sinobu had

42

collected a large pile of firewood. The old buck they had shot that morning was ready skinned and drawn, and Tojimoto had jointed it skilfully.

"We can scrape and stretch the hide and take it with us tomorrow. It'll come in handy for making bags," Hidaka said. "You can get the fire started now, Sinobu. Good and hot, but just a glow, please, no flames."

Of course, it was impossible to make a fire altogether without flames but Sinobu, the hunter, knew what was expected of him. Hard old pinewood was the most suitable fuel, once the bark and rotten parts had been removed. It burned with a small, bluish flame and quickly gave off a great deal of heat. The position of the fire-trench ensured there was enough draught.

The fire could not be seen from outside the hollow; the trench, about eighteen inches deep, concealed the glow. Any remaining flicker would be hidden by the brushwood. The dry hardwood gave off little smoke and the thin spiral now rising towards the night sky through the treetops was undetectable. However, anyone versed in woodcraft would be able to smell the smoke from many miles away. In a damp atmosphere wood-smoke would creep along the ground and linger in the brushwood for days.

"I don't know how long we'll be able to allow ourselves the luxury of hot meals; it's too big a risk," Hidaka said warningly.

The lieutenant was less worried.

"Really, Enzo, I think you're overdoing it. This country is completely deserted—I've never seen anything like it."

Hidaka grasped Yoshi's arm and bent over close to his friend's ear. "Never say anything like that again, Yoshi, never."

He spoke softly but in deadly earnest.

"We must become like ghosts, Yoshi. The earth must not feel our weight, and the birds must not see us. We must drill this into our men until it is in their blood. Once the Americans wake up to what we are doing, they'll move heaven and earth to wipe us out. They will *have* to silence us. It'll be a matter of life and death to them: incendiary bombs and high explosives dropped on their cities . . . Of course, they won't be able to mount a large-scale operation against us; the distance involved and the terrain will see to that. But they'll certainly send in small units by air, and sooner or later we'll come up against them. When we do, Yoshi, we must see them before they see us, we must!"

Tojimoto understood this only too well; he had no illusions about what lay in store for them.

"It'll be a long-drawn-out hunt, Enzo, and perhaps in the end not a single one of us will be left. We have volunteered for a mission which will give us death with honour. When the transmitter is silenced and all but the last bullet has been fired, we shall have done our duty and be free to join our ancestors."

"No, Yoshi, we must survive the transmitter. There is something else we have to do. The admiral gave me express orders not to tell you until we were actually here, and only two of us, I, as the commanding officer of the unit, and you, as my second-in-command, are allowed to know. If I become a casualty, you must tell Suda. He will have to tell his No. 2 if he has to take over from you."

Hidaka picked up his map-case and pulled out a sheet. As he unfolded it and spread it on the ground, Yoshi recognized north-west Alaska in the dim flicker of the fire. The captain pointed to a large river.

"That is the Noatak. It is almost unknown and even the Yankees have never explored it. All the smaller rivers coming down from the Brooks Range feed it and it flows into the sea at Kotzebue Sound. It would be quite a simple matter to float down it on a raft, in summer of course, from about the beginning of June to the end of

44

September. That's what we shall have to do, Yoshi, once our transmissions stop."

Tojimoto stared at the mouth of the Noatak on the map. "But we'd never make it to Attu, let alone Japan, from there, not in a hundred years."

"True, but we might make it to Igilchik."

Hidaka pointed to a small island, scarcely more than a dot on the map, in the mouth of the Noatak, not far from the open sea.

"It's bleak and barren, but it has some importance for the Yanks because hundreds of thousands of seals make their home there. The American Wild Life Service has a post on the island to protect the seals from poachers. A white man runs it, with the help of a few Eskimos and their families."

The captain stopped abruptly because Sinobu had come up to give the officers their venison. Hidaka praised his efforts; the meat had been well cooked. He formally invited the party to eat and wished them all a good appetite.

The Japanese do not tear at their food with their teeth. They first cut it into small pieces with a knife and then convey these morsels to their mouths with a pair of chopsticks. Only the two officers had brought their own, delicately wrought in ivory, from Japan; the men whittled theirs from willow sticks fresh for every meal.

"This white man I was talking about is very important to us," Hidaka went on to Tojimoto. "He is a Russian whose parents fled with him from Siberia to Japan during the Revolution. Later, he moved on to Alaska, and became an American citizen. We know him as Nizhinsky—Boris Nizhinsky."

"What do you mean, we know him as that?"

"He is one of our secret agents and has been for years. His wife and children live in Japan, at Hakodate. Nizhinsky's only job is to be ready for us in

45

case we need him. He is waiting for us now, Yoshi; that is, for any of us that may be left."

"I don't understand, Enzo. What good will it do the High Command, even if any of us do manage to get through to this Boris?"

"The good it'll do them is that they will get detailed topographical reports about the unmapped interior of Alaska which they can't get anywhere else. We cannot fight this war at all without a great deal of intelligence; or the next one, either. If any one of us gets through, he will be a mine of information of the utmost strategic importance. Should the transmitter fail, it is our duty to make for Igilchik. Nizhinsky has a powerful transmitter and he can call up a flying-boat from Attu. Yamada will move heaven and earth to recover an eye-witness from this mission. More than one, of course, if he possibly can."

"This makes everything quite different," Tojimoto said. "Our task is even harder than I thought, and we won't be allowed to die in peace when our strength is finally exhausted."

12

The first thing Allan had to do to prepare for his one-man war against the carcajou was to obtain fresh meat, which he did by shooting an old moose-cow the following day. He stuffed its entrails and the half-emptied stomach into a large sack full of holes, cut the meat up into hunks and stowed it in his rucksack, and then set out on a series of expeditions, dragging the evil-smelling sack behind him. If his enemy, also known as the glutton, or wolverine, picked up the scent, it would be compelled by its greedy nature to follow until it came upon something edible. That something would be the hunks of meat in Allan's rucksack. To eradicate all traces of human scent which would frighten the glutton from the trail, Allan tied pieces of hairy moose-hide to the soles of his oldest pair of boots with lengths of moose-sinew.

During the next few days he put in many miles, dragging his sack along in straight lines towards several spots along the bank of the stream where he had put out bait.

The carcajou did not take his first bait until eleven days later but soon after that reappeared at the same spot and, of course, found more meat. The predator was returning almost daily by now and Allan began to build his hide. About a hundred paces downstream from the bait was a stretch of banked shingle in the middle of the stream which gave a clear line of fire to the spot Allan and the carcajou had selected. He would have to camouflage the hide well and equip it for a fairly long stay. So as not to alarm his prey, he went carefully and carried over just a few branches at a time. Slowly a kind of moss-lined bower went up, almost invisible from the outside. Only a small loophole was left open to shoot through, directly opposite the spot where the bait was left. If Allan kept still, the carcajou would be completely oblivious of his presence. The air was filled with the sound of water gurgling all round his little island.

The glutton usually came in the early morning. Allan intended to spend that very night in his hiding-place; dawn would bring the animal's doom.

As the gamewarden, in high spirits, was about to walk back to his cabin, a small flying-boat flew above him towards Lake Nunalto. Captain William, the only passenger on board, had been detailed by Army H.Q. Alaska to contact Allan McCluire and talk to him. The babbling brook drowned out the sound of the aircraft, and Allan went on his way with no inkling of what was to come.

It was not until he left his stream and walked back towards the lake that he noticed the 'plane. It lay like a dragonfly on the surface of the water, its stilts stretched out to the floats. At first Allan thought Wilfrid Frazer had come to ask about the beavers, which were long overdue on Afognak. But as he hurried down he saw to his astonishment that a man in army uniform was sitting on the bench outside his log cabin. Captain William stood up and walked towards him.

It had been a lapse on the captain's part not to have gone into the cabin. It was a time-honoured custom in the forest to make free use of hospitality, and a visitor who stays outside merely because the host is out, casts a slur on his generosity.

Allan realized at once that the officer had one glass eye. A thin, jagged scar, evidently a war wound, ran from his hairline down to his chin. He looked like a man with courage and drive. He's out of a different world, Allan thought, but he liked the look of him and gave him a friendly grin.

"Mr. McCluire," the officer called out while he was

still ten paces away, instead of the simple "Hullo, Allan" more usual in the forest.

Allan opened the door of his cabin and motioned to his guest to come in.

"My visit is no doubt a surprise, but . . ."

"A drink?" Allan interrupted.

"I don't want to put you to any trouble . . ."

The host took out a bottle and two glasses. One match was enough to set the fire crackling in the hearth.

"General Hamilton sends you his respects, Mr. McCluire."

"Don't know the gentleman, I'm afraid," Allan said with a laugh. "But I've heard of him. I'm always glad to get regards from people, so give him mine, too."

William was nonplussed for a moment. He decided the best thing to do would be to go straight to the point.

"The general wants you to join a patrol of Alaskan Scouts which is being formed in order to track down a secret transmitter in the Schwatka Mountains. We would greatly appreciate it if you would accept the honourable and highly responsible post of Chief Scout of the patrol. The job seems tailor-made for you; we can't think of anyone better qualified."

William then told him about the mysterious transmitter sending messages every evening at a quarter-past six in a completely indecipherable code, and of how their first thought was of Japanese espionage.

"What on earth would the Japs have to spy on in such a desolate part of the world?"

"That's a good question. But radio messages *are* being sent from up there and by people whom we must assume are working for the enemy. They must be stopped."

Allan nodded. "That's obvious, Captain, but you don't need me for that. The Scouts will be able to manage all right by themselves. Finding a transmitter that sends out radio messages every day is quite a bit easier than finding missing mountain climbers."

"Oh no, it isn't. It's very much more difficult because the transmitter is constantly changing position. Also it is being operated by people who are quite determined *not* to be found, as opposed to people in trouble who do all they can to attract attention."

Allan could not argue with that.

"Think of it, Mr. McCluIre, we have only the vaguest idea of where the transmitter is actually located. Each transmission lasts only a few seconds. Before our direction-finding equipment can get a bearing on it, it's stopped. We shall have to comb an area of about fifty square miles."

"Like trying to find a needle in a haystack."

"Yes, the general mentioned that needle, too, and it's just because it will take exceptional skill to find it that Hamilton wants your help."

"How did he get on to me in the first place?"

"Through your Indian. Harry Chiefson has been saying wonderful things about you. According to him, you have a phenomenal tracking instinct."

"Harry? How did Harry come to be talking rubbish like that?"

Captain William laughed. "He's quite a character, that fellow, talks with the general as if they were old friends. Our general is a passionate sportsman, you understand. And when he happened to bump into your Indian, they soon found out what a lot they had in common. That's how the conversation got round to you, Mr. McCluire. You couldn't find a better P.R. man anywhere."

"I'll wring his neck!" The gamewarden was horrified.

"But why? The general got on to your boss, Wilfrid Frazer, and he confirmed every word Harry said.

Hamilton asked Frazer to release you for vital military duties and he agreed at once."

Allan said nothing.

"You would be doing us a valuable service," William went on. "We need you, we must have you; even your Indian realizes that. Without you, the whole mission would fail, he told the general. You will head the best scout unit in the whole of Alaska. And even I will be subject to a large extent to your discretion."

"So the patrol will be under your command, Captain? The search for the transmitter is a military operation, then?"

"Of course. After all we are at war. And it's a good thing we are dealing with an identifiable enemy. The scouts have been formally incorporated into the Army for as long as this picnic lasts. Only soldiers are equipped to fight soldiers."

"That's all very well, but I'm not one."

The captain gave a perceptible start.

"That can soon be remedied, Mr. McCluire; you can volunteer."

"Don't take this the wrong way, Captain, but as far as I'm concerned, I'd rather stay out of this."

"Stay out of it . . . ? You can't be serious!"

Allan put some more logs on the fire.

"I would only be a burden to a military operation. My business is with wild animals, not with strange human beings. Leave me to get on with my private war against the carcajou."

They stared at each other, the gamewarden with a look of calm indifference and the captain with bitter disappointment and mounting frustration.

"You actually refuse?" William said, an expression of disbelief on his face.

"I'm sorry, Captain, it's nothing personal, you understand. But it's just not up my street. I'm sure you'll find someone just as good for the job."

The officer put his hand to his breast pocket.

"Mr. McCluire," he said coldly. "As we had to be prepared for every eventuality, particularly after talking with Wilfrid Frazer, I brought your call-up papers along, just in case."

He put an official-looking document on the table in front of Allan.

"These are your orders to report for duty, McCluire. From now on, you are subject to military discipline and must consider yourself a soldier."

The gamewarden said nothing. He seemed stunned by the shock.

"Pack up your things, McCluire, and lock up your hut. We are off to Richardson in half an hour. Further orders will be given to you in person by General Hamilton."

13

Admiral Yamada was worried. His stock of explosives was running low, there was a shortage of all spare parts, and only with difficulty would he be able to eke out the garrison's provisions for another three weeks. The cause of his troubles was the group of enemy destroyers which had recently begun operations in the Bering Sea. The last convoy bringing supplies to Attu had suffered heavy losses: two heavily-laden freighters had been sunk and two others badly damaged. Only the sudden descent of thick fog had saved the rest of the convoy from total destruction. It had sailed without an naval escort because, up till then, there had been no sign of an enemy presence anywhere in the area. This happy-go-lucky state of affairs had now come to a end; the enemy had woken up to the situation and had begun to attack the life-line between Japan and Attu.

The Japanese Navy was stretched to the limit; the main body had to be kept in readiness for the decisive battles to come in the Pacific and it had also to escort convoys supplying the Japanese garrisons further south. Everywhere, generals were calling for reinforcements and Yamada knew that there was little prospect of his next convoy being escorted by a strong enough destroyer force. At the same time, he was being urgently pressed to finish the airfield on Attu. He had reduced the men's rations and made considerable fuel economies. Picks and shovels had taken over from the bulldozers, and human hands now shifted rocks from the tunnels. The work was harder and the working day longer, and all on insufficient food.

But the runway was still not ready and the hangars had not yet been carved deeply enough into the cliffs. Human hands were no substitute for dynamite in the tunnels, and the pneumatic hammers had run out of fuel. He was constantly being told that a new convoy would be sent out as soon as possible, but he needed more fuel now. A squadron of bombers was standing by in Japan prepared to take off for Attu. All they were waiting for was the news that the runway was ready for them to land. Hidaka's mission had gone well and his reports were coming in regularly. The weather situation in Alaska was no longer the impenetrable mystery to the Japanese Air Force that it had been. As soon as the work on Attu was completed, there would be nothing to stop the dreaded Shinzans dropping their incendiary and high-explosive loads on America's major cities.

The admiral cursed the delay. Every single day mattered, because every day that went by was one day less in the effective life of Hidaka's signals patrol. By now the enemy must know of its existence and be making every effort to track it down. From now on the patrol would have to change its position much more frequently; it would be on the run and would be forced to maintain radio silence for days on end.

All the supplies Yamada needed were on board six cargo ships at present lying off Hakodate. On several occasions torpedo boats or destroyers had been sent to escort them only to be withdrawn at the last moment because they were needed elsewhere. The Admiralty was not prepared to risk the convoy by sending it to Attu unescorted.

Yamada made up his mind to send a signal to the Admiralty proposing a bold course of action, of the dangers of which he was well aware. It involved a few obsolete submarines in the harbour of Kobe which were now used only for training purposes. He proposed that these should be put back into active service and sent straight through to Attu, as their range was too limited for them to accompany the convoy on its zig-zag course. They could protect the convoy where it was most at risk—in the Bering Sea—and if they managed to torpedo just one enemy destroyer, the surprise attack would distract the enemy long enough for some of the convoy at least to slip through to Attu.

Yamada's arguments bore fruit, both because they were well reasoned and because of the reputation he enjoyed. He received a signal the very next day that two recommissioned submarines were on their way and that the convoy at Hakodate had set sail for Attu. The admiral sighed with relief, quite unaware that he had set in train a chain of events which made a major contribution to the ultimate defeat of the Imperial fleet.

In the early morning of 16 July, a reconnaissance flight from a U.S. aircraft-carrier in the North Pacific sighted a surfaced Japanese submarine of obsolete design drifting with the waves. Its guns were silent when the aircraft approached it and it made no attempt to submerge. The pilot came down low and circled the vessel. He saw that the conning tower was shut and that the screw was motionless. He reported this strange find and before long a U.S. destroyer was drawn up alongside the submarine.

When the hatch of the conning tower was opened, a cloud of poisonous carbon dioxide escaped. The crew had suffocated from choke damp. Their bodies were still at their posts, blue-lipped and with bloated faces. Amongst the papers the boarding party found was the current Japanese naval code. By the following day, this invaluable prize was in Washington.

During the next few months, the Pentagon was able to decode every single radioed Japanese naval signal. A great many Japanese warships sailed straight into the open arms of the enemy. Operations which had been meticulously planned ended in disaster, and this chain of unprecedented naval defeats did not end until the Japanese Admiralty finally changed the code.

14

Allan McCluire had been in Fort Richardson for three days. His billet was Room 36, Barracks E, Block VI. All around him the place teemed with men in uniform, and new draftees were coming in all the time from the south. The huge camp resembled an ever-growing antheap. Prefabricated huts were being brought in by sea and were erected in a few hours. There was a smell of petrol, leather and gun-oil. Trucks and jeeps rumbled over the rutted roads. Gritty dust came in through the windows and doorways and it was impossible to keep anything clean. Tank-tracks rattled, engines throbbed and everywhere men were shouting. None of the newcomers could find his way around this military labyrinth.

Thousands of men had been posted to Alaska, together with all the equipment required to turn the amorphous mass of recruits into effective combat units. It had been decided to defend the territory, whatever happened; the American people would not tolerate the thought of the increasingly hated enemy setting foot on the mainland of their own continent. It was bad enough that he had established himself off-shore; the yellow peril must not be allowed any closer.

Anchorage was the very heart of Alaska. It was the largest city, the most important port and the starting point of the only road and railway that went up-country. Everything radiated from Anchorage, everything converged upon it. If the enemy were planning a landing, Anchorage was the obvious choice. Any other thrust would be into the void. And if the enemy were to launch bombing raids from Attu, as was now to be expected, Anchorage was the only possible target.

There was no other choice from a military point of view.

Anti-aircraft batteries had been brought up and trenches dug. Concrete gun emplacements had been established at the entrances to the fiords at Seward, Valdez and Cordova, and high-speed naval launches patrolled Cook Inlet day and night. Larger naval units had not been made available to Alaskan H.Q.; as General Hamilton had been told earlier in Washington, the Navy and the Air Force were needed more urgently for coming events in the South Pacific.

The Pentagon had been more generous with ground troops and their equipment, but most of them were raw recruits, and the hardest task facing the general and his staff was their training. There were too few instructors, and most of them had no combat experience. Everything, everywhere, had to be improvised so as to bring some semblance of order into the camp and among the recruits themselves. General Hamilton had so much to do all day that he had no time to devote to Allan McCluire.

That particular recruit sat on his camp bed and stared into space, his eyes half shut. The constant noise, both inside the barracks and outside, jarred on his every nerve. He was still as stunned as he had been that evening by Lake Nunalto when Captain William had press-ganged him. He felt hemmed in by the throng of countless men by which he was constantly surrounded. The waves of confusion breaking round him were sheer torture. He was incapable of picking out individual voices or faces from the crowd. To him it all seemed a shapeless grey mass of stamping feet, loud voices and smelly bodies.

Allan was still in civilian clothes. Since William had handed him on to others and he had arrived at the barracks, nothing whatever had happened. He only went to eat or wash when somebody nudged him, reminded him, and showed him the way. He could only find his own way to the latrine; the smell acted as a guide. Allan had no idea to which unit he belonged and did not ask. His room-mates wondered why he had not been allocated to any unit, but he was completely indifferent.

"For God's sake, do something about your get-up," somebody said to him. "There'll be hell to pay when we're ordered on parade and one of us is still in civvies."

Allan shrugged his shoulders. He had never wanted a uniform, so why should he make any effort to get one now?

"Why don't you pull yourself together and go along to the orderly room," somebody else suggested. "They're bound to know what you're supposed to do."

As this piece of advice was accompanied by a friendly nudge, Allan did his best to grin back.

"I don't give a damn what I'm meant to do."

His room-mates laughed; they thought Allan was a great character.

"What's the use of hanging around in here? There's a lot more going on outside." One of the young men pulled Allan up, pushed him out of the door and stood him at the end of a long queue of men. He did not even have to give his name. When his turn finally arrived, the sergeant sitting at the big table, and the two corporals, knew who he was at once.

"Get back to your barracks, McCluire. They'll call you when they're ready for you."

Anybody else would have noticed that the sergeant's tone was not unfriendly, and that his relative politeness presaged special treatment for Allan. He had been informed that Allan was an expert in something or other.

So Allan wandered back to Room 36, threw himself on his bed and picked up a garish magazine from one of the piles lying about. The cover portrayed a glamorous blonde whose well-filled blouse was in the process of being ripped open by a lasciviously grinning Jap. The poor creature had been tied to a chair and behind her other Japs with murderous faces were holding their bayonets pointed at her. The text revealed, however, that on the very threshold of a fate worse than death she was rescued by an intrepid young American. How simple-minded propaganda is, Allan thought, and reached for the next pulp magazine.

"Mr. McCluire, General Hamilton would like to see you now."

A lieutenant, impeccably uniformed, stood in the doorway. He had to repeat his message before Allan realized that he was being addressed.

His room-mates, impressed by Hamilton's name and rank, helped Allan to find his jacket.

"Hurry it up," one of them whispered. "The old man is in a fix. He needs you to help him win the war."

Allan buttoned up his shirt and put on his jacket. Then he followed the officer, who went out quickly in front of him. It was not until he was outside the barracks that he stopped and waited for Allan to catch up with him.

"You'll have to excuse the general. He's been pretty busy these last few days. All these new arrivals and nowhere to put them."

"Where are we going?" Allan asked.

"To the staff guardroom, Mr. McCluire. A car will pick you up there and take you to the general's private quarters."

A limousine of impressive length drew up. It was khaki on the outside, like a military vehicle, but inside it was luxurious. An ebony-coloured sergeant with an impressively large head sat behind the wheel.

The moment had come for Allan to receive his orders direct from the Commander-in-Chief, Alaska. He was resigned to his call-up now. After all, his own boss, Wilfrid Frazer, had surrendered him to the Army. But they could not ask him to perform any duties other than those of an ordinary private. These he would do, since there was nothing else for it, but he could refuse to command other men; there was no question of his taking on any position of responsibility. It would only give him feelings of guilt if he made a mistake and there were casualties as a result.

The car came to a smooth stop before the portico of a large white mansion. With its columns and gabled roof, it reminded Allan of the stately Colonial homes in the south of whose aristocratic air Americans were so proud, and the black butler at the door in his blue livery with silver buttons fitted well into the picture. However, the whole thing seemed rather out of place in Alaska, Allan thought.

The man led him at once into a large room off the hall.

"The general is changing and will be down shortly. He sends his apologies."

Allan stood still in the middle of the floor and looked around him with growing astonishment. He had never before seen such a collection of hunting trophies. His host must have gone shooting at one time or another in every part of the world where big game was to be found. He already knew that Hamilton was a passionate sportsman. He had also been told that only his marriage to a Texan oil heiress made it possible for him to pursue his hobby in style.

Elephants' tusks, stag, moose and wapiti antlers covered the walls. Lions looked down on him, and snarling tigers. The collection included chamois from Europe, yak heads from the Himalayas, eland and Cape buffalo from Africa. There were ibex, bighorn and Marco Polo sheep. There were even specimens of the rare bongo antelope and the sittatunga. The game-warden recognized them all and knew the strength of their horns and antlers, whether straight or coiled.

Though he had never seen this exotic game in the wild, he was familiar with it from books and illustrations.

The floor was covered with black, brown and white bearskins. A three-foot-long rhino-horn hung on the left doorpost; a pair of massive walrus tusks looked down from the right. In the background, there towered a lifelike stuffed gorilla.

In the course of inspecting all these treasures, Allan had slowly turned a full circle and, now facing the stairs again, saw the general coming down. He was in civilian clothes and looked just like a successful businessman.

"If you see nothing but uniforms all day long," he explained, "you are glad to dress like a human being in the evening."

He gave his guest a cordial handshake and made his excuses for keeping him waiting.

"I hope you weren't bored, Mr. McCluire."

His manner was enough to disarm any visitor, which was exactly what he intended. His ability to adapt to anyone with whom he came into contact was one of his great strengths.

"I did not have time to be bored, sir," Allan said, feeling very much at ease. He had expected a somewhat different reception. "I could spend hours looking at your trophies."

The general laughed. "Yes, Mr. McCluire, to some extent we're brothers at heart. Only you chose the right job to indulge your tastes and I didn't. Now, what will you have, Scotch, brandy, or plain beer?"

The butler offered Allan these alternatives and others on a silver tray. Hamilton had already taken a pewter tankard full of beer and Allan followed suit.

"I'm really pleased to meet you at last," the host said when he had taken his first swallow; his voice was slightly too loud. "I am only sorry, though, that they upset you with this crazy idea of handing you your

call-up papers. Complete mistake, and, of course, I
didn't hear about it till today. No wonder, with the tur-
moil we're in."

With a dismissive gesture, the general indicated that
the matter was now closed as far as he was concerned.

"Why don't you take this chair, Mr. McCluire? It'll
give you a good view of my most impressive tiger."

Allan, however, was standing stock-still, gripping his
pewter tankard.

"Would you mind repeating, sir, what you said just
now?"

Hamilton pretended to try and remember.

"Oh, of course, about your call-up. Complete blunder
. . . an excess of zeal on the part of an otherwise most
competent officer. Of course, I would have been delighted to have a man like you along, but only if he
came on a voluntary basis, and with unlimited enthusiasm. But I can see why you're reluctant. Individualists
like you don't fit into a team, I understand that."

He beamed at his guest so amicably that Allan did
not know what to say.

"Sit down, sit down," Hamilton said, with a wave of
his hand.

Allan found himself in the depths of an easy chair,
decorated along the arms with the tufts of zebra tails.

"I hope you don't mind, McCluire, devoting this
evening to me. If I can't go hunting myself, at least I'd
like to have a good yarn about it. William told me
about the carcajou you were after. I've never heard of
one of those beasts taking bait; tell me all about it."

Allan told him the whole story, starting with the loss
of his beavers, right up to the point at which there was
scarcely any doubt left that his quarry would meet its
doom. The general interrupted the narrative with a
number of questions which showed both his lively interest and his sound knowledge of animals and forest
lore. The two men were getting on well together and

Hamilton felt he had made a good deal of headway in these first few minutes.

"And what about the story about the Denali timber wolf?" the general asked. "Do you really think he savaged that child? I don't believe it; wolves are often accused of things they would never do."

In this particular case, Allan thought, the story was probably true; sometimes individual members of an animal species did behave out of character. He told the general this story in great detail as well.

"A great job, Allan, really a great job!" Hamilton exclaimed at the end, genuinely enthusiastic.

The coloured butler brought in a platter of cold meats and sandwiches.

"I don't suppose you hanker after the kind of trophies I've got." Hamilton indicated his crowded walls with a sweeping gesture. "And yet, Alaska is unsurpassed anywhere in the world as far as bear, or moose, or bighorn are concerned."

Allan had to look for the right words to express his feelings on the subject.

"For sportsmen of your class, sir, big game hunting *is* a sport, a very noble sport, admittedly. But for those of us who live here all the time, it's a simple matter of making sure of the next meal."

"But what about those moose antlers of yours, Allan, that Wilfrid Frazer sent to the New York Natural History Museum? They just about beat the world record, didn't they?"

"At the time, they beat the record," Allan said. "That made them special and somebody had to take them."

Hamilton filled their glasses again and drank deeply.

"So it's rarities that attract you, uncommon specimens, a new light on the chase?"

"Yes, that's about it, sir. And that's why I can understand about other people being keen on bagging their trophies. It's pretty much the same thing, when you come down to it."

The general nodded in agreement; he had been thinking along the same lines.

"Like your glacier bear. I'd have been just as keen as you on a remarkable pelt like that."

"Why don't you get one yourself, sir? It's not too difficult."

"Well sure, if you were to guide me I'd come like a shot."

Allan thought it was a good idea; he felt under an obligation to the general. After all, it was thanks to him he had regained his freedom. But in a moment Hamilton had recalled his professional duties.

"If only it weren't for this damned war: I'm afraid we'll have to postpone that trip till some other time."

"Don't you ever get any leave?"

"Yes, of course, but it wouldn't look too good if I went off chasing bears when we're in the middle of chasing something else much more urgently."

That's what you get from doing a top job, Allan thought. The more responsible the position, the more closely you're watched from all sides and the more criticism you have to take. Again he felt how fortunate he was.

"I can't get this damned transmitter out of my mind," the general said with deliberate candour. "I wish I could at least stop thinking about it off duty."

His guest was sympathetic. "I'd be just the same. When we put the musk-oxen out to pasture on Nunivak and they got fewer instead of more, I couldn't take my mind off them either."

"And what was the answer?"

"A poacher, an American hiding on the island; we had no idea at first."

At once Hamilton seemed to forget the transmitter. "I wouldn't have thought that a white man could last out that long up there. Nunivak is a cruel part of the world."

Allan disagreed. "The Far North isn't so inhospitable as you'd think. It's not bad country for people who know their way about. There are lots of Alpine polar hare and even more ptarmigan. The lakes teem with salmon and trout, and at times you get flocks of wild duck and wild goose up to ten thousand strong. There's plenty of timber about for building cabins and for heating them. If you've got the know-how, you can do quite well for yourself up there, if you want to."

"You could do even better in the Schwatka Mountains, I presume."

"Oh, yes, much better. The northern forests are pretty hospitable, really, but outsiders don't realize it, even those who decide to stay around for a week or so. They take along everything they need or think they're going to need, and that's no way to get to know the wilderness. In fact you can find all basic essentials there. A man who knows his way around can be quite independent of the outside world. He could hold out for years."

"You might be able to, Allan, but who else could, nowadays?"

"Oh, lots of people, sir. The trappers, for instance, and the scouts would be even better. It's part of their basic training after all."

The general looked doubtful.

"I've heard that; but what they'd be like when it comes to the point is another matter. Those characters, on the other hand, seem to know what they're about."

"You mean the men with the transmitter in the Schwatkas?"

"Who else? They're cunning devils up there. More difficult to find than the proverbial needle in a haystack."

McCluire suggested the general was being too pessimistic.

"I've got to be, Allan. Those bastards are in a different place every night. Even if anybody should come across them, they'd be able to shoot him down. With all our superiority in numbers and equipment, we're still at a disadvantage."

"They just mustn't get the idea that anyone is after them," Allan said, taking the bait. "What's more, they mustn't know if anyone finds their tracks. The element of surprise will do the rest."

"You may outwit wild animals like that, Allan, but not thinking human beings."

"It all depends whose thinking is better."

"You just try finding a needle in a haystack by taking thought," the general said ironically.

"The analogy doesn't work, sir, because they aren't needles. You said yourself just now they were human beings. They've got to eat, drink, sleep, keep warm, and protect themselves from the climate. On top of that, they've got to beam out their little message at the same time every day. So you can work out roughly how and where they must be doing all that and that leaves you with a limited number of places where they could be. And that's where you look."

The general was visibly taken aback.

"I don't quite understand, my friend. What are you trying to say?"

"The Brooks Range stretches right across northern Alaska like a huge fish-bone. The highest peaks represent the backbone running east and west. The foothills on either side are joined to the backbone at an angle like the little bones, and include the Schwatkas in the west. That's where they're supposed to be hiding out, isn't it?"

Hamilton nodded. "That's what I've been told."

"I don't know much about radio, but I believe there

shouldn't be any higher peaks lying between the transmitter and the receiver."

"That's right. And if there were, we wouldn't be receiving them either."

"It follows that you can restrict your search to a certain type of terrain. Their camp will always be on the edge of the forest, about half-way up the mountain slope."

"Why only half-way up? That would mean that they'd have to climb the rest of the way every single day."

"Yes, they would. But they'd have to go down to the river every day, as well."

"What river?"

"There's a river or a stream in every Alaskan valley. As a hunter, you must know that game goes down every morning and every evening to the watering places in the valleys. That's where the grass is juiciest. People who have to live off the land must also find their food down in the valley, particularly if they have to do it stealthily. Instead of firing off a lot of ammunition, they will lay traps, dig holes, and use snares. They can only do that at twilight or in the dark, and it has to be down in the valleys, not up in the mountains."

"That makes sense," Hamilton said with satisfaction.

Allan nodded. The general seemed to be following his argument so far.

"We must assume these people know all that as well as we do. Otherwise they wouldn't have been sent on such a mission. They are compelled to go up to the top as well as down to the valley at least once a day. They're probably divided into two parties, one to look after the transmitter and the other to forage. They'd meet at their camp half-way and rest up there, well hidden."

"And how many of them are there, do you think, Allan?" the general asked eagerly.

67

"To have an idea of that, I'd have to know how much a transmitter like that weighs and whether one man is enough to operate it."

"One man could operate it but he'd need to have a relief for carrying it up steep mountains. I think we can exclude the possibilities of it being powered by batteries or a generator: it's probably operated by a treadle or crank. So it wouldn't weigh much, but it would still be a considerable burden. I should think the transmitter alone would need at least three men to look after it."

"I would expect, sir, that they'd have two or three men to forage for them in the valley, one or two men to guard the camp and a patrol commander, as well as one or two reserves. I should think there'd be ten to twelve men up there."

"You know, Allan, we could do with a man like you on our tactical staff."

Allan was beginning to enjoy the planning of the whole operation, treating it like one of his hunting-trips.

"When our friends move camp," he went on excitedly, "they'll go along the edge of the forest. That would mean they'd still be under cover but would be able to keep the terrain above them in view. So our search can be confined to a small strip of forest near the top of the range. And we need only consider mountains that have no higher peaks to the south of them."

The general rang for more beer. When the two men were settled again, he said. "That's all very well, but we've still got a lot of country to cover. Let's assume, though, that we get on to them, what trick are we going to use to capture the secret transmitter?"

"No trick, sir; we just put ourselves in our quarry's position and work out what they'd expect us to do."

"They'll certainly be expecting us to do something."

"Of course, sir. But what they'll be expecting first of all is an aerial reconnaissance. And there isn't going to be one. The next thing they'll expect is a mass ground reconnaissance with troops combing the forests, because they think we'll use our enormous superiority in numbers and our capacity to fly in any number of men. But we won't do that either, and so add to their confusion."

". . . and so add to their confusion," Hamilton repeated.

"Yes, sir," Allan rushed on, more and more confidently. "They will expect us to do all kinds of things and we won't do any of them. They'll be baffled; they'll have no idea of what's going on. In that kind of situation people become nervous and make mistakes."

"What kind of mistakes?"

"Well, they'll get the idea we're slow, so they'll feel safe and won't move camp. That way, we'll get on to their track sooner or later."

"They might just as easily get on to *our* track," Hamilton said, confident that Allan had not considered this.

"Not at all, sir; we have the advantage of knowing roughly where the enemy is. He knows nothing at all about us."

Hamilton was satisfied. He nodded and sipped his beer.

"Regular soldiers wouldn't be any good for this kind of thing, of course," said the gamewarden. "You need lynx-eyed men who are able to move about without making a sound. After all, their job will be to pick up tracks without being discovered themselves. Men from the forest, skilled since boyhood in the tracking down of wild animals, are the only ones who could do it. That means only the very best of the Alaskan Scouts, and Captain William told me the other day you had thought of using them yourself."

"That's right. I did think of them. But I still wonder if we'd find the right people, and be able to be absolutely certain they didn't give themselves away."

Again Allan found himself allaying the general's doubts. He felt himself in command of this problem.

"There are lots of things by which men betray their presence. Our sense of smell isn't up to much, but wild animals can pick up a scent from miles around and they move out in a hurry when there is something strange in the air. It's possible we might see them doing that and draw our conclusions. When a wild animal has been shot, there's always some offal left over. A fox will dig it up after it's been buried, and take it to his den. If you cross his track, you may find the hunter's track as well. When an animal has been killed, scavenger birds will hover over it; when it's been wounded, other animals will follow its trail. The presence of man will always be noticeable in some way or other; it's quite unavoidable."

"All right, so we'll use the scouts, but they'll have to have one or two competent regular soldiers along to give them a bit of backbone."

"No, they won't, sir; that'll only make things more difficult for them. The scouts know their way about and make a good team. Their principal job is finding people and they've traced hundreds of missing and injured men in the course of their existence. Let them do it by themselves, without the help of any soldiers."

The general poured more drinks, reflecting on the best direction to steer the conversation now. He was fully aware now of Allan's excitement.

"I agree, as far as the search itself is concerned. But if there's going to be any fighting, we'll need men with a lot of combat experience. Have any of your forest people got that?"

Allan could not think of one, and the general continued:

"Under fire, at the decisive moment, everything depends on the leader. He's got to have an iron nerve

70

and, above all, experience in such situations. When there's a bang out of the blue, he has to react like a well-oiled machine, get himself and his men behind cover and then lead a counter-attack. You know as well as I do, Allan, that there isn't a man like that in the scouts. We'll have to provide one."

"You've got someone I know about for sure. Captain William."

"Yes, I've got him," the general said with emphasis, "and there's no better man for the job in the whole of Alaska. You had some bother with him but that was on an administrative matter. William has sense and courage; he's the ideal man for a thing like this. He has proved himself often enough in the past."

Hamilton told Allan of the captain's astonishing exploits behind enemy lines: surprise raids in the jungle, daring reconnaissance patrols and sabotage of enemy ammunition dumps. The Japanese had hunted him through a tropical wilderness for a whole week, but he had returned with most of his patrol, even though he had been severely wounded and had lost an eye.

"Don't you think a man like that would make the most suitable leader for the scouts?"

"Sure, if there's going to be any shooting," Allan agreed. "But he'd have to adapt himself to them."

"Every man-jack of them will have to adapt to the others," the general said with more severity than he had shown before. "A good deal is at stake here."

Allan took the point and hoped the scouts would, too.

"I think it's the best solution, don't you?" Hamilton said, pressing home his advantage. "Of course the scouts don't need to worry that they're going to be ordered about. They'll have their own chief scout, to whom they'll be responsible, and he alone will be in charge of the search. Captain William will be guided by him. Only when there's any shooting will the captain be

71

in absolute command, no matter who starts it. I don't think we can make a more sensible arrangement, or can you think of one?"

Allan looked down at his toecaps and then at the other man.

"No, sir, I can't."

The moment had come. The general rose and went over to him. "Allan, you're a man with the hunting instinct. I can tell. I don't want you to make a decision that goes against the grain, but I am absolutely convinced that this job would fit you like a glove."

Allan got up too. He felt constricted in the armchair.

"Perhaps you're right. I'm beginning to believe it myself."

The general raised his glass to him.

"Delighted to make your acquaintance, Chief Scout McCluire."

15

The loveliest time of the year had begun—early autumn. No Japanese had ever seen such a glorious riot of strong and delicate shades in nature; it only existed in the wilds of Alaska. The spectrum ranged from the palest green of the poplars to the very deep dark green of the black pine. Snow white cotton-grass gleamed, and small, bright-yellow bells hung on the arctic broom. Willow-herb still bloomed and the mountain slopes were covered with dark crimson cranberries. Every breath one took was a delight; everything smelled of autumn and damp earth. Squirrels hopped right into the camp and crossbills perched in the branches above them.

The Japanese had now moved camp six times. There had been ideal flying weather, but the runway on Attu was still not finished, and everything depended on the arrival of the convoy. If only a part of his supplies arrived, Yamada expected to have his airfield ready in a few days' time.

"I hope the weather holds that long," Sergeant Tsunashima, the meteorological officer, said. "It will soon be time for the equinoctial gales, and then the barometer can plummet from one hour to the next. We'll have to radio twice a day then."

They were up in the mountains, covered by their camouflage net and waiting for the scheduled time of their transmission.

"No other country has heroes like Japan," Hidaka said. "My thoughts are often with those men who are going to fly our bombers deep into enemy country and who will never return. They will die but their heroic spirit will ascend to the gods."

All four Japanese remained silent as they contemplated such heroism. Only the Oshone did not understand. "The gentlemen not flying back?"

"No, Noboru," answered Hidaka. "The journey is much too long. They will drop their bombs on the Yankee cities and then they will smash their aircraft and themselves to pieces on the houses."

Noboru was incredulous.

"So, Japanese comrades must die, Hidaka-san?"

"They do not have to: they wish to. But first they will do enormous damage and all Japan will be proud of them; the whole world will ring with their names. This is what the Japanese are like, Noboru, they go to their deaths gladly for the good of their nation."

"What I don't understand is why the Yankees aren't doing anything about us," said Tsunashima.

"The longer they take, the more thorough their preparations will be, you may be sure of that," Hidaka said. "But I am surprised they have made no attempt to reconnoitre from the air ... It would have been the obvious thing to do."

"They probably think it won't do any good," remarked Watanabe.

"Perhaps they don't want to alert us. Make us think they don't know of our existence. But we won't fall for that. On the contrary. Omaé-tachi, we'll redouble our caution."

Sinobu, daring to intervene, said apologetically that he thought they were cautious enough already.

"So far we have been, Sinobu, that's true. But we'll have to move into different country now, at least thirty miles from here."

He looked at his watch again; the time was drawing close.

"Sinobu, start cranking."

Sinobu swung the handle and after only a few turns the little bulb glowed.

Hidaka looked at the second-hand of his watch. Watanabe had Tsunashima's message in code in front of him. Noboru extended the aerial so that it protruded from the camouflage net.

Hidaka began the countdown.

"Five, four, three, two, one, now."

The key-sender clicked faster than ever, and it took a bare six seconds to tap out the message. Now Watanabe was waiting for acknowledgment.

Instead, there was a relatively long message from Attu. The radio operator covered two pages of his notebook with the text. Watanabe confirmed that he had received it loud and clear and reached for his cipher book. Patiently and silently they sat round, watching him. Finally, he lifted his head.

"It's from Kaigun-Taisho himself, Taiji-dono. The admiral signed it." Importantly, he read out the message.

CONVOY ARRIVED PRACTICALLY NO LOSS-
ES STOP SEVEN SHINZANS PLANNED TAKE-
OFF IN SIX SEVEN DAYS STOP YAMADA
END MESSAGE

Hidaka threw down his forage cap.

"They've made it! They've made it at last!"

The others were beaming at each other.

"Pack everything up and wait for me here," he ordered. "I'm going further uphill to spy out the land for tomorrow. Noboru, come with me."

They travelled silently up a gully, almost completely filled with tangled undergrowth, and headed for the nearest peak. At the top they found a small plateau with a hollow in the middle where they had room to stretch out. There were cranberry bushes all round and Hidaka thrust his head through them in order to have a clear view.

He drew a quick sketch-map of the contours of the

northern slopes and made a few notes, lying on his stomach. There seemed to be a crevice in one of the massive, soaring slopes of the Brooks Range which led deep into the centre of the massif. It was worth noting against the eventuality that, one day, the whole patrol would have to vanish into the mountains. It was possible that the crevice went right across the range. He had just finished making notes, when Noboru's hand touched his.

"I think I hear flying-bird . . ."

The captain was alert at once. "Get further into the bushes, Noboru." Their bodies slid down flat among the reddish-brown plants.

"You hear, Hidaka-san?"

The captain shut his eyes and held his breath.

"Sounds more like an insect; it's too high-pitched for an engine."

They listened again. Hidaka could hear nothing now.

"Is flying-bird," Noboru insisted.

Hidaka knew that the Oshone's hearing was much more acute than that of any Japanese, and so he believed him.

"Where is it? Show me where."

Noboru pointed south.

"Flying-bird there, Hidaka-san."

If he was right the aircraft was coming in from the coast, from Anchorage. Both had raised their heads and were listening intently. The drone became a low buzz.

"Coming closer. Towards us."

Hidaka was quite certain now that the aircraft had two engines, perhaps even four. However, it seemed quite slow; perhaps a transporter.

"No more hear," the Oshone said. "Flying-bird quite still."

"It's touched down, Noboru, on a lake, perhaps."

"What flying-bird want to do there?"

76

"It's brought some Yankees to try and find us."

The Oshone suggested that they should go and kill them at once.

"For the time being, it's better to trick them than to kill them," said his captain.

16

Captain William and Chief Scout McCluire had agreed to make Lake Clifton the starting-point of their operation in the foothills of the Schwatka Mountains. They had decided to move all their men and equipment in one go, so as to reduce the danger of being spotted by the enemy. If the enemy heard the sound of aircraft engines once only, he might take it for a routine supply flight to the Arctic coast.

The lake was framed by larch forests. They had pitched their tents and stowed their baggage while the flying-boat was still on the water. They were going to have to leave most of the gear by the lake, taking only the bare essentials into the mountains with them. If need be, a couple of men could be sent down later to fetch additional supplies.

Allan McCluire had chosen twelve of the best men from among the large number of Alaskan Scouts who had volunteered, all of them keen and enthusiastic. This would be the first time they would look for men who would be doing everything they could to avoid being found, and also for the first time, they were going to meet with resistance, and fierce resistance at that.

The chief scout counted the crates and checked them against his list.

"They've sent half a hospital," he said to Slim Wortley. "I only hope you'll know what to do with it all."

Wortley was a final-year medical student. Allan had selected him, rather than a fully qualified doctor, because he had already proved himself on search parties looking for mountaineers on Mount McKinley.

"What else is left in the aircraft, Mr. McCluire?" William asked.

"Only the transmitter and the generator. They'd better stay in their crates."

Allan went over to lend a hand. The men had already taken the transmitter out and put it away inside a tent.

"Have we got everything now?" the captain asked.

Allan confirmed that they had, but William went aboard once more to make sure.

"We could do without that clumsy bastard," Charlie Stewart grumbled behind his back. "He looks at you sometimes as if you were dirt."

"We've all got our ways, Charlie; we'll just have to get used to him."

The pilot was ready for take-off. The four-bladed propellers began to spin. Up to their waists in cold water, the scouts helped to turn the flying-boat round, the slipstream blowing into their faces. The aircraft skimmed towards the northern shore of the lake, making a thunderous noise and leaving two glittering streaks behind in its wake. The fourteen men on the bank waved briefly, and the great grey bird disappeared over the forest.

Bert Hutchinson, a forty-year-old trapper and the oldest member of the patrol, came over and said, "The captain wants to speak to the whole lot of us."

Taking their time, they sauntered over to their commanding officer's tent. William saw them coming and stood a little straighter.

"Well, I've got news for you," he began, taking trouble to make his voice sound friendly. "The general didn't want it to be known before now, and in any case, he only heard yesterday himself."

He paused, to emphasize the importance of what he had to say.

"Come on, tell us what's up," Dick Hamston said impatiently. "We can take it, whatever it is."

The captain was taken aback at being spoken to in

79

such a way, but quickly said: "Well, the first thing you'll have to take is that we know now it's Japs up there."

"That's what I thought," Randall said, "Haven't I said so all along?"

"Who says it's Japs?" Mike Herrera never believed anything he had not seen with his own eyes.

"They don't just say it: they know it for a fact," William replied. "Somehow we've got hold of the Japs' naval code and we can read all their radio messages. We've decoded every single thing that's passed between Attu and the Schwatkas."

"How many of them are up there?"

"Probably ten or twelve men. We even know their commander's name. He's called Enzo Hidaka."

"Pleased to meet him," Randall said cheekily. "It'll be a pleasure."

"No, Randall, it won't be such a pleasure; he's a pretty exceptional fellow. Altogether I think it's a very efficient and dangerous crew we're up against."

"And what are the bastards up to?" Branson asked.

"They're a meteorological patrol and they've probably been parachuted in. Every day they send weather reports to Attu. The Japs want to launch a long-range squadron from there, but they're waiting to complete their big runway. They're at it night and day. If we don't manage to smash their transmitter, we'll have bombs raining down on America. At the moment, we're the only defence against it. It's in the Brooks Range that the weather for the whole of Alaska is cooked up. And even the Japs won't launch a valuable bomber squadron without knowing what the weather's going to do. That transmitter has got to be knocked out and we've got to do it."

His brief speech was well received. For the first time, the scouts were favourably impressed by their officer, who seemed to stick at nothing, or so it appeared from the long scar across his face and his glass eye.

"That's all I have to say. We start at half-past six in the morning."

The captain withdrew quickly into his tent. It was Allan McCluire who had been put in charge of search operations by the general himself. The scouts already knew that they would be operating in small groups. Allan explained once more why the enemy would have to keep to the tree-line. He suggested the best way to cover all the ground was to send two small search parties into every valley. The two parties would then meet at a predetermined spot at the top of the valley.

"How many days will that take, Allan?"

"We can't tell till we've had a look at the terrain. The routes aren't all the same length. But however long they are, we can cover four valleys simultaneously."

"How d'you work that out?" Hamston asked.

"It's simple enough, Dick. There are fourteen of us altogether. That's twelve men to cover three valleys, each with two groups of two men. Leaves one group of two men. Those two will make their way right through the whole of the easiest valley."

"What do you mean, the easiest valley?"

"The nearest. All the other groups will have to go some way before they reach their particular valleys. The best thing to do would be for the captain and me to cover the shortest route because then we'll probably be the first to get to the rendezvous. In the process, William can get some lessons on how people like us act in the field. After all, it's a bit different here from the jungle in the Philippines."

"So I've noticed, chief scout. I hope you won't be disappointed in your pupil's willingness to learn."

None of the scouts had noticed William come up behind them. Allan was not at all non-plussed; if anything, he was pleased that William had heard what he had been saying.

"Any questions?"

"Yes, I've got one," the captain said. "Why has it got to be groups of two, Mr. McCluire? If everyone was on his own, we could reconnoitre a much bigger area in the same amount of time."

"Well, our experience in these parts has shown that accidents, whether it's broken bones, concussion or wounds from falling stones, or being dragged away by river currents, invariably happen to one man only. His mate can then help him or get help. And if neither of them turns up at the rendezvous, we can assume they've both fallen into enemy hands."

William was convinced.

"I should like to emphasize once more, Mr. McCluire, that there must be no shooting. When we've discovered where the group is hidden, we'll wipe them out in one concerted action, all of us together. Until that moment, they must be kept in complete ignorance of our existence."

Allan felt embarrassed for the captain. It would never occur to any scout to draw attention to himself unnecessarily. Their self-conscious silence showed William how much he had underrated them. He changed his tone at once.

"I think your plan is excellent, chief scout. But I am worried about the transmitter. I hate being cut off from the outside world."

It was the one sore point between them; they had debated it at length in Richardson.

"Believe me, captain, the transmitter would be more trouble than it's worth. The men would have to take turns carrying it and the entire patrol's mobility would be gone."

"But we might need help one day."

"We'll manage on our own," Fortier threw in.

Allan insisted: "Please take my word for it. All an invisible line to the outside world like that does is to cramp initiative."

The scouts agreed unanimously.

"All right, then," the captain said. "Let's hope we won't have any reason to regret it afterwards."

17

"Taiji-dono, look at the birds up there."

Sergeant Suda pointed to a hummock in the valley above which two bald eagles were circling. It was unusual for eagles to be seen over the valleys; they usually kept to the heights, among the lemmings and the ptarmigan.

Hidaka ordered his men to take cover in the undergrowth and lay down himself to observe the birds through his field-glasses.

"They must have found something, but they don't seem to want to go in too close."

The eagles glided through the air effortlessly; their wings showed no noticeable movement. They flew in diminishing circles and gradually came down closer to the ground.

"There must be a dead animal there," the sergeant said.

The captain piled a few stones in front of him as support for his field-glasses. He was not as interested in the birds of prey as he was in what they might have discovered. If it were game, it must still be alive, or the eagles would have picked its body to pieces long ago.

He turned to his men. "Inaki, run down to the camp and get the telescope from Lieutenant Tojimoto."

The two birds seemed to pluck up courage. Their wings spread out like fans, they now flew down close to the green hump and hovered above it.

The lieutenant brought the telescope up himself, Inaki following with the tripod.

"I want to know what's going on down there, Yoshi," Hidaka said. "It could be a moose—perhaps it's been gored by its rivals in a fight."

Inaki spread the tripod and pressed it firmly into the

ground; the telescope's sixty-fold magnification required steady support. The field of vision was very small and it had to be sighted accurately like a rifle.

"There's pretty tall grass with bushes in between," Hidaka said.

He slid backwards and pulled his forage cap over his face to rest his eyes.

"One of the birds is swooping down, Enzo!"

When Hidaka looked again, the second eagle had joined the first.

"They're dragging something white out of the bush."

"It must be a Rocky Mountain goat or a bighorn," the lieutenant said. These were the only white animals in their part of Alaska.

"I must sce the head first. It's certainly dead."

Hidaka tensed suddenly: noticing this, his companions moved closer.

"Didn't anyone hear a shot?" he asked, to his men's astonishment.

"The wind is in the west," Kurakami ventured, "and it's strong enough to carry away any sound of a shot."

"It's been decapitated. There's no doubt about it, somebody killed it."

"You know that lynx sometimes bite off their prey's head and take it away with them," said the lieutenant.

"Yes, I know, Yoshi, but the eagles wouldn't have waited that long if that's what happened. They saw something unfamiliar. But what I can't understand is why a man should take away the head and leave the best part of his booty behind."

Suda and Tojimoto both brought out the answer at the same time: it must have been a trophy hunter and the animal must have had particularly impressive horns.

"Of course, he was after a trophy, I can see that myself. But it couldn't have been one of the Yankees that are after us. It would be sheer madness for them to fire off ammunition round here."

The only possible solution was that there must be a genuine sportsman in the valley who had brought his own food along with him and did not need any fresh meat.

Hidaka pooh-poohed this theory. "It's most unlikely. What would a trophy-hunter be doing in these parts? There are better hunting-grounds within easier reach."

Tojimoto suggested they go down and take a closer look. The tracks would tell whether the hunter had been alone.

"No, Yoshi, it might be a trap. We must get away from here, as soon and as far as possible."

They waited for darkness to fall before they rolled up their camouflage net and crept down to their camp in the faint starlight. Hidaka would not let them build a fire.

"We won't break camp till first light. We might cross the tracks in the dark without seeing them."

All traces were removed before they left. The débris of their evening meal was buried a good eighteen inches deep to prevent hungry foxes digging it up and revealing where they had been. Noboru straightened the bushes again and strewed leaves over what had been their camp. They marched cautiously on fallen timber, bare stones and along the gravel beds of dried-up rivers. Noboru brought up the rear. He was the most meticulous in the whole patrol about picking up leaves that had been torn off or wiping away soil which a boot might have deposited on the stones. He was a past master at this but he had to be given time to do his work. This meant that the patrol did not make as good progress as their commanding officer would have wished.

To begin with they walked along the edge of the forest. The valley was on their left, the mountain peak to their right. When the wind dropped, they could hear the rushing of the river. The further they walked, the quieter it became; the river was now a stream.

They entered an overgrown birch wood with hundreds of loose stones lying between the trees. The spring thaws brought tons of stones down every year. Progress was becoming increasingly difficult. The springy branches had to be held to one side with every step, and as soon as they had passed by, would snap back again, catching on the men's packs which had then to be disentangled before they could move on.

Towards noon, it became lighter in the grey-green wilderness; the wood had come to an end. Hidaka parted the last branches and pointed out to the patrol their destination at the foot of the bare mountain which he had discovered some days ago through his field-glasses. In front of them was open country as far as the base of the sheer cliff walls. The white peaks above were shrouded in constantly shifting cloud. Hidaka looked at them with satisfaction.

"It couldn't be better. It looks as if the clouds will be coming down to shield us. We'll climb up to that ledge there, the one that looks like a dog's head. It'll be high enough to radio from, and tomorrow morning we'll go under the wall of the cliff into the next valley and disappear into the forest again."

Tsunashima could tell from his barometer that this period of fine, clear autumn days was now over. The clouds would admittedly be very useful for covering their march. But when Yamada's airfield was ready they would need clear weather again.

When the grey swathes of cloud were low enough, the Japanese moved off again. Progress was now much easier, through knee-high shrub.

"Don't lift up your feet," Hidaka said, "and make sure you don't tread on any plants. Push them aside with your boots."

He showed his men how to do it. Because no stem had been snapped or bent right over, the plants sprang back up in place straight away, and the patrol marched in fan formation so as not to touch any tuft more than once. It was remarkably effective. A few moments after the eleven heavily-laden men had passed through, no trace of them remained.

After a while, there were no more plants or grass; with fog swirling about them, they walked over soft cushions of moss. Hidaka ordered them not to step on protruding rocks, so that any particles of moss stuck to their boots should not be transferred. By early afternoon, they had reached the dog's-head ledge.

Captain Hidaka ordered the men to pitch the tents and told Tojimoto to let no one break cover until darkness fell. They had no food yet for the following day but nobody was worried. Cranberries covered nearly every slope in great profusion.

As there were no mountains to the south-west to interfere with their transmission, they could operate the transmitter from quite close to their camp that day.

"The barometer is down and the humidity is up," said Tsunashima, the meteorologist, "but I think the depression will pass. If there were going to be a serious break in the weather, I would get more dramatic readings."

The captain was not so confident. "Experience elsewhere is irrelevant here, Tsunashima. This is where the worst weather in the world is cooked up."

Kurakami had already encoded the message and was trying hard to make radio contact. It took longer than usual; there seemed to be a thunderstorm over the Aleutians and reception was poor.

Attu had a message for them today, too. Kurakami listened intently and had to ask for it to be repeated several times. While Lonti cranked the machinery, the captain held the radio operator's notebooks for him, so that the wind would not blow over the pages.

"Let's get back to camp. We'll do the decoding there," Hidaka said after the last signal had come through.

Parts of the message were mutilated and it was not easy to decode. But Kurakami finally managed to fill in the gaps.

"Good news, Taiji-dono!" he said.

The captain quickly looked through the decoded message and then read it out:

THREE SHINZAN SQUADRONS STANDING BY HERE STOP IF WEATHER CONDITIONS FAVOURABLE FIRST ATTACK POSSIBLE IN FORTY-EIGHT HOURS STOP HENCEFORTH EXPECT TWICE DAILY WEATHER REPORTS STOP YAMADA END MESSAGE

Hidaka heaved a sigh of relief. At last the war was being brought to the enemy's own country.

18

Captain William and Allan McCluire were the first to reach the scouts' rendezvous. They had got on well together. William still needed to become more used to walking along the smooth pebbles of river-beds and had fallen several times, but had never asked for a rest. They now looked for a sheltered place to make camp.

The river, whose course they had been following for the past two nights, had narrowed into a raging torrent. A mass of melted snow was rushing from higher up into the mossy green chasm below them. A cloud of spume lay over the water.

"It's pretty wet," the captain said, "but we can afford to make a fire. The spray will absorb all the smoke."

Allan agreed.

"We can roll up a few rocks and plug the gaps between them with moss, to hide the fire."

They dropped their packs onto the ground and set to work, forming a semi-circle of stones quite soon that shielded the flames adequately. When the fire had caught, William took dried egg, flour and fat out of his haversack to make pancakes.

"Shouldn't we save that, Frank? I'm sure we could get a few fish."

"What, as high up as this?"

"Sure, there's lots of salmon up here."

Allan took out a soft, tuber-like plant from his pocket.

"What's that?"

"It's the root of the monk's hood, pretty poisonous but a boon to a hungry ranger all the same. You crush it and throw the pieces into the nearest pool. All the fish within a radius of ten to twenty yards are paralysed and come to the surface; they float as if they were dead. But the poison doesn't do any harm; the fish are still good to eat."

They pulled their packs up to the fire and started to undo them. Allan had worked out what each should contain after asking the men and taking their varied experiences into account. Everyone had a short axe and a hunting-knife; every third man carried a field spade. Each scout had three hand-grenades dangling from his belt. Their waterproof sleeping-bags were filled with the lightest down, which kept them warm however cold it was outside. Each man had his own tent and could camp alone if necessary. The tents, however, were so narrow that there was room only for the man himself, his rifle and his pack.

The scouts had brought their own rifles with telescopic lenses. It had taken a good deal of effort on William's part to persuade them to take along four sub-machine guns. They did not think much of these unfamiliar weapons: their range was small and the spread of fire too wide.

Each scout had his own binoculars and stormproof matches in a water-tight tin. In addition to the army mess tin, he had his own frying-pan, without which no ranger ventures into the wilds. Most of them carried a roll of fine wire to make the snares and traps they would be using, and also carried fishing-gear and light fishing-nets.

They had sewing implements with them and some of them had even taken cobblers' awls and linen thread to resole their boots, if necessary. Oilskins and sou'westers were part of their normal equipment as well as fur hats and a good many woollen garments for the cold nights. Their iron rations, packed in aluminum containers, consisted of raisins, lard and dried meat, weighing ten pounds altogether, and for use in emergency only.

"The lighter we travel," Allan said to William by the fire, "the better. The enemy has got to lug his transmitter along wherever he goes and we haven't. Nobody who would have had to carry a load like that would have thanked you for it."

William shrugged.

"Maybe. But I'm not used to operating without some line of communication open to base."

Allan suddenly sprang up and reached for his rifle. He had not actually seen or heard anything; he had just sensed that there were people near. A moment later Jeff Pembroke and Mike Herrera walked into the camp.

"We're just in time for supper, are we?" one of them said.

They threw down their packs and sat down by the fire. They both looked exhausted. Allan passed them the frying pan with the first pancake.

"First get your strength back, then make your report."

"There's nothing to report; absolutely nothing."

William said that a negative report was valuable, too. If the Japs were not in that valley, then they had to be in another.

Next morning, Stewart and Fortier arrived, with Will Branson and Slim Wortley following soon after. Towards lunchtime only Hutchinson and Ted Miller were missing. Nobody had found any tracks.

"We've only been here four days, after all," Allan said reassuringly. "We can't expect to pick up the track that fast. If we haven't got anywhere after four weeks, then we can start to worry."

He took Herrera with him to help him catch the salmon. They did not find a pool but there was a small backwater of a stream. Allan crushed the root in his hand and scattered the pieces over the water.

"Go to the other end, Mike, so they can't get away."

Herrera took a twig and beat the water with it. The salmon were swimming desperately in circles and after only a few minutes they surfaced. Their fins seemed to weaken and soon stopped moving altogether.

"O.K., Mike, let's bring in the harvest."

They were able to gather up their catch in their hands. The stunned fish appeared to be dead. They collected enough to feed them all for one day.

Shortly before they got back to camp, they met Miller and Hutchinson, who were sauntering along as if they hadn't a care in the world.

"Look what I've got," said Hutchinson with a cheerful grin.

He turned round so that they could see the head of the Rocky Mountain goat he had tied to the pack on his back.

"What d'you say, Allan; have you ever feasted your eyes on anything like it?"

Its horns were unique; their size and spread were quite fantastic.

"Magnificent," Allan agreed. "Where did you find it?"

"Where did I find it? You must be joking. I don't go round just finding horns. There's no sport in that!"

The chief scout was horrified.

"You didn't shoot it, did you?"

"Well, of course I did."

"He wouldn't be stopped," Ted Miller said.

"You must be out of your mind, Bert. You were expressly ordered not to shoot unless there were compelling reasons to do so."

"Listen to me, Allan. What hunter could let an animal like that get away? I would have dropped dead on the spot if I had done that. So it was a matter of life and death. And when it's a matter of life and death, we were told we could shoot."

"Let Allan have a word with William first, Bert."

"I don't need anyone to put in a good word for me."

But Allan had already gone.

The captain was sitting by the fire, tin mug in hand, and surrounded by scouts.

"Miller and Hutchinson have arrived, Frank, but I want to tell you something first."

William stood up and joined Allan.

"I wanted to ask you, Frank, to do no more than reprimand Hutchinson just this once. He was carried away by hunting fever."

Allan told him the whole story and just then Hutchinson came up with a crowd of men around him. William could see for himself what he had brought along.

"Just take a dekko at that," Hutchinson boasted to his friends, so loudly that the captain could not help hearing.

"Let him cool off first, Frank, then he'll see how stupid he's been," Allan said, but William was already walking up to the culprit.

"Scout Hutchinson," he said in so cutting a voice that everyone fell silent. "In ordinary circumstances you would be court-martialled. Your lack of discipline has endangered the entire operation."

He walked to the centre of the little crowd of silent scouts.

"Each one of you is in the Army now. The enemy may be anywhere. If anyone else reveals our position to the enemy, I'll shoot him down on the spot."

Nobody knew if he really meant it. But the cold scorn with which he had spoken silenced any protest. With the eyes of the scouts following him, he picked up the trophy, took it to the waterfall and tossed it far into the rushing waters.

19

Captain Hidaka wondered whether he dared pitch camp so close to the river. But he had to get enough food in to last several days. The barometer continued to rise and on Attu the bombers were standing by. If the weather improved enough for them to start on their mission, then reports would have to go out every few hours. The slightest change would have to be reported, especially once the squadron had taken off. It therefore seemed best for the weather patrol to find a suitable spot and stay there for the next few days.

"I've never seen so many fish in a mountain stream," he said to Tojimoto. "Just the spot to get enough food in for a whole week. Then we'll move to the next valley and look for a good place to hide. During the crucial period, we can leave the transmitter up in the mountains while we camp down in the forest."

"I am afraid it will take us far too long to catch enough salmon," Lieutenant Yoshi said. "We should have brought a net, Enzo."

"We can use the camouflage net. Then it'll only take a few hours and we'll smoke the fish straight away over a good fire."

That afternoon they made preparations for their great fishing expedition. Hidaka made the men dig a trench, and build a grill of green willow twigs over it. Dry branches were brought up for the fire. Inaki and Inoué came from a fishing village and knew all about nets. They were put in charge of river operations and Sinobu and the Oshone were detailed to bring the catch back to camp.

"Ten or twelve pounds per man ought to be enough," Hidaka said.

"We won't have to forage for a whole week. We'll

wrap the salmon up in leaves and twigs, and tie the bundles to our packs."

Sergeant Tsunashima seemed particularly happy about the captain's plans. The more readings he could take and the more often he could report, the less the danger of Attu not being warned in time of sudden changes in the weather.

20

Early winter had arrived overnight, raw, and with a biting wind. The clouds swirled together and drew apart, squirrels and chipmunks bustled about filling their larders. Whistling swans and grey geese, cranes and wild duck began to fly south in formation. Golden needles rained down in the larch woods, the cloudberries turned yellow and the cranberries darker red. Black bears browsed on the slopes, now rich in a variety of sweet berries. The grizzlies made their way to the nearest river, and gave themselves up to the joys of fishing.

The scouts had made camp in a copse of aspen and mountain-ash; it was like an island, surrounded by scree. Nobody could approach without being spotted, and William had decided that they would spend the day resting.

After their fruitless search of the first few valleys, they had decided on a new move, this time in the opposite direction, from the foot of the Brooks Range through another network of valleys and back again to Lake Clifton.

Most of the scouts used the time for sleeping; others were busy putting their equipment in order. There was no fire because the wind was blowing down the valley and the smoke might have reached the lurking Japanese.

"How is Hutchinson?" William asked. "Has he calmed down yet?"

Allan was not sure.

"He's hardly said a word since the incident, and he's been keeping himself to himself. It had quite an effect on him."

"It's ridiculous, Allan, we need every man ... we can't afford any sulks at this stage of the game."

The chief scout was aware of that but was worried about Hutchinson.

"Bert's always been his own master, he's worked as a trapper for years, completely on his own; that makes a man very independent."

"What would you have done in my place, Allan?"

"Exactly the same, Frank."

Harry Chiefson wandered towards them and sat down without ceremony between them. "Boss, how about a little walk tonight? The salmon are rising, and now is a good time to go fishing."

"We've got enough to eat, Harry. If we need salmon later, we'll get it then."

"It's easiest to get it from the river in the valley," the Indian persisted, "and you can spread a net in the dark."

"Yes, Harry, we'll do it, but some other day."

"I'm not talking about us, boss, I mean the Japs."

"Looking for the enemy when it's pitch black," William said doubtfully. "I wouldn't think much of our chances."

"But it might work, Frank, and it's not a bad idea, at that. We know how crazy the Japs are about fresh fish. Their camp's in the forest, they'll come creeping down through the woods and make for the river. They wouldn't let the chance go by!" said Allan. He had made up his mind to take Harry's advice.

"You might blunder right into them. What then?"

Harry made a face. "We won't blunder anywhere, Mister. We'll see them before they see us."

William was still not keen.

"The search is your business, Allan, but I'd be a bit worried."

"We're not, Frank, and there's just a chance we'll find something."

"Perhaps you're right," the captain said. "We're going to have to take some risks sooner or later."

Allan waited for dusk, and then set off with Harry. They crossed the scree, ploughed their way through the bush and reached the edge of the forest. They found a small gravel gully, and climbed down. It was dark now, and they had to step with great care. They had cut themselves long sticks and used them to feel their way forward.

A grey owl screeched in the forest and small animals scurried by. Somewhere they could hear something heavier pounding through the thickets; it was probably a moose that had caught their scent. Allan and the Indian stopped in their tracks; animals fleeing through the night might easily alert the enemy.

When they reached the torrent, they stepped into the gurgling water and made their way downstream, still using their sticks. The water came straight from a glacier and was numbingly cold. They managed to stop their legs from becoming completely frozen by keeping on the move at a steady pace. However, wading through the stream did have its advantages. Its gurgling drowned the noise they could not help making, and floating logs and branches were trapped by boulders in the stream and freed again by the current, covering the movements of the two men.

After hours of painful groping the stream narrowed, and the current grew so strong that they found it hard to keep their balance. Allan could actually feel the violent thrashing of the fish fighting their way upstream. Their slippery bodies brushed past his knees as they hurled themselves out of the water to leap over the rocks barring their way. In a brief moment of moonlight, the salmon resembled nothing so much as silvery flying saucers.

It became impossible to fight the water any longer.

"There's nothing for it, Harry, we'll have to get out and walk along the bank."

They pulled themselves up by overhanging bushes, and felt the soft ground of the forest underfoot again.

"We'll leave tracks, boss," the Indian shouted above the noise of the water.

"We'll take our boots off, then they won't be so obvious."

They were wearing two pairs of thick socks because of the cold, and Allan stuffed some leaves between his to give his footprints a large and indistinct appearance.

"You do it too, Harry. Someone who has never seen real bear tracks might take us for bear cubs!"

The going was very slow now. Often they were forced to bend double under low-lying branches and most of the time they scrambled over slippery, moss-covered rocks. The slings of their rifles caught on the trees and their hands hurt from their continual contact with rough wood.

Allan straightened up by the trunk of an old black fir tree, and pulled the Indian to his side.

"Stand still a minute, Harry!"

He turned towards the forest and sniffed the air. The Indian too took a deep breath through his nose.

"Is that smoke . . . or am I just imagining it?" Allan whispered at last.

"Yes, boss, I think it is."

"I'm not a hundred per cent certain yet; we've got to make absolutely sure."

A few yards farther on they came upon another stream roaring down out of the forest, falling steeply to join the river. The smoke could now be smelled clearly. It occurred to Allan that the enemy must have travelled along this very mountain stream to hide their traces on the way down to the river. In that case, their camp would be in the forest higher up, and it was only because of the damp air that the smoke had drifted down to them.

"They can't be far away," the Indian whispered. "You can even smell the fish they're cooking."

"I expect they're smoking salmon."

Harry touched his arm. "Boss, let me go and creep up on them . . . I'd like to get a good look and see what they're like."

Allan grasped his arm. "Are you mad? If they notice anything, we'll have messed up our chances for good!"

The Indian felt sure he could steal up undetected, but he was used to taking orders, and the two men slipped back without a sound, unable to reconnoitre further.

"And the captain didn't want to let us go!" the Indian said after a while.

"Well, it was an extraordinary piece of luck, finding them tonight. What gave you the idea, out of the blue, like that?"

"Just a hunch, boss. I felt something would be up."

They had found one end of the thread that led to the needle in the haystack, but they would need much cunning to turn it to advantage, much more cunning than the enemy.

21

The scouts were making good progress. To judge from Allan's report, the enemy was planning to leave the area, and everything depended on keeping up with him.

"We have the advantage," the chief scout told them. "All we need to do is keep a good look-out ahead; it doesn't matter about leaving tracks now. The Japs are on the move and we're after them."

The scouts made good use of the flat ground along the valley floor. They were in high spirits; the quarry had been found and the search had become a chase. They quickly reached the narrow part of the river where Allan and Harry thought the enemy had smoked fish. Where just a few hours before ten or twelve men must have camped, there now seemed no trace of their presence. Loose foliage covered the ground, and the surrounding bushes appeared undisturbed.

At first the captain was not convinced that the Japanese had in fact been there, but Harry Chiefson pointed out the slight traces that remained. Here, a small patch of leaves was lying damp side up, the dry side against the ground, and there, where branches had overhung the camp-fire, the bark had burst open with the heat.

"Can you tell which way they went, Allan?" William asked.

"No, but if I were Captain Hidaka, I would keep to the stream."

So they followed it through the forest, as it gurgled over boulders and fallen tree trunks. Higher up, where the stunted Alaskan willows began and the stream became very narrow, Allan warned them all to be very careful.

"From here on, our friends will have begun to look for a safe spot to leave the stream."

"How about that landslip over there?" Randall suggested.

The spring floods had eroded the soil from a broad stretch of the bank and laid bare the gravel beneath, which had been washed clean by the rain until the pebbles shone. The scouts spread out along the stream and started examining the stones near the edge. If any had been trodden on, they would lie lower in the ground than the rest.

Harry Chiefson was the first to find a clue. Blood and tiny fragments of flesh were stuck to the bottom of a large pebble.

"Squashed worm, boss. Happened this morning."

A moment later Will Branson found a round leaf crumpled on a stone.

"Winter cress," Allan explained. "It only grows in the shade and damp. Someone carried it here on his boots."

There was no doubt that the enemy had crossed the stretch of gravel. Reaching the top of the bank, the scouts stopped and scanned the slope on the other side. Practice and long experience enabled them to pick out a very faint line in the coarse sedge, no more than a shadow, made by the boots of men treading very carefully.

In common with all the valleys in the Schwatkas, this one too had a wide belt of willow, alder and dwarf-birch thickets between the forest and the bare slopes. There the scouts took cover, well concealed among the light, yellowy-green trees. The farther they went, the more careful they had to be, taking care at every step not to snap dry twigs underfoot. The chief scout went first, Dick Hamston keeping a look-out above them and Harry Chiefson below. The rest of the men followed in single file, with the captain bringing up the rear.

Allan heard the call of a nutcracker and stopped, bringing the column to a halt behind him. The call came again, and Allan answered with that of the female. Dick Hamston approached silently through the brushwood. "I've got on to their tracks again," he whispered. "They've gone up the bed of a dried-up stream."

A robin had betrayed the enemy's route to him. It had been pecking so busily between the stones that Dick had taken a close look and discovered a tiny piece of smoked salmon no bigger than a crumb.

As they went on, the slope levelled off. The bed of the stream began to fill with water and marshy ground took the place of gravel. The bootmarks left by the Japanese were clearly visible now.

When they reached the edge of the black pines, the chief scout called a halt.

"It could be they're camping quite near. Harry and I'll go ahead."

William suggested he go along too, but was turned down.

"Sorry, Frank, but this is strictly a scout affair."

There was nothing the captain could do about it, so he posted men to keep a look-out and gave the rest of the scouts permission to rest. Allan and Harry vanished into the forest.

The black pines crowded so closely together that no sunshine could penetrate the gloom. It was damp and mouldy under their feet and thick fern grew chest-high, but the ground was level.

They had gone about half a mile into the forest when they saw a glimmer of light through the trees. They moved soundlessly forward, and saw a clearing with a pool surrounded by reeds in the middle.

The two men stayed hidden behind the friendly cover of the bushes. Nothing disturbed the midday stillness except a few wild duck quacking in the reeds. It would make an ideal place for the men to camp that night. If they put enough snares in among the reeds, they would have at least a dozen duck by morning. Watching them, Allan noticed that they seemed to favour certain places. And suddenly he noticed something else.

"One's been caught already, Harry!"

"What do you mean? What with?"

"It looks as if it's in a snare ... it's flapping about like mad but it can't get free."

"A snare, boss? Can you see it?"

"No. I can't see the duck either, but I can see the movements in the reeds and I can hear it flapping."

The Japanese were already well provisioned, as Allan knew. If they had put snares in the pond here all the same, it must have been because doing it cost them neither time nor trouble. Their camp must be very close indeed.

However, everything lay in complete silence around the pool. The two scouts examined every blade of grass they could through their field-glasses to see if any had been broken off. But nothing betrayed the presence of strangers.

"They must be there, Harry; that duck didn't get snared of its own accord."

Suddenly Harry's head went down, and he pressed his body closely to the ground. Allan followed his example instinctively. The Indian inched his way towards the chief scout until he lay beside him with his mouth against the other's ear.

"Over there ... a man standing ... other side ... behind the reeds."

It must be the man who had set the snare. Allan raised his head, infinitely slowly. On the other side of the pond he saw the back of a man bending low in the reeds to pick up his catch. He wore a brown Japanese forage cap with a wide peak to shield his eyes against the sun.

He killed the duck, very expertly and without making a sound. As he straightened up, they could see through their binoculars his broad, reddish-brown face with its hooded, almond-shaped eyes. He looked like an Indian, Allan thought, or perhaps an Eskimo in strange disguise.

After a little while the man waded into a marshy part of the pool and made for a flat rock which jutted out into the water. When he had reached it, he pulled himself up and disappeared, creeping through the fern. Beyond, there was a dense, dark copse of spruce. If Allan had had to choose a camping-site for his scouts by the pool, that would have been the very spot.

"Still," he said to Harry on their way back, "this Hidaka can't be as clever as I thought."

Harry agreed.

"How could he be so careless, letting someone leave their hide-out in broad daylight just to catch a duck!"

22

Hidaka did not, in fact, deserve Harry Chiefson's stricture. At the time Lonti was setting his snare, the captain was up at the top of the ridge looking for a good place to camp with the transmitter for the next few days. Tsunashima, the meteorologist, and Kurakami, the radio operator, were with him, as well as Sinobu and Noboru to help carry their gear. Only about half the patrol had stayed by the pool with Tojimoto. The lieutenant had had strict instructions to maintain complete silence, not to light a fire, and to avoid leaving the slightest trace of their presence around the camp. When Lonti asked permission to set some snares in the reeds, it did not seem to run counter to Hidaka's orders. It would make no noise and would leave no trace.

The captain planned to stay up in the mountains until the first bomber mission to the south had been completed. The range consisted of a rocky ridge with deep fissures and sharp escarpments, and they were forced to do a most strenuous climb. Hidaka was very particular and looked around for a long time before he found a suitable spot for a stay of some days.

Beneath some beetling cliffs was a dry place concealed on all sides by scree and bushes. In a hollow below there was a natural reservoir of rain water, so they would not have to rely solely on the contents of their water-bottles. The transmitter and its operators could all be concealed at the base of the cliff, and only the telescopic aerial need be exposed.

Tsunashima waited until shortly before six o'clock to take his readings so that he could give Attu a completely up-to-date weather report.

"It couldn't be better, Taiji-dono; the west wind has

died down, and the ground is as dry as in mid-summer."

Hidaka was pleased. "If it keeps up like this, Kimitachi, we will have a great day tomorrow."

Again the cranking-handle was swung and the little light on the transmitter glowed. Hidaka squatted down beside the operator and watched as he tapped out the weather report.

They could see Kurakami's tense expression when the radio station on Attu replied. He was receiving three short identical signals only.

"T . . . T . . . T . . ." the operator repeated. "I don't understand, Taiji-dono."

"But I do," Hidaka said with a smile. He and Tojimoto were the only ones to know what this secret signal meant. If the weather held, the Shinzans would take off within twenty-four hours.

23

The scouts huddled close together so as not to miss a word of Allan's report.

"We'll wipe them out!" Jim O'Hara said excitedly. "They won't know what's hit them!" He had leapt to his feet, almost beside himself in his eagerness. The general excitement was so intense that it was all Allan could do to calm them down.

"Shut up, now," the captain said authoritatively. "Let him have his say."

"The Japs aren't caught yet," Allan reminded them, "and remember, they'll have posted look-outs. If we can, we must strike while their forces are divided. Do you agree, Frank?"

"Of course. That's only basic tactics."

"Right, then, we'll tail the radio section first, when it goes up the mountain in the afternoon to send its weather report. They are sure to follow the stream again, so we can't miss them; they'll walk right into our arms. If fourteen men suddenly jump out of the bushes at them, those little yellow Nips will just have to put their hands up!"

"Japanese never surrender," the captain said. "It's against their code of honour."

"Well then, it'll be their fault if we cut them into little pieces," said Hank Fortier with determination, but Allan ignored him.

"The radio section will have the transmitter with them, that's for sure," he went on, "and that's got to be knocked out first."

"I'm with you completely," said the captain. "Our main job is to stop those weather reports." He looked at his watch. "Quarter-past three. Our friends will set off between four and five."

The attack was planned with meticulous care. The best place for the ambush would be along the river-bed where the enemy would have to clamber over the rocks on all fours, and the scouts deployed themselves in a semi-circle twenty yards from the spot, out of sight behind bushes and boulders. If the Japanese put up a fight they would be caught in the cross-fire of fourteen rifles.

By four o'clock their preparations were complete. Rifles cocked and straining every nerve, the fourteen waited for the enemy to appear. They waited for half-an-hour, an hour, an hour-and-a-half. The sun was sinking, twilight fell, and the normal transmission time was now long past.

Frustrated and angry that the Japanese had dashed their hopes by failing to make an appearance, the scouts retreated into the willows to camp for the night.

"If the bastards don't feel like transmitting tonight, there's nothing we can do about it," Jeff Pembroke said.

"No, Jeff," the captain told him, "the whole object of the exercise is that they must radio weather reports daily; that's all they're here for. We can only assume that they took another route up. We acted on false assumptions today, but tomorrow we shall rely on the only thing we're sure of."

"What's that?"

"We know where their camp is."

It was now so dark that they could not make out each other's features. They moved up close to each other to keep warm.

"We'll attack them in their camp tomorrow and take the whole lot of them by surprise, in one fell swoop."

"Why not tonight, captain?"

"You've got to be able to see them; I don't hold with creeping around in the dark."

The chief scout disagreed.

"Wouldn't it be better, Frank, if we followed them as soon as they make a move, try to overtake them and then lie in wait for them somewhere well camouflaged?"

Bert Hutchinson, who had not spoken for a long time, suddenly exploded.

"For God's sake, Allan, shut up with all your clever tricks. Let's go and get them!"

He seemed to reflect the general mood of the men, whose patience had been exhausted by the disappointments of the long afternoon.

"Bert's right. I'm beginning to feel ashamed of myself," Randall said to the chief scout. "Anybody'd think we're a bunch of cowards."

Allan could not argue. His plans had misfired today, and his companions were determined to prove their mettle. Their anger had been roused, as had the captain's.

Allan reminded them of the sentries; there would be at least two look-outs constantly patrolling the perimeter of the camp.

"All the better," said the captain. "What moves can be heard. The look-out men will have to be dispatched with a knife in their backs. Who'll see to that?"

Harry Chiefson volunteered.

"I can throw a knife, captain, and hit a dollar piece at ten yards."

"Better to jump him from behind, Harry. Do you think you can do it?"

"I could do it to the biggest grizzly there is, if I had to."

The captain took him at his word, and Harry beamed with pleasure and pride.

"Don't show off like that," Allan said severely. "You've never stabbed a man in your life."

"I'll polish the Jap off, boss, you wait and see!"

William was satisfied; his only concern was to have the sentries eliminated without a sound.

"Allan, will you take care of the other one?"

"No. I'm not trained for that sort of thing."

He would have added that he regarded it as murder, but he did not want to offend anyone who might be prepared to do it. Branson, Stewart and Herrera volunteered. Herrera was chosen because he was a judo expert. Although he had never practised with a knife, he knew all the holds.

24

Enzo Hidaka had awoken before daybreak and watched the rise of the red, glowing sun, the symbol of his nation. Dawn, the moment the sun rose majestically on the horizon and heralded the glory of early morning, was a time of consecration and spiritual renewal to the Japanese.

"Amateras will be with us; a day of victory has begun." Sergeant Tsunashima stood reverently to attention for a minute, and then, remembering his more immediate duties, began to take readings from his instruments. The captain noted down the figures.

"Wind direction: 45° E.; speed: 4 knots; air pressure: 1.012; temperature: 6° C.; sky cloudless; outlook settled."

Kurakami put the information into code while Sinobu began turning the cranking-handle.

Contact with Attu was established immediately, and the report transmitted at 0815 hours precisely. The radio patrol waited in growing excitement for Yamada's answer.

Again three identical symbols came back.

"X ... X ... X ... What does it mean, Taiji-dono?"

The captain was so moved that he had to swallow hard before answering.

"Our comrades are in the air, Kimi-tachi. Our great day has begun."

Leaping to their feet, they threw their caps high in the air.

"Banzai . . . banzai . . . banzai!"

Then, as was the custom, they turned in the direction of the Emperor's palace and bowed low.

"They'll be overhead in about four hours," Hidaka calculated.

"It could be longer than that, Taiji-dono, the wind is against them."

"I thought conditions were ideal?"

"Almost ideal ... unless a depression follows after the wind."

"And do you think one will?"

"Not really, the glass is too high."

Nevertheless, Hidaka insisted that he take repeat readings constantly.

The captain had lifted the camouflage net over their hideout in the rocks just enough to enable him to look down the hillside through a gap in the bushes. About five hundred yards below the belt of willow trees began, and below that the forest itself.

"Down there they don't even know that our birds are on the wing," Kurakami mused.

They sat in silence, each thinking of the bombing mission. By next morning the news of the devastation would be echoing round the world.

"Taiji-dono, the glass has fallen a little. The clouds over the Brooks are strato-cumuli now, and that's usually a sign of change."

But the light, peaceful-looking little clouds which Hidaka could see floating high and far away on the clear horizon appeared so harmless that he did not worry.

"Radio the new readings," he ordered, "though I don't think they'll have any effect on the admiral."

"Neither do I, Taiji-dono, things would have to get a lot worse before they did."

While Tsunashima went to work with the radio operator, and Sinobu turned the cranking-handle, the captain looked down the hill once more, hoping to spot some moose. Suddenly he gave a start. Just at the place where he knew the pool to lie in the middle of the clearing, a few dozen wild duck were flying over the trees. No fox or lynx would go hunting in broad daylight; only strangers could have scared the birds away.

"Be prepared to fire!" Hidaka hissed. "There are men down by the pool."

The three men round the transmitter were so preoccupied with their work that they did not at first understand what Hidaka was saying. But the look on their commander's face jerked them into action as their training and experience came back to them. Hidaka ordered them to pull in the aerial and to replace the camouflage net in front of their hide-out.

"Has the transmission gone out?"

"Yes, it's just been acknowledged."

They hurried over the boulders to the grassy slope, worked their way across it on their stomachs so as to gain maximum cover, and then slipped and tumbled down to the willows. They raced through the trees to the alders, from the alders to the twilight of the black pines, and began thrusting through the mass of soft, damp fern which reached up to their chests.

"Careful now," Hidaka whispered. "Get your grenades out and safety catches off!"

He caught sight of a glimmer from the clearing and thought he could see someone moving. It might be one of his own men . . . they had to make sure.

"Much quieter," Hidaka hissed, "and get further under cover! We mustn't be seen."

But caution had ceased to be necessary.

Sudden explosions rent the air, and rifle fire tore through the trees. There were screams, yells, curt shouts of command, and the sounds of clashing metal, splintering wood, heavy running and loud groans.

The three men around their leader immediately started in the direction of the mêlée. Hidaka held them back.

"It's too late now! Spread out fan-wise!"

115

It was not easy to channel the overwhelming urge to save their comrades as quickly as possible into a silent hunt of the attackers, but there was no alternative if they were to have a chance of turning the tables on them. Hidaka hurried ahead. He could only hope that the enemy now had more to do than to listen for the snapping of dry branches and the rustling of leaves.

They were tramping now through mud, high reeds barring their way ahead.

"Left round the pool," the captain panted. "Keep close behind me."

His men crawled through the undergrowth, pulling themselves along by roots and branches. A clod of rock-hard earth rolled noisily down the slope, the barrel of a gun clanked against a stone. But nobody noticed down below, where the sound of curses and shouts could still be heard. Hidaka assumed that they were looking for the transmitter and could not find it.

The four Japanese wriggled snake-like through the bushes and carefully approached the camp. Hidaka flattened himself against the trunk of a pine tree, his men pressing close behind.

The Yankees were still searching. They had separated into groups and were apparently preparing to search outside the camp-site. Hidaka and his men would be discovered at any moment.

Hidaka leapt out.

"*Sah . . . hajimero!*" he yelled and hurled a grenade into the middle of the camp.

A split second later his men followed him; grenades spiralled through the air, rifle-shots rang out. Fountains of mud spurted up and broken branches fell to the ground. Hidaka stumbled and was blinded; he heard men shouting around him. Boots trampled through the undergrowth; there were three, four more single shots, then everything was still.

Hidaka wiped the mud from his face and could see again. Tojimoto helped him to his feet.

"Are you hit?"

"I don't think so, Yoshi . . . did we make it?"

"The Yankees have fled . . . they're running like rabbits."

"What are our casualties?"

"Watanabe has been killed, Inoué is wounded. That's all I know."

"Sergeant Suda," the captain ordered, "take Noboru and go after the Yankees. Don't let yourselves be seen, and above all, don't shoot."

Both hurried off.

"All right, tell me what happened, Yoshi."

"They stabbed Watanabe from behind . . . he was on watch. We didn't notice anything. But the knife missed Inaki by a hair's breadth over on the other side. He hit the Yank on the head with his rifle-butt and gave the alarm, but they were all over us in a flash. We didn't have a chance. If you hadn't come . . ."

Hidaka pointed to an American lying motionless on the ground.

"He's dead," the lieutenant said. "Inaki killed him. They've left two of their wounded behind, too."

The captain went over to Watanabe's body, saluted and bowed. Then he turned the dead man over and pulled the knife from his back.

"Perfect throw, must have hit the right ventricle of the heart," he said.

He dropped the bloodstained knife and looked at Inoué, who was covering his face and trembling violently. Hidaka kneeled down beside him and pulled his hands away. Inoué's face appeared to be one great, raw and bleeding wound. Gently, the captain replaced his hands.

He saw Tojimoto pull out his pistol and go up to the wounded Americans. One was bleeding from a hip wound, and the other had lost his left foot and was binding the stump himself with his belt. Both looked up at the Japanese with horror.

"Come back, Yoshi," Hidaka cried, "come back at once!"

Tojimoto hesitated. "But Enzo, we have orders . . ."

"Not from me, you haven't. I give the orders here!"

He took the pistol from the lieutenant's hand, uncocked it and shoved it back into his belt.

Tsunashima pushed between them and reminded them of the bombers in the air. They ought to be thinking of their weather reports.

"Later, we've got a good three hours yet," Hidaka said. "The weather doesn't change that quickly."

It was impossible to take Inoué with them, and his fate was therefore sealed. The captain took the wounded man in his arms and explained gently that he had lost his sight.

"Tenno-heika will pray for you, and your soul will rise up to join the immortal heroes."

The blind man nodded and asked Hidaka to convey his last greetings to his family. Then he asked to be helped up. The captain handed him his own pistol. His comrades said nothing and lowered their eyes. Inaki, who had marched, eaten and slept beside Inoué, and loved him for so many years, began to sob. The man with the mutilated face lifted the pistol to his right temple and fired.

Inaki caught the falling body and laid it gently on the ground. Hidaka and the other survivors stood beside it for several minutes in complete silence.

Jeff Pembroke and Ted Miller, who had also witnessed Inoué's end, could not believe their luck in still being alive. No one paid any attention to them.

Sergeant Suda and the Oshone returned.

"The Yankees have gone into the river and are making off downstream," Suda reported. "They are carrying one man and another one has to be helped along."

Tojimoto wanted to go after them straight away.

"We must take advantage of their panic, Enzo."

"Get this into your head once and for all!" Hidaka shouted furiously. "We are not a fighting unit, we have other things to do . . . our bombers are in the air!"

He hesitated for a moment. "But we'll get them in the end, anyway."

The lieutenant looked at him. "What have you got in mind, Enzo?"

"We'll go and look for the Yankees' last camp!"

He told them to fill their pockets with ammunition.

"Leave the rest of the stuff here, we'll be back soon."

Before following his men out of the camp, Hidaka went over to the wounded Americans and threw a packet of bandages on the ground between them.

25

The scouts had been beaten. No one had realized that only a few of the Japanese were in the camp when they stormed it. No one had foreseen the possibility of the transmitter, together with the commanding officer and a second party, being up on the ridge during the daytime.

Captain William had been badly wounded, and Charlie Stewart had been shot in the right thigh.

As soon as they reached the bottom of the valley, they quickly made a temporary stretcher, using branches and their rifle slings. Branson and Hank Fortier carried the captain, and Slim Wortley walked beside him, arranging his blood-spattered bandages. Charlie Stewart tried to walk unaided, but cursed at every step.

Chief Scout McCluire ran to the head of the column, which was being led by Hamston.

"Dick, we must get into the water, otherwise they'll find us and attack when it gets dark!"

"But what about all our stuff, Allan?"

"Can't help that, we'll just have to try and fetch it later."

"Where are we going now?"

"Don't know yet ... somewhere safe for the night, to start with."

The river was broad and shallow, but deep channels had been worn away in the middle of its pebbly bed. Here the water reached up to their waists, and sometimes even to their chests. The stretcher supporting the captain had to be carried at shoulder-height; Stewart, hopping on one leg, was helped by two of his comrades. The current was very strong and dangerous, and Bert Hutchinson lost his footing and was almost swept away. Soaked to the skin and shaking with cold, they managed to reach the shallows.

It struck Allan that the Japanese killed all wounded who were no longer able to walk. He remembered the force with which one of them had brought his rifle down on Mike Herrera's head, but Pembroke and Miller had still been alive when he had last seen them. He had only just managed to haul the captain away in the confusion, after William had fallen into some bushes concealing him effectively from the Japanese. They had lost the use of five men in this short engagement and were now burdened with two wounded. The Japanese had suffered casualties as well, to be sure, but at that moment they had the advantage. They would rid themselves of all the wounded, and they still had all their equipment intact. They would be free to take whatever action they chose, and their choice was unlimited.

The sky was darkening, and an icy wind blew down the valley and whistled in the trees. A northerly storm was about to break over the Schwatkas.

"We'll have frozen feet by morning," Hamston warned, "if we don't get a fire soon."

Allen knew this. The storm would bring freezing temperatures with it and perhaps snow as well. Their sleeping-bags and tents had been left at their last camp, and they had no chance of surviving the night without a fire. They also needed a shelter before the towering clouds opened over their heads. If the enemy did discover their hide-out for the night, the approaching storm would provide an excellent opportunity to take the scouts by surprise. They were not, of course, leaving any tracks at the moment, but would be unable to avoid it once they got out of the water. Allan was pinning his hopes on the shingle banks. The river was becoming wider all the time and downstream the shingle islands were larger and more numerous.

Everything now depended on their reaching one of

these islands, but they must not be seen doing it. They desperately needed the friendly cover of darkness or the thick Alaskan mist.

26

The Japanese had no difficulty in finding the trail to the scouts' deserted camp. McCluire's men had made little effort to cover their tracks, so confident had they been of success. However, the captain still took every precaution and insisted that the patrol remain together.

"There are only nine of us left now, and we'll need everyone if we meet up with the Yankees again."

Their opponents had lost three men and had two wounded with them, but numbered as many fit men as the Japanese. However, they had no equipment, just their guns, and a few axes and spades, and their ammunition was probably running low, too. All the Japanese had to do to make themselves undisputed masters of these mountains was to destroy the Americans' equipment.

They found the camp quite soon. The Japanese had never seen such compact, lightweight tents and equipment before, and examined everything with amazement.

"All right, we haven't got time to stand around looking at this rubbish," Hidaka said finally. "Build a bonfire and burn the lot."

With no sign of regret, the men threw the sleeping-bags into the fire. The tents quickly followed, and everything else, boots, thick woollen sweaters and other clothes, joined the blaze. This done, they systematically smashed every tool they could find.

The meteorogist used the time to have a look at his instruments. No one else had noticed how quickly the sky had clouded over.

"Taiji-dono, there's a sudden change in the weather coming!" Tsunashima exclaimed. "The barometer is falling faster than I've ever seen before, over an inch in under two hours . . ."

For a moment all activity ceased.

"That quick? It can't be!" cried the captain, horrified.

"I've only got my pocket barometer on me, but it's quite reliable. We must go back to the transmitter. The admiral will have to recall the bombers!"

Hidaka turned to the others. "Yoshi, finish breaking up everything here; you'll have time for that. Kurakami, Tsunashima and Lonti, come with me. The rest of you, go back to the pool when you've finished and stay there!"

Tojimoto saluted briefly and turned back to the demolition work.

"Hajimero," Hidaka shouted to his three companions, "let's see what our lungs are made of!"

Behind them, the Americans' ammunition store blew up, everything containing gunpowder caught up in the explosion.

The men's lungs held out as they raced up, but their blood roared in their ears, and it seemed as if their skulls would split. They fell so often that they no longer felt the pain, and their hands and shins were bleeding but they did not notice. They scrambled up the steep and rocky mountainside through thick brush, tangled undergrowth and over treacherous gravel. The threatening storm drove them on; unawares, the bombers were flying straight into it.

An icy, biting north wind whistled across the heights, and a great mass of lowering clouds, black as night, rolled over the mountain peaks. To the west, the sky was sulphur-yellow.

Hidaka was the first to pull himself up on to the ridge. His exhausted companions panted behind him and crawled under the net to their transmitter.

124

"Get the aerial out!" Hidaka yelled. "Lonti, turn the crank."

Tsunashima grabbed the large barometer and bent over it.

"It's even worse now, Taiji-dono . . . it can't go any lower!"

Nowhere else in the world would such a dramatic change in the weather have been possible. It was the water-shed of the Brooks Range, towering into the sky, that had held off the northerly storm for so long. Now it would burst upon them all the more violently.

"It's crackling like gunfire," Kurakami said desperately.

"You must get through," the captain shouted. "You must, whatever happens!"

His face covered in sweat, Tsunashima scribbled down his readings. Even here, where they were protected from the wind, the leaves were fluttering down onto his notebook.

Suddenly Kurakami made contact with Attu, but the weak signal was lost again in the crackling interference. Hidaka stood leaning over him to act as a windshield. The aerial arched and vibrated in the wind, making a singing noise.

"I've got Attu," the radio operator shouted out. "They can hear us!"

"We'll send it clear, just as it is."

Hidaka held the piece of paper from Tsunashima's notebook in front of Kurakami so that he could read it.

"It's gone again, Taiji-dono. I can't hear anything at all now!"

"Never mind, Kurakami, just do it over and over again, ten times running. They'll get the message all right in the end."

The radio operator bent closer over the transmitter. He hammered on the keys without pause, repeating the same five figures: wind strength, wind direction, cloud height, temperature, humidity.

The warning went out, over and over again. Kurakami was making a noise like machine-gun fire, while Lonti continued to turn the crank; they had forgotten to relieve him. Over a thousand miles away the radio operator in Attu must be listening intently. He had replied to them twice, briefly and very faintly, so he was aware that they were trying to reach him.

At long last, Kurakami leaned back. Lonti let go of the crank and for a while it went on turning of its own accord. The four men sat on the ground, utterly weary, and in a state of nervous exhaustion. The camouflage net flapped over their hide-out and the wind blew in under it. The clouds above moved across the sky in serried ranks, with an occasional break to reveal a brief patch of blue. They seemed to be in a headlong rush, driven on by the great grey mass that followed. It could not be long now before they burst and let loose a deluge over the mountains and valleys.

"It's an equinoctial storm, Taiji-dono, marking the end of the long autumn . . ." Tsunashima began.

Lonti interrupted him with a violent gesture.

"The Shinzans, I can hear the Shinzans!"

They fell silent and now they could all hear the drone of aircraft engines above the roar of the wind.

"They're coming, Taiji-dono! They're coming straight into an inferno!"

The four men hurried outside and searched the southern sky but found nothing.

"It's all been no use," Hidaka groaned. "None of our warnings reached them."

There was nothing more they could do now; their transmitter was tuned to Attu, and the bomber squadron would keep on its original course, even though it led to disaster.

A grey mist had come down over the ridge. The four

126

men turned their heads towards the noise as it grew rapidly as loud as thunder. It had come from the south before, but was now clearly to the west. Then the droning seemed to recede and stay put, returning after a short while straight towards them.

For a fraction of a second, a long, wide wing became visible through a blue gap in the clouds, and the great 'plane roared over their heads. They had all recognized the bright red ball on the white background. They stared as if transfixed at the clouds into which the apparition had vanished, and slowly it dawned on them that they were facing south once more.

"They've turned back, Kami-tachi, they're flying back!"

Hidaka unbuttoned his collar and took a deep breath. Their warning had got through. Nothing had been lost after all; the big attack had only been put off for a few days.

27

The blanket of cloud came down, mingling with the swirling mist, and the scouts drew closer together in the obliterating grey damp.

In front of them was the outline of an island. Thick brush reached as far as the water, and wet rocks, slippery and covered with algae, lined the coast.

The men forced their way to the middle of the island through a wilderness of bulrushes and willows. They came first to a juniper thicket and then reached a copse of old larch trees. Behind them, some fifteen feet high, rose a sheer rockface.

"Suits us fine," Pete Randall said, "it'll make a good windbreak for the stove."

They put down the stretcher and Charlie Stewart relaxed, easing his injured leg.

The first flames crackled and the men held out their hands to them. There was a good supply of dry wood, and the fire grew bigger and hotter.

The air was unbearably close and oppressive: the thunderstorm would break at any moment. Building a shelter became a race against time. The scouts sharpened two large stakes, drove them into the ground, and found a thick branch to place across them. Against this crossbar they leaned a number of thinner sticks, and, taking some leafy twigs, wove them into the structure. Harry and Jim O'Hara tied up bundles of reeds with which they covered the slanting wall to windward in overlapping layers. The result was a round openended hut with a watertight roof, one wall towards the cliff and the other towards the wind.

They brought in the captain and laid him on a bed of leaves. Slim Wortley had to give him morphine while they changed his bandages, but Charlie Stewart was in better shape; the ice-cold water had staunched the bleeding and eased the pain. His was only a flesh wound and he had no broken bones.

The scouts threw off their sodden jackets and removed their boots and socks. Each collected a pile of leaves for his bed and lay down, feeling surprisingly snug and relaxed.

"So far so good," Fortier said. "Now the weather can do what it damn well likes."

Allan got up and looked out.

"This won't last longer than half-an-hour at the most. Then all hell will break loose."

He put on his boots and jacket again.

"I need a couple of volunteers to go with me and see what the sons of bitches have done with Ted and Jeff."

It was a tough assignment, but it had to be done and now was the time—only under cover of the approaching storm could they hope to reach the Japanese camp undetected. And even if the enemy had withdrawn, he would certainly have left the wounded men behind.

"Hell, we'll all go," Randall said.

They reached for their things, fatigue evaporating at the thought of how they would feel if they abandoned their comrades.

"I only want two of you," Allan insisted.

"Well, pick them yourself, then."

"OK. You come, Dick, and you, too, Harry."

Dick Hamston and the Indian said nothing while they got ready.

"Allan, I still think we should all go," Branson said. "Perhaps the yellow bastards are still there and we'll be able to settle up with them."

"Have you had a look how much ammo we've got left? Next to nothing, I bet, and the grenades are all used up. Anyway, we can't leave the captain and Charlie Stewart all by themselves and somebody has to keep the fire going."

He was right, of course. The three men went out together into the biting wind.

28

Rolls of thunder accompanied by flashes of yellow lightning reverberated through the valleys like a heavy artillery barrage. Hailstones, hard as bullets, bounced off the rocks. Branches snapped overhead and torrents of water swept through the gorges with a deafening roar.

Five men fought their way through the deluge. At last Tojimoto and his companions gained the foot of the ridge, but dense undergrowth now barred their way and their rifles caught on the bushes as they stumbled past. Completely exhausted, the men reached their captain's shelter, and collapsing outside, had to be dragged in by their comrades.

"It's bad," Tojimoto gasped. "Our camp is deserted and the Yankees have stripped everything. When we got there, Enzo, we couldn't find anything except an American's grave. They must have rescued the others while we were gone."

The captain took a moment to grasp what Tojimoto was saying.

"We might have known what the Yankees would get up to. They went to our camp to get their wounded, saw we'd gone, and decided to stock up."

"No, Taiji-dono." Sergeant Suda had got to his feet. "They took nothing away; they dumped the lot in the pool."

"They didn't realize we'd wiped out their camp," Tojimoto said.

So the Americans had gained very little, and would have to lie low, biding their time.

"We must try and salvage the stuff."

"We can't, Enzo; we've tried already. That little

stream's a raging torrent now, and is sweeping in mud and stones. Everything's been buried long ago."

The captain nodded as he tried to take stock of the new situation. Their radio equipment was intact, and there were nine of them, all strong, able-bodied men. For the rest they had only what they stood up in, and their sleeping-bags.

"On top of that, we've each got a rifle," Hidaka said, "but we've got to keep the ammunition for the enemy, especially those last grenades."

He stood up. "We've suffered another blow, but we will do our duty to our last breath."

Afraid that their clothes might freeze solid, they did not undress that night. They only took off their boots, and wrapped their feet in rags. The storm would last some time yet, and while it did they were safe from the enemy who was busy with his own problems.

The captain spoke to Tojimoto.

"We have to make the best of a bad job. Remember, we are travelling light now, so we can go much farther."

"But in which direction, Enzo?"

"Crossing the streams or maybe up a gully. I thought I spotted a good one the other day. The storm has wiped out all our tracks. If the Yankees—another lot, perhaps—come looking for us again, they'll have to start from scratch. For the time being we won't have to transmit weather reports. They know very well on Attu that we can't do anything right now. We'll go on a forced march, Yoshi, and camp somewhere a long way away. Then we'll start sending in reports again, and just hang on till the big push is over."

Tojimoto agreed eagerly. "What will happen later, though, when Yamada has no Shinzans left?" he asked.

"Then we'll start on the second part of our mission, the march to Boris Nizhinsky's island. It'll probably take us the best part of a year."

132

"Do you really think we'll make it?"

"Some of us will. And even if in the end only one of us gets through with a report, that's all we need."

29

Although the reed roof over the scouts' heads had now been shaken by the storm for hours, their hut had been designed with the storm in mind, and it swayed and shook before the gusts of wind with no sign of collapse. The rain poured down in increasing amounts but the trench which they had built round the hut drained most of the flood harmlessly away. The front of the storm had now rolled away farther south.

It was warm in the hut, with the glow of the fire reflected from the rock wall. The clothes on their backs were now dry and the scouts felt much more comfortable. The badly wounded man was still unconscious, but Charlie Stewart lay gazing up at the ceiling.

"I think I'll survive," he said.

"Sure, your leg will be all right," Slim agreed. "But if the captain doesn't get proper surgery soon, he won't stand much chance of becoming a general."

Pete Randall leapt to his feet. "Footsteps . . ."

They reached for their weapons but saw that it was Dick Hamston who was lifting the reed bundles on the roof and looking inside.

"Make room, men, we're bringing Jeff in."

Five pairs of hands stretched out to help. Dick pulled the stretcher in behind him with Allan pushing from outside. The injured man was fully conscious and even attempted a grin.

"How's it going, Jeff? Where'd you get hit?"

"His left leg's gone below the knee," McCluire answered for him. "You'd better get to work, Slim."

Allan was utterly exhausted. He sank down by the fire, and O'Hara and Fortier had to help him take off his wet clothes.

"Where's Harry?" they asked.

"He's just coming, and he's got a couple of things to tell you."

"What about Ted? What happened to him?"

"He's dead. We buried him there."

There was silence and all that was heard was the crackling of the fire and the pelting rain outside until Harry returned, heavily laden with a scout pack and other gear.

"Well, look at that, he's brought my pack!" Hutchinson exclaimed joyfully.

"It's not as good as it looks," Hamston said. "Your stuff was all that was left."

Dick began to tell them what had happened. The three men had battled their way through the storm and the pouring rain, and had reached the camp, finding it seemingly deserted. Then Jeff had called out to them, and they had recognized him in the flashes of lightning. After they had buried Ted, they had had the idea of dumping all the Japanese equipment into the pool.

They had improvised a stretcher for Jeff, and Harry Chiefson had offered to fetch the first aid kit and some ammunition from their old camp above. When he reached the camp, he had discovered the destruction the Japanese had wrought there. Luckily he had remembered that Hutchinson had camped a little apart from the others, deep in a clump of osiers. And sure enough, his things had escaped unharmed. Harry had also discovered three fur-lined anoraks, tied together in a bundle and buried under some branches.

No one said anything when the storm was over. They waited for the chief scout to pronounce on this new development, but Allan was almost too tired to speak and was finding it difficult to keep awake.

"If the Japs start looking for us in earnest, they won't have any trouble finding us here. We'll stay until just before first light, and then move off fast. We'll be warm enough if we keep on the go."

135

None of the scouts could think of a better plan.

"In two or three days," Allan continued, "we'll be able to give the wounded a chance to get some proper rest. The others will make their way back to Lake Clifton as fast as possible, and report to General Hamilton so that he can decide on the quickest way to bring up help."

He was about to turn his back and go to sleep when Hamston said, "You'll still be chief scout, though, won't you, Allan?"

"No, Dick, I won't."

The men were shocked.

"What, you're going to give up?"

"On the contrary, I'm going to stay here."

Pete Randall leaned forward quickly.

"What did you say, Allan? What are you going to do?"

"I'm going to track the Japs until I find out where they decide to hole up for the winter. We'll arrange a rendezvous somewhere; then we'll be able to start afresh."

Hamston shook Allan's knee.

"Are you out of your mind, man, going after that murderous bunch now, with winter coming on and without any proper equipment?"

"OK, I'm out of my mind, Dick, but leave me to sleep in peace now!"

"Well, I'm crazy too. Let's do it together, Allan, we stand a better chance if there are two of us . . ."

"Three," Harry said from his corner.

"And I'll come too, with all my stuff, then at least we'll have something," Bert Hutchinson joined in.

The chief scout pulled himself up by a branch in the roof.

"That's enough volunteering. The first thing is that the wounded have got to be taken to safety, and we'll need at least five men for that. I can manage my part on my own."

Charlie Stewart thought that if he could make some strong crutches, he would be able to get along without help. Then only four men would be needed to move the wounded.

The chief scout would not discuss it any further.

"Sleep on it, fellows. The choice is between forty degrees below or your warm beds back home."

30

Captain Hidaka and his eight companions were marching straight into winter. The ground was frozen hard, the grass and club-moss covered in hoarfrost. A cold wind swept down from the mountains. The sky was overcast and a huge procession of black clouds still threatened the landscape.

They had long since left the forest and the willows behind, and were crossing open slopes, moving towards the precipitous mountain faces where they hoped to find the gap that Hidaka had sighted earlier. As they walked they left clearly visible footmarks on the rough terrain.

"Are you absolutely sure that no one is tracking us?" Tojimoto asked anxiously.

"Not absolutely, but it would be nice to know."

"Why do you want to make it easy for somebody to find our tracks?"

"So that he'll give himself away, Yoshi. That's why I want the tracks to be so obvious. In fact, I don't think anybody is following us. But I would like to be certain."

From close to, the Brooks Range did not present the unbroken front it had from further away, and the rockface was cleft by ravines and valleys. One of these, towards which Hidaka was making, led steeply upwards to a deep col.

"There's nothing but snow up there," Tojimoto objected. "I don't see how we'll get through that."

"You can always get through where the snow has settled, Shoji-dono," Sergeant Suda said. "You can tell it's too steep when the rocks are bare in winter."

Suda ought to know; he was one of the best mountaineers in the Japanese Army, and had had climbing experience in the Himalayas.

They clambered over boulders and through brush, higher and further into the virgin land. A rushing mountain stream roared over a bed of pebbles worn dangerously smooth by the strong current. They had to form a human chain to withstand the force of the water, and the cold bit into them with an icy sharpness.

On their left a large valley opened up, sheltered on all sides and very quiet. Dwarf birches and an occasional stunted alder had taken root there. Soon Hidaka ordered a halt.

"There are polar hare droppings all over the place. We'll stop and Noboru and Sinobu can put out some snares."

There was a stretch of ground between two great boulders that was carpeted in soft moss and here they spread their waterproof groundsheets.

"We'll carry on taking no precautions," the captain said, "and make a good fire. The smoke will carry to the river, and that's what we want."

He ordered his men to pitch camp, and quickly retraced the half-mile back to the river. He was frozen through, but resisted his longing for warmth and dryness. A quick run would soon get his blood circulating again.

On the river-bank he found a pile of stones behind which he could hide. A few willow twigs, covered over with moss and handfuls of grass, protected him from the cold ground. He built a low wall in front of him from loose stones, leaving a small loop-hole to watch through. Lying down behind it, he waited; if someone was following the Japanese patrol it would be easy for him to trace them up to the spot where they had entered the river.

A long-legged polar hare came up to nibble at the club-moss, unaware of the presence of a human being.

A mink slid smoothly through the slate-grey moss. A russet salmon, having finally reached the end of its long journey, lay in the shallows barely moving its fins. With two quick bounds the mink reached it, stretched out its claws and pounced on the scaly body. The sharp daggers of its tiny teeth buried themselves in the pink flesh.

Suddenly, the polar hare pricked up its long ears and fled. Hidaka reached for his field-glasses. The mink, noticing something too, dropped its booty in fright, and vanished with lightning speed.

Hidaka cocked his gun and pushed the barrel through the loophole. There must be a reason for the animals' flight. The captain carefully scanned the landscape downstream, and picked out a grey dot moving cautiously through the bushes, making use of every bit of cover. It was about three hundred yards away and was undoubtedly a man, wearing a fur hat and quilted, camouflaged clothes. He was almost certainly following the Japanese tracks but with far greater caution than Hidaka had expected.

Earlier, Hidaka and his men had taken a curving path to the river bank. Their pursuer would hit upon this path at any moment, and would follow it to the stream, at which point Hidaka would have him in his sights, at a range of fity or sixty yards. Unfortunately, it was already twilight and beginning to get dark.

The scout's next two moves brought him within range. As the Japanese put down his glasses and carefully aimed his rifle, the scout dropped down into the undergrowth again, and disappeared from sight. Hidaka could follow his progress by the swaying of the tall ferns, and settled down to wait for his enemy to reach the bank opposite him.

With a sudden leap the American broke cover, raced across four or five yards of open ground and threw himself down behind a clump of club-moss, scarcely big enough to conceal him. Hidaka could make out his shape quite clearly, but because of the bad light decided to wait until he had the figure in front of him again, out in the open.

After a while the man seemed to be satisfied that no danger threatened from the other bank and with a quick movement raised himself to his full height. Through his sights Hidaka could see a determined face with steel-blue eyes, a jutting chin and thin lips pressed firmly together. He wore no badges of rank and despite the cold his collar was unbuttoned and his anorak was open at the neck. He carried his rifle loosely in the crook of his arm, his right hand on the lock.

Now the scout had discovered the place where the Japanese had entered the stream, and went up to it, gazing through his field-glasses at the far bank.

Hidaka slid the cross-wires of the graticule over his opponent's body, hesitated for a moment at the button on his top left pocket, and then lowered the sights fractionally to the point where the bullet would enter the heart.

The captain had already crooked his finger round the trigger and was about to squeeze when the figure in his sights made a sudden sideways movement and beckoned to someone behind him.

The scout was not alone, a possibility that Hidaka had not envisaged. He had been concentrating so hard on the first scout that he had failed to notice the others behind him. They jumped out from cover, and hurried up to join their leader. There were five men now, each armed with a rifle and hunting-knife.

Hidaka withdrew his gun and uncocked it again. He would have to be satisfied with observing the enemy. Even if he fired as quickly as possible he would not be able to knock out more than two men, and the rest of them would immediately spread out and cross the river both above and below him in order to surround their

141

hidden enemy. He had to avoid action if possible; his patrol's task was more important.

Hidaka watched as all five men now looked across the river through their field-glasses, and ducked down even lower. The enemy had smelt the smoke but could not see the fire. They were obviously discussing how best to cross the river, and various suggestions were apparently being put forward.

Finally the scouts retreated. Hidaka continued watching until their heads and shoulders had disappeared from view down the mountainside into the bushes.

He stood up, stiff and almost numb, and soundlessly returned to his men to tell them what had happened.

"We'll keep the fire going all night with a lot of damp wood. But we'll go on ourselves further into the mountains."

"Will we catch the Yankees tomorrow, Enzo?"

"No, we'll move off again at first light. But we'll leave them a little present."

31

Allan McCluire and his men marched back from the river for an hour and then chose a good place to camp. The trail the Japanese had left behind made it appear that they wanted only to cross the mountains as quickly as possible.

"The Japs want to hole out somewhere," Allan said, "before the heavy snows come. It won't take nine strong men long to build a log-cabin."

Allan had made it clear to his companions when they separated from the rest of the patrol that their sole task would be to find the enemy's winter quarters. There was to be no attack; his small group of five was far too weak and badly equipped for that. The plan was for two of the scouts to hurry down to Lake Clifton as soon as the Japanese had been located and inform the general from there. Allan and the remaining two scouts would find a suitable landing ground and mark it out so that it could be seen from the air.

The scouts had again laid their fire so that its heat was reflected by the rocks and they were warmed from all sides. They discussed the game the Japanese would be able to find to eat during the winter.

"It's a funny thing, you know," Hutchinson said, "the moose are moving further and further north. They hardly ever used to come up as far as the Brooks Range in the old days, and now they're well beyond the other side."

Dick Hamston suggested this might have something to do with the gradual warming-up of the northern hemisphere.

"I've not noticed much warming-up," Bert said. "Round my hut on the 68th parallel the birch trunks split open with the cold. I don't mind because the colder it gets the better the furs are."

They had all heard wonderful stories about Hutchinson's spoils, but Hamston complained that he never told a soul where his hunting-grounds were.

The trapper grinned. "Do you think I'm mad, my friend? You keep that sort of thing to yourself."

He was full of pride and enthusiasm as he talked about the gleaming gold of the pine-marten, the shining pelt of the mink and the thick, silky-soft furs of his white and blue foxes.

"I could have been a very rich man if those crazy society women didn't want different colours every year. Their damned fashions change all the time, and those fine ladies don't spare a thought for the likes of us—seven months of nothing but snow and ice, forty degrees below zero. No Indian could stand that! A few half-caste Eskimos come up there, but you never catch sight of them."

He meant the Nunamiut, the only inland Eskimos. They were shyer than wild animals, and hardly anything was known about the way they lived.

"They don't have any homes or houses," Bert said, "and they're always on the move. You might come across the remains of their fires sometimes, or pieces of a broken sled, perhaps, but you'll never catch a glimpse of them."

The night passed quickly even though it now became light much later. When they set off in the morning, Harry took the lead with McCluire bringing up the rear. They paused when they reached the spot where the Japanese had entered the river and Allan went first to test the crossing. When they had all reached the other side it took some time before they picked up the enemy's tracks again.

"There's still some smoke in the air," Harry said. "Perhaps the Japs are still here."

"They'll have gone, you can bet on that," said Allan. "Hidaka and company are in a hurry these days."

They moved on in the same order as before, the Indian spying out the land with the rest of the scouts following behind.

At last Harry stopped and waved; the others came up to him. In front of an untidy-looking clump of birch trees was a small pile of glowing ashes, thin wisps of smoke still curling upwards.

"Better approach it from the other side," ordered Allan.

They fanned out, forming a semi-circle round the far side of the fire. "They were really in a hurry," said Harry. "They've left a cartridge pouch behind."

It was half hidden under the cranberry bushes and could easily have been overlooked. As soon as Harry touched it, it exploded, tearing off his right hand. Half his face was laid bare and pieces of shrapnel flew into his ribs and hip.

The scouts ran for cover, certain the Japanese were mounting an attack. It took Allan a few moments to realize what had really happened: the enemy had left behind a vicious booby-trap which had been laid with diabolical cunning.

"The bastards," Randall swore, "the dirty bastards!"

Harry's hand was hanging from his arm by its sinews. Hamston and Randall could not bear the sight and turned away.

"You'd better keep a look-out!" Allan shouted at them. "Watch out on all sides, this is a perfect chance for them to attack us!"

Hutchinson had already bound the stump of Harry's arm with a leather strap. "There's iodine and bandages in the pack," he called out to Allan. "Right at the bottom!"

Allan emptied everything out of the pack, grabbed

145

the box with the red cross on it and kneeled down beside Harry, who stared at him with wide-open eyes.

"There isn't any morphine, Harry, nothing to kill the pain."

"It doesn't matter, boss. Get on with it!"

"Do the face first, Allan. I'll hold him."

Everything was hanging loose from his chin to just below the eye, and his jaw and cheekbone were exposed. Allan sewed the skin together with the needle and thread intended for mending their clothes. The Indian fainted.

"That's better. Now you can help me, Bert."

Using their fingers and sharpened pieces of wood they removed as much shrapnel as they could from Harry's hip. Allan poured iodine over the wounds.

Then he blew the fire up again and held his knife over it until the blade was red-hot.

"We'll do his hand now, Bert. I hope to God he doesn't come to."

The sinews were cut and the stump bandaged. Allan's hands were shaking as he wiped the knife clean and he had difficulty in putting it back in its sheath. He waved to Randall and Hamston to come back. There had been no sign of the Japanese while they had been seeing to Harry, and the enemy was certainly nowhere about.

"Is he . . . is he dead?"

Allan's lips tightened and he said nothing.

"He's not dead, he'll probably survive," Bert answered for him. "But we're stuck here now, we can't move! The bastards got what they wanted with their dirty low-down trick!"

"No, they haven't!" Allan McCluire shouted in a sudden burst of fury. "They'll pay for this! I'll have Hidaka's guts if I have to hunt the louse to the ends of the earth!"

146

32

The nine Japanese had crossed the central massif of the Brooks Range and turned westwards. Many days of hardship lay behind them. The landscape had changed: the mountain peaks were no longer so high and the forests had thinned out. The temperature never rose above freezing-point even during the day. The Japanese had sewn hare-skins together and wore them under their clothes to protect themselves against the cold; they lined their socks with down from the winter-duck and used bear-cub pelts as blankets.

On the fourth day Hidaka re-established contact with Attu. The weather had improved and his report was favourable, but the answer that came back was a bitter disappointment. Admiral Yamada did not have enough fuel for the 'planes. The last convoy to Attu had had to turn back to Japan, having sustained heavy losses. They were hoping for a fast blockade-runner to get through to them, but for the time being the Shinzans were grounded. Hidaka was instructed not to make contact for the next few days so as not to give away his new position needlessly.

The Japanese patrol marched rapidly towards a range of mountains that lay on the far western horizon, where Hidaka hoped to find a wooded valley, plentifully stocked with game, in which to stay for the rest of the winter. But when they reached the unnamed range two days later, they found themselves standing before the steep, unbroken face of a towering rock wall.

The captain decided to split the patrol up for the time being. Tojimoto and four men were to march along the rock-face to the south while he and the rest of his men would push on to the north. The reconnaissance would go on for three days at most, Hidaka de-

cided. Afterwards, they would rendezvous at their starting-point.

"We'll find a way in somewhere," he said. "There
are no mountains without valleys!"

They hid the transmitter and most of their food and
set off. The captain was accompanied by Sergeant
Tsunashima, Corporal Inaki and the Oshone, Noboru.
Lieutenant Tojimoto's group consisted of Sergeants
Kurakami and Suda, Corporal Lonti, and Sinobu.

Hidaka urged his men to hurry; he wanted to cover
as much ground as possible in the short time available.

He climbed up every rise in the ground, scanning the
mountains with his field-glasses for a gap in the rock-
face. But he could find no valley and there seemed to
be no breach in the great, grey wall.

"Taiji-dono, sled tracks!"

All that could be seen were faint grooves in the
hard-frozen ground.

"They must have been made before the last rains,"
Hidaka said. "Just before the frost came."

They followed the tracks and in a hollow found
traces of men and dogs.

"Those weren't white hunters," Hidaka decided.
"They were wearing moccasins with soft soles, and
their sleds didn't have metal runners, but wooden ones,
fairly battered, by the look of the tracks."

Inaki squatted down and felt the grooves with his
fingers.

"These aren't sled tracks, Taiji-dono, they're made
by something being pulled along. These people were
dragging their belongings behind them on a couple of
poles."

The captain kneeled down to have a look and had to
agree with Inaki. "Yes, you're right, the distance between the two runners isn't always the same."

It was difficult to imagine what kind of people had
made the tracks. Eskimos did not penetrate so far in-

land, and Indian tribes never travelled as far as the tundra on their hunting trips.

The captain shut his eyes and covered his face with his hands to help him concentrate. Somewhere in all those books and reports he had read while preparing for this expedition he had come across a reference to an ancient people roaming the depths of Alaska.

"I can't remember," he had to admit to himself, "but the author didn't really know anything, either. He was just repeating a legend current among the West Coast Eskimos."

Soon after Noboru found a similar track, and then Hidaka found a third. In the end they had found half a dozen of them, all leading northwards. A community of several families must have passed through, taking all their worldly possessions with them.

"They ought to be leaving the tundra now," Hidaka said, "but the tracks are going north towards the Barren Grounds."

"But always along the side of the mountains, Taiji-dono. Perhaps they know of an opening somewhere leading to forest and game."

When darkness fell they camped in a river valley, concealing their fire. During the night snow fell and covered the sled tracks. Even Noboru had difficulty in finding them again.

"We'll go on just as far as that hill," Hidaka pointed ahead, "and then we'll give up."

The outcrop of rock was further than they had thought, and they did not reach it until the sun was at its height. Hidaka sat down at the highest spot and scanned the rock-face with his field-glasses. It looked as impenetrable as before and seemed to stretch to the north forever.

"Over there!" Noboru cried. "A tent!"

The captain spun round. Its outline showed in the distance as a small dark patch and they would certainly

149

not have seen it had there not been snow on the ground. It stood completely alone, and there seemed to be no sign of movement anywhere near.

It took almost an hour for them to reach the tent, and there was still no sign of life. It was made of old caribou skins sewn together and supported by birch branches. Beside it were the cold embers of a camp fire, some charred bones and fragments of wooden crockery.

"There must have been at least twenty people here," Tsunashima said. He pointed to a number of large circles made with stones, each of which had been used to weigh down the sides of a tent in strong winds.

Noboru wanted to look into the skin hut, the only one left standing, at once. But Hidaka urged caution. There could still be people hiding who might be frightened into using their weapons if anyone came too close.

The captain called out in English, saying they came as friends and no one need be frightened. There was no answer. He stepped closer and shook the poles. Then the folds of skin on the ground moved and a small, wretched-looking little dog appeared and whimpered pitifully. Tsunashima picked it up and realized at once that it was close to starvation.

Hidaka pulled the skins apart and peered inside, but immediately withdrew. "There's someone lying inside. He's either dead or in a coma."

They tore away part of the roof and saw a pair of feet in moccasins protruding from a pile of shaggy pelts. Hidaka crept into the tent and began to free the inert figure from its cocoon of furs.

"Looks like a boy of fourteen or fifteen," Tsunashima said. "Is he alive, Taiji-dono?"

Hidaka fetched his compass out, wiped the glass and held it in front of the boy's lips. He had to do it several times before he got a result.

"The glass is clouded. He's still breathing."

He replaced the furs.

"Perhaps it's an infectious disease," Tsunashima warned. "We'd better get away from here!"

But the Oshone knew better; he had had a look around, and had examined the charred bones outside.

"Not ill, Hidaka-san. Hunger, much hunger!"

"I suppose it could be hunger," Hidaka agreed. "The game has all vanished from the tundra now. This boy seems to have been left behind."

Hidaka knew that it was the custom among primitive peoples to abandon the old and infirm in times of hunger. Nobody was allowed to become a burden on the group as it moved on.

"We must let him die," the sergeant said, "and then he won't be able to tell anyone about us."

They had to return to the rendezvous as quickly as possible, and the wide, empty tundra depressed them, as did the thought that these wild people, whose home this was, somtimes died of hunger.

"Inaki, build a fire," the captain ordered. "We'll make a good meat soup."

Later, Tsunashima was still holding the dog in his arms. Unable to bear its whimpering any longer, he pushed a few small pieces of his meat into its mouth.

Hidaka chewed his helping slowly and, leaving the nourishing stock in the bowl, crept into the tent with it. He lifted the starving boy's head and let the liquid run between his lips, drop by drop. After a time he felt a slight movement: the boy was beginning to swallow.

"Inaki, get the tent poles out," Hidaka called. "We need a sled. Noboru knows how to make one. We are taking the boy with us."

33

Harry Chiefson could not be moved. Any sudden movement caused him great pain and might easily re-open his hip-wound. Allan's suggestion that Hutchinson should stay with him while Allan himself, Hamston and Randall tracked the enemy was turned down by his companions. They felt that the injured man would one day recover enough for them to take him back and they could only do this if they stayed together.

The scouts built a strong lean-to surrounded by a wall of stones, and kept a fire burning constantly so that there was always a ready supply of hot water to wash the bandages. On the third day the swelling in Harry's face suddenly went down, and his wounds appeared to have stopped festering.

There was snow next morning, and since animal tracks could now be so easily seen, they caught more hares than they could eat. However they did need the soft skins, for they had nothing to fear from the worst of the cold with enough of them under their clothes.

On returning from fishing in the river, the scouts were startled to see Harry, bent double and dragging his feet, collecting fresh wood for the fire.

"Are you crazy?" Allan shouted. "If your hip breaks open again we'll be stuck here for God knows how many more weeks!"

"Three . . . four . . . five days . . . then . . . I . . . can . . . walk," Harry said thickly, his face not yet healed.

They set to work making a stretcher. Poles were bound together with strips of skin, over which they placed a layer of springy branches and dry moss. On the litter, wrapped in furs and tied fast, Harry would neither freeze nor fall off. They stuffed the small tent and the only sleeping-bag into Hutchinson's pack, together with the other implements they still had with them. If the weather held, the best plan would be to move off next day.

But next morning the sky was overcast with pale grey clouds, and snow flakes drifted down onto the roof of their shelter. It was no weather for setting off on a journey. They had to have a clear day, or it would be impossible for them to find their way through the mountains.

"We'll turn the extra day to good use and stock up with food," Allan said.

Hutchinson agreed to stay behind with Harry. Allan, Hamston and Randall went off for a day's hunting.

Towards midday they found a moose-run with fresh droppings and soon afterwards Randall, who was in front, heard the galloping hooves of a large bull. They turned away from the run so that the animal should not get their scent and moved in silently towards a clump of willows where they were sure they would find it. Dick saw its wide antlers between the branches and whistled. The animal raised its head, and was hit almost instantaneously.

"It was worth the bullet to get so much meat," Dick said as Allan came up. "We've got plenty of ammunition back at the base-camp."

They were able to take only the hind-quarters back with them. With the heavy load of meat on their backs they did not reach camp until darkness was falling.

"Hey, Bert!" Dick called out when they were just within earshot. "You might come and give us a hand!"

No one answered.

Allan quickened his step through the snow. "Something's happened . . . there's no fire!"

For several minutes they stood under the lean-to and looked around the empty camp.

"The Japs . . . ?" Hamston asked after a while.

At that moment Allan caught sight of a piece of

153

white paper stuck on the back wall, and tore it down. By now it was so dark that they had to light a match to read it by. The message was from Hutchinson: *Harry was set on walking. Could not stop him. Best of luck!* That was all.

"Harry's out of his mind!" Randall shouted.

"Perhaps Bert agreed with him," Hamston said. "Maybe he thought it would be best for us to be able to go after the Japs straight away."

"That's why Harry wanted to go, that's for sure. But not Bert—he was always for us keeping together!"

Pete had made a fire and taken a look around.

"It's a hell of a business, Allan, they've taken the pack with all the stuff in it!"

This was puzzling, too, as Bert had known how badly those things were needed.

All they had now was what they had taken with them that morning. In addition, there were tin cooking utensils, and axe, and some sewing things lying about on the ground.

"But remember," Allan said when he had completed the inventory, "we are in good health, and are willing and able to live off this fertile bit of the world!"

"Maybe we could catch them up?" Randall suggested.

"Not a chance," Allan said, pointing outside. "It's still snowing and their tracks will have been covered up long ago."

"Do you think Harry can possibly make it to Lake Clifton in his state? Bert won't be able to carry him," said Dick.

"I'm pretty sure," Pete said, "he won't survive the journey."

The chief scout had already made his decision.

"Harry's sacrifice won't be for nothing. I'm going on!"

Hamston smiled broadly. "What a coincidence, Allan, so are we!"

The three scouts broke camp as the sun came up. In spite of the sunshine it was colder and the snow crunched beneath their feet. Every branch and blade of grass was covered with glistening hoarfrost and the silence was complete.

There was no doubt that the Japanese had gone to the west. They could not go too far to the north or they would lose their radio link with Attu and end up in the tundra. Their need for game and fuel would force them to keep to the timber-line. Moreover, they could not keep on the move indefinitely. As soon as their leader felt relatively safe he would concentrate on finding a suitable place to spend the winter. Then, with luck, it would be possible to discover their tracks again, or perhaps see the smoke from their fire.

Allan chose the easiest route; Hidaka would have done the same. They left the steep rock wall behind and travelled through less mountainous country. With the glaciers of the Brooks Range to their right, the scouts were moving across a gently undulating chain of hills towards a long valley filled with snow-covered forest that stretched out in front of them.

Allan stopped on the last hill and lowered the load on his back to the ground. He wiped his field-glasses clear of snow and raised them to his eyes.

"They won't light a fire in day-time," Pete Randall said.

"Not as long as they're on the move," Allan agreed. "But once they settle down for the winter, they won't do without warmth. And in this cold weather and with the still air that would mean a thread of condensation, as well as smoke, rising for maybe a mile in the sky."

All three stood and scanned the frozen, petrified landscape.

"Not a thing, Allan. Later on, perhaps."

34

The Japanese did not make much progress with the motionless boy on the improvised sled they were taking turns to pull along. It was dark by the time they reached the rendezvous, seven hours later than agreed. A fire was burning there, which had guided them along the way for the last few miles. Only Sergeant Kurakami and Sinobu were waiting for them but they had good news. Tojimoto's party had discovered a gorge in the cliff face with a fast-moving river flowing through it. The water had frozen over at the sides and so they had found it possible to edge past the sheer cliffs.

"All of a sudden," Kurakami reported enthusiastically, "the walls opened up and we were looking into a wide, flat valley, big enough to build a city in, Taiji-dono. There are caribou everywhere and you can see their tracks going all over the place in the snow. There are magnificent forests all around, going halfway up the slopes, and the lieutenant has even found a fair amount of herbs and other plants to eat."

Hidaka asked if it would be difficult to reach.

"Not at all, Taiji-dono; it won't take more than an hour. It's a really marvellous piece of luck. We can live in a large cave. There are lots of caves in the mountainside; it's as full of holes as a sponge."

They had examined all the caves and the lieutenant had selected the best for their winter quarters.

"Most caves are damp," Hidaka said doubtfully but the sergeant assured him that the cave they had chosen was completely dry.

"It's like a large vault with crannies and smaller caves branching off on either side. Dozens of families could live there comfortably."

The lieutenant, together with Suda and Lonti, had

stayed behind to get the cave ready. Hidaka decided that they would stay where they were until the next day, and told the men with him to gather as much fuel as they could.

As there was now no wind, a tent was unnecessary. They put the skins and sleeping-bags round the fire in a circle, and Hidaka carried the boy up to the warmth. He tried to give him meat broth with a spoon but had to hold the boy's mouth open again and feed it drop by drop. The boy made swallowing movements but his eyes remained shut, though the lids began to tremble a little.

"The little dog's appetite's better, Taiji-dono."

Inaki held his mess tin out to the dog and in a few moments it was empty.

"It's unbelievable how quickly an animal like that can recover," Hidaka said, "but the boy will get well, too."

His four companions nodded but said nothing. They had drawn closer to the fire; the night was the coldest they had yet spent. The slender branches from the trees that grew on the edge of the tundra burnt quickly and did not give out much heat.

"Sinobu, go back to the river with Noboru, there are a few stunted firs there. Chop off the biggest branches and bring them back."

The two men set off at once; the night sky was full of stars and the moon was rising. The cold became steadily more severe. In the distance, they could hear the long-drawn-out howls of wolves.

The sound of hurried footsteps pulled Hidaka out of his doze. The men snatched up their rifles and rolled away out of the light of the fire, but it was only Sinobu, panting as he ran up.

"Wolves, Taiji-dono, they are howling with hunger!"

The captain seized him by the arm.

"Where's Noboru?"

"By the fir trees . . . he's still by the fir trees."

Sinobu stopped beside the fire, his whole body trembling. Hidaka shook him by the shoulder.

"What do you mean by this, deserting a comrade?"

Sinobu did not answer, his face distorted with fear. The captain shook him so hard that his fur hat fell off.

"I'm sorry, Taiji-dono. The wolves were howling so horribly. I have never heard anything like it before."

Sinobu covered his face and began to sob. His comrades gazed at him in disgust, but Hidaka felt more than that. This was the first of his men to lose his nerve; it could prove infectious and have disastrous consequences. They had heard wolves a number of times but nobody had ever taken any notice before because it was very rare for a half-starved pack of wolves to attack human beings. In spite of knowing this Sinobu had simply deserted Noburu. In normal circumstances, he would have been court-martialled. But circumstances here were not normal and the best thing would be to ignore the incident.

Noburu came back quite soon, dragging an entire tree-trunk behind him.

"Very much heavy," he said pointing to his load, "one man walk slow with that." He threw a meaningful look at Sinobu. The men chopped up the trunk and stacked the logs by the fire. The howling of the wolves was now clearly audible but the smoke, which they hated because of instinctive memories of prairie fires, kept them at a respectful distance. Sinobu's shoulders quivered each time the wailing of the hungry pack started up again.

They set off long before daybreak. The captain told the men to make a litter from poles and skins. Sinobu picked up the front end at once but Hidaka had to wait a moment or two for a second volunteer, Inaki finally taking the rear.

The river ran free in only a few places but could be

heard roaring away under the ice. The six men kept as close as possible to the rock-face and picked their way with great care over the snow-covered gravel. If anybody crashed through the ice into the river he would be dragged under and never seen again.

They followed the river round a bend and then stopped in amazement. Suddenly, the mountains had fallen back and they could see before them a large plain, covered in snow.

"Where is the cave?"

Kurakami pointed to the left where the gray outline of a sheer cliff rose above the tops of the firs.

"We'll reach it in half an hour."

Sinobu and Inaki picked up the stretcher again and went more quickly. Tojimoto was waiting for them in front of the cave.

"Everything's ready for the master of the house," he announced.

Hidaka was greatly impressed; a better refuge for the six ice-bound months could not be imagined. The sandy floor was as dry as a bone. Inside the cave was a welcoming fire with the smoke rising straight up to one of the cracks in the vaulted roof. The place was pleasantly warm and lit by the flickering fire. Only the back of the cave was in darkness.

"We've collected stones," Tojimoto said, "so that we can wall up the entrance. Bears seem to like the cave too, and it might be a bit inconvenient to share it with them."

Sinobu and Inaki brought in the stretcher, and Hidaka settled down by the fire. Tojimoto sat down beside him and Hidaka told him how he had found the boy, apparently dying.

"What will you do with him if he recovers?"

"Well, I think he might be useful to us. He knows the country and what possibilities it has to offer. We could use him as a guide when we go west, and he can show us how to fish and hunt and cook the way his people do it. We shall have to live more and more like natives and he'll help us, you'll see."

Tojimoto did see but he was worried about the difficulty of communicating with the boy.

"To begin with, it won't be easy, but we've got plenty of time to give to the problem."

"All right, but there's something else. I think it might be a bit of a risk for us. As soon as he is up and about, he will run away and look for his family and his tribe. The news of our whereabouts will spread like wildfire and the Yankees will be bound to hear it, too."

Hidaka shook his head. "No, Yoshi, he won't run away. His people had left him to die and I saved him."

Tojimoto wondered whether a primitive boy's reasoning would work like that.

"We are strangers to him and to a savage that's the same as being an enemy. He'll be frightened of us just because our faces look different."

"Not all that different, Yoshi. Look at me. Look at my eyes, my mouth, and my nose. Look at my cheekbones and my hair. We are Mongols, all of us; our origins are the same as the Indians', the Eskimos' and the Aleuts'. Our appearance doesn't distinguish us from them at all. The boy will see that; he will feel we're related."

"You're right, Enzo; I'd never thought of it like that before."

Hidaka stood up to take off his parka and his hareskin waistcoat; the cave was as warm as a well-heated house. They did not even need to keep their boots on, since the fine sand was soft, like a pile carpet.

The captain asked Kurakami for a mug of his herb broth.

"I'll look after the boy myself. Then he'll always know who he belongs to."

He knelt down beside the unconscious figure and removed some of the many furs that were covering him. At this, the boy's face showed some movement, his lips trembling a little and his nostrils quivering with each breath.

Hidaka put his arms round the boy's narrow shoulders and sat him up. He looked for the strings of his fur hood, undid them and pulled it back. A cascade of gleaming black hair fell over his hand.

Hidaka knocked over the mug but took no notice. He had eyes only for the beautiful soft hair, very shiny and wavy and almost reaching to the ground. It was a girl he was holding in his arms but he had not yet taken it in.

Her eyelids trembled and opened. Hidaka felt the small frame give a jerk; waking, she evidently wanted to free herself but her weakened body lacked the strength to do so. Two black eyes stared up at him, widening with astonishment.

"Ikanga deska?" Hidaka asked softly, although she certainly did not understand his language.

She opened her lips but could not bring out any words. Her face had lost some of its pallor, now appearing charmingly feminine, and to Hidaka she looked just like a lovely Japanese girl who had been woken too early in the morning.

Hidaka pointed to himself and said his name. He did this four times, repeating slowly and distinctly, "H-i-d-a-k-a." He thought she must know what he meant, and pointed to her face, saying: *"Anato no namei,"* and then, in English, "Who are you?"

Slowly she raised her thin fingers to her chin. Hidaka saw what effort it cost her just to utter her name and waited patiently. And then it came, very softly but quite clearly:

"Alatna."

35

The Japanese had been living in their cave for two weeks. Flickering pine torches had been pushed into cracks in the rocks, and the smell of woodsmoke filled the room. Shaggy moose and caribou hides were spread in the sleeping area, and on the benches, and carpeted the floor. A low table stood in the middle. Bundles of brushwood covered with hareskins were scattered around and served as cushions. The whole place was spotlessly clean and tidy. Most of the entrance had been walled up, all that was left being an opening the size of a door which was covered with a windproof curtain of skins.

There was work for everyone; the captain had seen to that. Traps and snares had to be made, and pelts, needed for clothing and for making bags and overshoes like the Eskimos wore, were scraped and stretched. Kurakami was working on the transmitter which had not generated enough electricity the last time they had used it.

Alatna was chewing the edge of a fox skin. The hide had to be made soft and pliable or the bone needle could not pierce it. She had already made two pairs of mukluks, the finest kind of fur moccasin, only made by women. Hidaka sat facing her and was giving her a language lesson.

"*Ichi, ni, san,*" he said raising one, two, and three fingers, and she had to repeat after him. She smilingly did everything he asked of her. Alatna was never tired of learning and quickly mastered the words for all the objects that were shown her. She had made a good recovery, and moving nimbly now, was ready for any task at hand. It did not seem to worry her that she was the only female among nine men, but she always tried to stay close to Hidaka.

He had seen to it on the very first night that she had a place to herself divided off from the rest of the cave by a fur curtain. The little dog never left her side and slept in her arms. She called it Kinmek.

Hidaka thought her eyes her most attractive feature. They had very long lashes and beautifully arched brows. Her skin was copper-coloured with a pink sheen and set off her snow-white teeth. Her jet-black hair was tied in a knot which hung down her back.

"Taiji-dono, I think the transmitter's working now," the radio operator called out.

"Right then." Hidaka stood up. "We'll try it. Get ready."

Sinobu picked up the cranking-handle and Tsunashima shouldered the transmitter; Kurakami would relieve him later. Tojimoto and Hidaka took their rifles.

Alatna wanted to go along as well but Hidaka told her it would be more use to them if she went out and caught some ptarmigan. The birds lived under the snow-covered bushes in tunnels they had scraped through the snow. Alatna had a sure instinct for finding these runs. She was also good at finding pine-wood for the torches in the forest. None of the Japanese could match her in finding just the right branches, so saturated with resin that they burned for a whole hour.

It took them almost an hour to reach the forest, where the spreading branches were weighed under with snow. They stopped in front of a bear track.

"What's that?" Tsunashima exclaimed. "I thought bears hibernated at this time of year."

The track was quite fresh and could only have been made that morning.

"Sometimes they are about until November," Sinobu

163

said. "When there's still a lot of food to be had outside, they don't hibernate until later."

"Perhaps we've taken his cave," Kurakami said. "When we first moved in, there were piles of bear droppings in there."

Hidaka put his foot in one of the pad marks. "He must be a huge fellow."

"A good ten foot, I should think," Sinobu said.

"He would provide us with a fine carpet for our cave, and a mountain of fresh meat."

"I wouldn't recommend the meat," Tojimoto said. "Old bears like that often have parasites called trichinae. If one of us were to get trichinosis, he'd die a horrible death here where we haven't the proper treatment for it."

It was hard going through the alder scrub and they were up to their waists in snow. It was over an hour before they reached the top of the hill. Hidaka wiped the snow off a flat rock and the transmitter was set up there. Tsunashima took his measurements and Kurakami prepared the transmitter.

"You have to be very careful with the crank in this cold weather. It isn't gripping properly."

Sinobu began to turn the handle very slowly. It was more than ten minutes before the little red bulb began to glow. Hidaka knelt down beside the radio operator, who tapped out his message without taking his eyes off Tsunashima's notebook. There was a long wait for the acknowledgement.

"They can just about hear us, Taiji-dono, but they can't make out the message. We haven't got enough power."

Hidaka nodded to Sinobu to swing the cranking-handle faster.

"Attu is coming through. Quiet, please."

Tsunashima held the notebook for him but it was so cold that Kurakami could scarcely hold his pencil. Suddenly Sinobu was holding the cranking-handle up in the air.

"It's no good, Taiji-dono. The catch has broken off."

"Kono yaro . . . that's all we needed. Had Attu finished?"

"I don't think so."

Tojimoto helped to decipher what they had. The message was garbled but it appeared that the admiral was still short of aviation fuel. Attu had not been able to make out any of their readings that day, or their weather report, and they were instructed to proceed to Nizhinsky's island if their transmitter was damaged beyond repair.

"Then the whole thing will have been for nothing, Enzo."

"Oh, no, we're not giving up yet! We'll fix the damned thing. You can do it, Kurakami, can't you?"

"Taiji-dono, if anyone can, I can. It's a matter of fractions of a millimetre, though."

"Do your best. We need you, Kurakami."

Hidaka was the last to go down the hill. Half-way down he suddenly stopped and called Tojimoto back.

"Yoshi, come here! We've been looking at this gift of the gods for days without realizing it."

Hidaka stood with arms outstretched and laughed out loud as he looked down on the plain lying before them, framed in mountains.

"There's the best air-field imaginable for our bombers."

Tojimoto looked down wide-eyed and had to agree. Even the heaviest aircraft would be able to take off and touch down there.

"Transport 'planes could bring in the fuel, which would be stored in the caves. Then the bombers fly in, refuel and take off again for the south. The *kamikaze* won't need to die when they have strafed the enemy. They can return here, and go out, again and again and again. When Tokyo hears of this, they'll get the aviation fuel to Attu, no matter what it costs. And the whole thing depends on one tiny part of our transmitter!"

The others had gone on ahead and the two officers did not catch up with them until they reached the wood. They were at the spot where they had seen the bear track on their way up.

"It's been back, Taiji-dono, and had a sniff at our footprints."

Hidaka could see the impression of the bear's muzzle in the snow. "I am afriad we'll have to use up one of our bullets on this fellow. Nobody is to leave the cave without his rifle from now on."

He was thinking of Alatna, who went out unarmed to inspect her snares every day.

Sinobu pointed to the trunk of a fir tree nearby. "Those are its marks. They're there to tell would-be trespassers to keep out of its territory."

Shreds of bark were hanging from the trunk but so high up that none of the five men could have reached them. This was the grizzly's way of showing what a mighty opponent they had to deal with.

"Well, what do you think, Sinobu?"

"I'm not frightened of bears, Taiji-dono. I wouldn't mind taking a shot at that one. It's only when the wolves howl that I feel bad."

"Well, if you like, you can go and look for it tomorrow. Perhaps I'll go with you."

When they were still a hundred yards from the cave, Kinmek announced their return. He had become a reliable watch-dog.

Alatna ran towards them, her eyes shining and her hair blowing in the wind. She stopped face to face with Hidaka, stood on tip-toe and touched his nose with hers. The others laughed with embarrassment. To the Eskimos, this was a kiss, but to the Japanese it was not

166

proper to display one's feelings in front of other people, and such an intimate gesture was particularly out of place since it involved an officer in the presence of his subordinates. So Hidaka pushed Alatna away brusquely and sent her back to the cave. She was startled but obeyed immediately.

Inside, all was bustling activity. Hidaka left it to his second-in-command to tell those who had remained behind what news had come through from Attu. He himself went over to Kurakami to see how he was getting on with the transmitter.

"Perhaps there's a loose connection somewhere," he suggested.

"I don't think so," Kurakami said. "It's the condenser, Taiji-dono."

"Why isn't Lonti helping you? What's he been trained for?"

"He lacks the touch, somehow. I'll have to do it by myself. Lonti wouldn't be much help."

Hidaka looked round for Alatna but could not see her. Suda said she had run into her room and pulled the curtains across.

The captain realized that everyone was looking at him. Tojimoto brought over a mess tin full of a greenish meat stew and a pair of chop-sticks.

"Enzo, we'll have to have a word about this," he said as he sat down. "The men are getting restless, as if they had just noticed that Alatna . . . well, that Alatna is a woman. In the long run, you won't be able to protect her from so many men."

Hidaka looked down at the floor.

"You have first claim on her, obviously," Yoshi went on. "Nobody's going to question that. But if you don't want what you're entitled to, you must leave it to the others."

Hidaka's head jerked up.

167

"You must be out of your mind. All hell would break loose."

"That's what I'm saying. And that's why it's your duty to have Alatna for yourself—it's the only solution."

For a short time, Hidaka did not move. Then he stood up and walked quickly over to Alatna's alcove. He pulled her out from under her rugs and walked with her to the middle of the cave, where they both stood in the full light of the fire. Alatna clung closely to her protector.

"Listen, all of you," Hidaka called out. "This woman is mine, mine alone. No one is to touch her or come too close. Do you understand, all of you?"

The eight men stared at him with astonishment.

"Shoshi itamishata," they answered together. "Yes, sir. Orders understood."

Hidaka took the girl back to her alcove. She had understood what had taken place and stood beside him obediently. Her radiant look of happiness touched him, and he leaned forward, brushing the top of her nose with his. This gentle contact and the slight friction it caused aroused him, but it was neither the time nor the place for such thoughts. Hidaka released her, stroked her hair briefly, and left the alcove. His men were bent over their work.

"All right, Yoshi?"

"Fine. They all understand the position now."

Hidaka went up to Kurakami, who had dismantled the transmitter and spread all the parts out in front of him. A pinewood torch was stuck in a crack in the wall above to give him light for his work.

"How are things going, Kurakami?"

"It's as I thought, Taiji-dono, but I'm hoping . . ."

Suddenly the dog tried to give a warning bark but was too young to do it properly. He ran whining and

168

yelping through the cave, and vanished behind Alatna's curtains.

At the same moment, the big skins draped over the entrance were brushed aside and a huge grizzly lumbered in.

Noboru was the first to recover from the shock. He snatched a burning log from the fire and threw it at the enormous beast's shaggy chest. This enabled the bear to single him out as an obvious enemy and it made a rush for him. An instant later they were both rolling on the floor. Two or three of the men grabbed their rifles, and Suda fired at the animal's broad skull with no noticeable effect. He could have hit Noboru, who was clutched tightly in the bear's paws, and Hidaka shouted:

"Don't shoot! Use your knife!"

The captain had already driven his own into the bear's back. He pulled it out and stabbed the creature again. It wheeled around, drew itself up onto its hindlegs and struck out with both paws. Knives and axes flashed.

"Get back, Omaé-tachi! Don't let it get near you!"

The bear had now seized Kurakami and was squashing him up against the wall. Hidaka pounded on its back with his rifle-butt and Inaki broke a log over its head. Nothing was of any use. Screaming horribly, Kurakami was being crushed to death.

Then Alatna slipped soundlessly through the men and drove her tiny bone knife accurately into the bear's spine. It released its victim and turned, bellowing. Sinobu had his chance: he stabbed it in the heart with his steel-tipped wooden spear. The bear swayed and sank to the ground.

Kurakami died that night. Noboru had multiple fractures of his right arm and shoulder, and Suda and Lonti had flesh wounds. Tsunashima's knee had been dislocated, but they were able to manipulate the joint back into place. The bear had seventeen stab wounds and had clung to life tenaciously.

"If the Yankees had any idea what a loss Kurakami's death at this moment is to us," Hidaka said later as his radio operator's mutilated body was carried out, "they'd put up a statue to that bear—in a place of honour at the Pentagon."

36

The scouts had spent three days in the hole they had dug in the snow. Large branches braced the walls and the floor was covered with twigs. The space was so confined that they could not even sit upright but it kept the warmth in and protected them from the intense cold outside. They were able to use their hands, and worked on the snowshoes which were essential if they were to get away. Pliable willow twigs formed the framework of each shoe, bent into an oval shape like that of a tennis racquet, and then strung with moose-sinews. As there were no buckles, they had to be tied to the men's boots with more sinews. The snowshoes could not only support the weight of a man but also ride safely over any obstacles, and they lasted for several weeks.

A blizzard was raging over the forest. Surging waves of snow swept through the trees, branches snapped in the wind and huge fir trees were uprooted with a sound like gun-fire.

The scouts had been travelling for weeks but they had almost lost hope of finding the Japanese patrol. All they could think of now was surviving the storm. Even with their snowshoes on they only managed to travel a few weary miles a day through the bitter cold and the deep soft snow.

One more night and almost the whole of the following day passed before the blizzard gradually abated. Allan decided to look outside, and began shovelling the snow away with both hands. By the time his head finally emerged above ground, all that could be seen of him in the hole was the worn soles of his boots.

"It's not too bad out," he shouted down, "but it's too late to start now; it'll be dark soon."

Next morning they set off, trudging through the ravaged forest, and reached the river towards noon. Dick Hamston suggested they have a rest and do some fishing.

"We're in no great hurry any longer," Allan agreed, "and I wouldn't mind a change."

The wind had swept the snow off the ice covering the river at several places, and they decided to make an ice hole. Allan laid half a dozen logs together, making a little raft, on which he lit a fire, slowly melting the surface beneath. The logs sank and began to float on the melting ice, so that underneath the wood was wet and would not burn. The melted area grew larger and larger and the three men had to work hard to bale out the water.

The layer of ice was almost three feet thick and it took some time for the fire to do its work and lay bare the dark waters beneath. Allan lifted the raft out of the hole and laid it carefully on the bank. He did not want to use up any more matches and the fire had to be kept in for cooking their catch.

They dropped two fishing-lines down the hole. The opening in the ice, a bright circle in the dark water, attracted large numbers of fish. After a few minutes, Dick pulled up the first grayling and soon they had a small pile of different kinds of fish.

They grilled a few of the trout on thin willow spits and had just finished eating when all three raised their heads simultaneously.

"Was that a shot?"

"Perhaps the ice has broken somewhere," Pete said. "Or maybe it was a tree splitting."

Allan told them to keep quiet. If it had been a hunter's shot, a second might follow. The air was quite still.

The men listened with bated breath.

There was a second crack and then a third.

"Those are shots for sure!"

"I don't believe the Japs have got that much ammunition to waste. Anyway, game doesn't usually move away from its runs and they wouldn't need anything more than a halfway decent trap to get it."

The scouts were sure they would come across the hunter's tracks sooner or later. Anybody else wandering about in this wilderness would make use of the river, just as they had done.

Allan stopped at a bend in the river and raised his field-glasses. "There it is!" he exclaimed.

A line in the snow ran down from the forest and then along the river. The scouts forced their way through the bushes, scrambled over the snow-drifts on the slope above and stood before the ski trail. It was partially obliterated, and the lone skier must have dragged an animal carcass behind him; there were traces of hair and blood.

Dick examined the hairs. "He's got a wolf."

"He's got proper skis, with steel edges, too, you can tell by the sharp profile they make in the snow. If that was a Jap, the bastards have had a supply drop since we last saw them."

"They could have found a trapper's cabin and be using it," Pete said.

"Where do you expect to find a cabin anywhere round here?"

"I can't imagine a Jap going about all by himself in broad daylight, shooting off ammunition. They used to be so damned careful, and yet this one goes around as if he were all alone in the world."

The ski-trail followed all the turns in the river. The man could have shortened his journey by going further inland but it would have been difficult to drag the dead wolf through the undergrowth.

It was not until they had followed it for some hours and it was beginning to get dark that the ski-track turned towards the forest. Here they found another track, which Allan examined carefully. It had been made that day and by the same skis as the first.

"It's the same man. But there could still be a hornets' nest swarming with Japs the other end."

They soon discovered that the track went past a number of traps. They had been taken out of the snow and put up in the trees, probably because of the blizzards. They were not big enough for large game and were meant for trapping small animals, like lynx and ermine, for their fur.

"What on earth do the Japs want ermine for?" Dick asked.

"Perhaps their emperor wants a new coat." It was now completely dark. Allan had to bend down several times to feel the track with his hands. After a while they could smell smoke.

"We'd better get rid of some of our stuff," Allan said. "It can't be much further now."

They hid their skin bags and their furs in a snow drift and crept on cautiously. A glimmer of light winked through the trees.

"Careless people," Allan said. "Take your time now!"

They left the track and approached the light from the side. It was coming from a narrow window and they could make out the outline of a small log-cabin. They tried to look through the window with their binoculars but there were curtains drawn behind it.

"We'll have to do our reconnaissance through the door, then," Allan said. "Pete, you throw it open and Dick and I will cover you."

The scouts went carefully, step by step, up to the door. Inside they could hear the crackling of a stove and the clatter of plates, but no sound of voices.

Pete examined the door to see which way it opened and found the handle. Allan and Dick took off their gloves and aimed their rifles.

"OK, Pete, we're ready. One, two, three!"

The heavy door flew open with a crash and bright yellow light poured out on to the snow. A man was standing at a sink and, mouth wide-open in terror, he dropped the plate he was holding and raised his wet hands.

"Bert!" Dick Hamston exclaimed. "It's Bert Hutchinson!"

Allan put down his gun, cut the straps of his snowshoes in one quick movement and rushed up to the trapper. "Where's Harry?"

Hutchinson was too dazed to answer.

"Tell me or I'll smash your head in."

He seized him by the shoulder and threw him onto the unmade bed. Hutchinson, grimacing with fear, clung to the bedpost.

"Tell me where Harry is or I'll kill you!"

"I don't know! I went to inspect the traps. When I got back, he'd gone."

Dick and Pete picked him up from the bed and stood him up against a wall.

"You didn't leave with Harry?"

"No . . . no, I didn't."

"But you said you did! You wrote it on that piece of paper."

"Yes, I know. But I couldn't follow him. He'd gone, gone by himself. It was snowing and I couldn't find his footprints."

"Why didn't you stay? We were there."

Now Hutchinson was angry.

"Because I was sick of your bloody manhunt, Allan; because I didn't want to be ordered about by you any more. And because I didn't want to freeze to death!"

It took the three scouts a little while to sort out what must have happened. It seemed to be true that the Indian had made use of Hutchinson's absence to steal away. He had taken only his pack, two skinned hares and a parcel of moosemeat with him, as well as his knife, his small axe and a box of matches. With these few possessions, one-armed and with his wounds barely healed, he had set off for Lake Clifton. Hutchinson, who had not returned for some hours, had regarded this as a heaven-sent opportunity to make his own getaway. He had never told anyone where his hunting-grounds were and none of the scouts had had any idea that his home was not far away. He had brought a fully-laden sledge drawn by twelve dogs to his cabin the last time he had been there, and he could have held out in solitude for years, or at least until his disappearance had been forgotten. When he surfaced again one day with a large supply of the finest furs, people would believe whatever story he told them.

"You bastard!" Allan shouted when Bert had finished his account. "You left us in the lurch. You even took Harry's rifle. If the general got his hands on you, he'd have you court-martialled. You'd be lucky not to be shot and get away with ten years inside!"

In his fury, Allan hit him again and again, until Dick and Pete finally managed to drag him away.

"Stop it, Allan! That won't bring Harry back to life."

Allan had to leave the room to calm down. The two scouts followed him outside.

"I'm sorry, but I just had to do it. I couldn't control myself."

"Sure, Allan, sure, and he deserves much more. But on the other hand it's an incredible bit of luck finding somewhere like this to stay."

"Yes, you're right. He's got everything we need. It's only the man himself we could do without."

"We'll just have to do our best to get on with him, Allan."

The chief scout nodded and went back into the cabin. Politely, he asked Hutchinson, who was still

176

shaking, whether he had seen any signs of the Japanese patrol.

"Nothing! No tracks, no smoke, no shots. I haven't seen a thing!" he shouted.

Allan told him to calm down, and that nothing more would happen to him if he behaved himself.

"We're going to be your guests until the spring, but I think we'll have one or two excursions to make in the meantime."

37

One morning the caribou were gone; they had left the valley overnight and moved over the mountains to the south. Nobody knew what had made the herd leave the safety of its native valley so suddenly in the middle of winter.

"It can't be because of us. We didn't get many of them," Tojimoto said.

Sergeant Suda suggested the smoke might have disturbed them. Sometimes it would be blown downwards by the wind and would drift along the bottom of the valley. Alatna came up and heard the news with widening eyes.

"Arshakpuluk has called. Caribou go," she said.

Hidaka explained what she meant. Arshakpuluk was the great earth spirit to whom everything was subject. Any inexplicable event that took place was accepted as Arshakpuluk's doing.

Alatna had her sling with her and was going hunting. She never brought home anything bigger than a raven or a jay, but with the addition of herbs, they made good, nourishing soups.

"Don't go too far," Hidaka warned her, "Sinobu has heard wolves again."

Alatna was pleased at his concern. Never had a man been so good to his woman! No man amongst her people ever addressed so many kind words to his mate. Only once had her man been angry, and then she had not understood why.

On that occasion Alatna had been busy cooking the thighbone of a moose before extracting the marrow. She had unaffectedly taken off her skin jerkin to work and had worked over the fire naked from the waist up. The Nunamiuts invariably did this when it became too warm in their cramped dwellings, but Inaki, excited by the sight of her fine bare breasts, had stared long and hard, breathing heavily. At that moment Hidaka had come in and dragged Alatna away. He did not begin to scold her until they were behind the skin curtains of her alcove, and she had not understood all he had said, although it was now clear to her that she must not reveal any more of her body than her face and hands. This was a strict law amongst his race, Hidaka had said.

Nobody had been present when Inaki had stared at her so shamelessly, but he told his friends about what he had seen, and the others began to look at the young woman in a new way, vividly imagining her firm, youthful breasts under the loose skin jerkin. Only the captain and Lieutenant Tojimoto had no idea of what was now the men's most frequent subject of conversation.

Now Alatna ran through the snow. Near the gorge there was a thicket of tangled willow-bushes interspersed with a few black firs, where the skeletons and entrails of two caribou that Sinobu had speared had lain for the last two days. Alatna wanted to try for one or two of the large ravens that had been tearing at the remains.

The skeletons, caked in blood, were still in place, but the entrails, which had been scattered around, had long since been devoured by numerous scavengers, so there did not seem much chance of raven soup. Nevertheless Alatna stayed for several hours with the habitual patience of the native hunters, who were accustomed to wait for their quarry to come to them. Finally a blue fox with a thick, shining coat darted from the bushes. With its sharp nose pointing ahead and its bushy tail streaming, it raced through the snow.

Alatna had never before tried to kill a fox with her sling, but its fur would make an excellent collar for the parka she had been working on for several weeks. She would have to make sure to hit it in the head, that being the only place not well protected by thick fur.

The blue fox had reached its objective and, forgetting caution, began to gnaw busily without noticing the shadow which soundlessly moved from behind the trunk of a fir tree.

The stone hit the animal right in the middle of the small forehead, and it fell at once. Alatna rushed over to it, picked it up and slit its throat neatly with her knife. Proudly she laid her beautiful catch on a snow-covered bush and stepped back to admire it.

As she watched, a strange hand reached out from the bushes and pulled the dead animal away. Alatna froze with terror. There was complete silence in the wood and she had noticed no movement. But now the bushes parted and two figures stepped out, clad in furs from head to foot.

The taller figure carried a spear and the other a bow and arrow.

"We have been looking for you, Alatna," said the man with the spear, going up to her.

He was enveloped in new winter clothes, and Alatna did not recognize her father until he spoke. The other man was Sissuk, her eldest brother.

"Come, Alatna, we must be quick."

But she could not move.

"We saw the strange men who took my skins and my daughter," Tunak growled; he was the *tonjon* and chief of all the Nunamiuts. "We will kill them and take their possessions for ourselves."

This threat gave Alatna the strength to resist.

"These people are good! Without them I would be dead and the wolves would have taken your skins."

Tunak and Sissuk looked at each other. Never before had a woman dared to contradict them.

180

"Where do these strangers come from? What do they want here?"

Alatna remembered the explanation given to her by her man.

"They are fighting the *kablunas*. They want to drive the white man from our land!"

The *shaman* of the tribe had spoken of these white men. Without asking permission they came to hunting-grounds which were not theirs, and they were greedy for furs which did not belong to them.

"These ones here are not white men," Alatna assured them. "They have faces like ours. Only they speak a different tongue and have different customs. They have great power, Tunak. These men come flying through the air. Arshakpuluk gave them a great bird for them all to fly on."

Now it was the turn of Tunak and his son to be frightened.

"I am the wife of their *tonjon*," Alatna proudly declared, "and I am carrying his child."

That decided the two Nunamiut men. When a woman became pregnant, her father lost his power over her and she became a full member of her new family. Tunak gave her back her fox. "Take your catch to your husband."

Alatna nodded and placed the dead animal across her shoulders.

"We saw the tracks of the strangers, going up into the valley of the caves. Sissuk hid above their camp and watched. You came out and we followed."

Alatna's only wish now was to get away from them.

"The strangers will leave the valley in the spring, to go on fighting the *kablunas*. You must not come here again until then. These are my husband's and his men's hunting-grounds now."

The two Nunamiuts stood hesitating for a moment in the snow. Alatna pulled out a small bag made from ermine skins which she had made for Hidaka. "Give that to Babuk," she said to her father. "It will show her that all is well with me."

Babuk was Alatna's mother, the only person in the whole tribe for whom she had any real feeling. The fact that she could give her mother a present without having to ask her husband's permission would prove that all was well with her.

Tunak tucked the bag inside his parka and without more ado the two men turned and went away. The snowy bushes closed behind them and no trace of them remained.

Alatna wasted no time on the thought that she had probably seen her father and brother for the last time, but set out for the camp.

In the cave, great preparations were in progress. Hidaka was planning to look for the herd of caribou with Tojimoto and Sinobu. The rest of the patrol was to accompany them as far as the end of the valley where there was a lake full of fish, except for Noboru who was to stay behind to collect firewood and do other light work.

Hidaka went into the alcove, where Alatna sat alone. He took her in his arms, laid his cheek against hers and spoke to her gently.

"Alatna-kimi, don't work too hard, you must get enough rest."

Never had a man been so kind! She was so happy that she found herself crying for the first time since she was a little girl. Hidaka rubbed his nose tenderly against her damp cheek.

"I'll be back soon, Kimi, tomorrow or the day after."

He tore himself away and hurried out. The men had already tied on their snowshoes. Hidaka quickly did the same and they set off.

Sissuk sat above the cave, hidden in the snow-covered undergrowth, and watched the men as they moved

182

off. When they were far enough away, he stood up and with hand-signals told his companions at the mouth of the gorge how many Japanese there had been.

Soon after, Noboru left to inspect the traps which he had set before his arm and shoulder had been injured.

For the first time Alatna was now completely alone in the cave. She could have a bath in privacy, the invigorating steam bath which the Nunamiuts took occasionally to stimulate the circulation and keep the limbs supple.

Alatna fetched an armful of thick willow branches which she sharpened at one end. At the entrance of the cave, where the hot water used for washing was thrown out, there was a space free of snow. Here she drove the willow branches into the ground, making a circular fence about two paces across. In the middle of the circle she hacked a hole a foot deep in the ground with an axe, and threw out the loose earth. Then she tied the branches together at the top and covered them with caribou hides, which she weighed down with stones, leaving a small opening just big enough for her to creep through. The structure was now shaped like a dome. Taking burning logs from the fireplace in the cave, she started another fire with them at the entrance to her bath-tent, threw a dozen stones into the fire and covered them thickly with more wood.

The Japanese stored their water in a sack made from moose-calf skin. Alatna took it from its peg and propped the lightly filled vessel against the inside wall of her small tent. A branch, forked at the top, and the water-dipper, made the arrangement complete.

Everything was now ready. Alatna peeled off her furs and crept naked into the circular tent. Once inside, she used the forked stick to roll the hot stones from the fire at the entrance into the hollow. When she scooped up some water and poured it over the stones, the water hissed loudly and the tent immediately filled with hot

183

steam. She rubbed her body from head to foot with a ball of moss. Her skin began to redden and smart, but she paused only to take more stones from the fire and pour more water over them.

Meanwhile Noboru's snowshoe had broken, and he had had to turn back and trudge home because his injured arm prevented him from mending it. Inaki, who had been sent back by the captain to fetch the dog, fell in beside him. The caribou tracks had been blown away by the wind, and Kinmek's nose was needed to find them.

At the sight of the steaming dome at the entrance to the cave, the two men stopped abruptly. The structure looked sinister, like a monster curled up in the snow pouring forth smoke from its jaws.

Inaki took his rifle in his hand and ventured a little closer. They could see neither the opening in the structure nor the little fire in front of it because they were approaching from the other side. "Noboru, go and pull the skins off. I'll be ready to shoot."

"All right, then, but make sure you cover me!"

Terrified, the Oshone crept gingerly up to the steaming tent. He looked around to make sure Inaki really had his rifle at the ready and, when he was satisfied, grabbed the skins and tore them down.

The whole structure collapsed at once and a huge cloud of steam billowed upwards. As it rapidly evaporated in the cold air Alatna was revealed in all her nakedness. She tried hurriedly to hide behind the rest of the bath-hut, but stumbled against Noboru, who immediately seized her with his good arm.

Aroused by his close contact with her naked flesh, he held her body tightly to him. Alatna kicked out against his legs, freed her hands and pummelled him in the face with both fists. Inaki ran up, in two minds whether to rescue her or join Noboru in ravishing her.

Because of his injured arm, the Oshone could not

stop Alatna tearing herself free. She tripped over the remains of her bath-hut and fell sprawling into the snow, but as she was about to pick herself up, Inaki reached her and violently held her down. Alatna could tell from his distorted features that he had lost all control of himself.

At that moment a blow struck him in the back; he threw his head up, screamed shrilly and collapsed forwards. Alatna wriggled out from under him, scrambled to her feet, and saw a spear quivering in his back.

Sissuk, followed by a band of other Nunamiuts, came up.

"These are bad men," he cried, "worse than rats and wolves!"

Alatna quickly picked up her parka and pulled her fur clothes over her head. As she was putting on her mukluks, she noticed Noboru squatting motionless in the snow. A long arrow protruded from his neck.

"We saw everything from the beginning," Sissuk said. "Then we came and killed them."

He threw back his head and gave the victory cry of the Nunamiuts to the spirits above. His companions followed his example and their wild howling could be heard as far as the bottom of the valley where Suda, Lonti and Tsunashima sat fishing on the ice. They threw down their tackle and hurried off at once to the camp.

The Japanese were not far from the cave when they were ambushed by the Nunamiuts. All three of them were killed.

38

The captain and his two companions had waited a long time for Inaki and could not understand why the dog came alone. Kinmek's whole body trembled. He leapt at Hidaka, breathlessly trying to bark and tearing at his parka. Then he ran back a little way.

"He wants us to go back," Tojimoto said. "He doesn't like this expedition."

"Dogs are often like that," Hidaka said. "They always want the people they belong to to stay together. It's their herding instinct."

"Kinmek wants to tell us something," said Sinobu, who knew more about dogs than his captain.

"Perhaps he's seen a hare; that's important enough to him."

The dog was running back once again and Hidaka had to call him firmly to heel.

"We'll go on," he said. "Inaki will just have to follow."

The three men continued their march over the hills, Hidaka making the dog run on ahead. Although the wind had blown away the herd's tracks Kinmek could still pick up its scent; only twenty-four hours had gone by since it had moved off.

On the other side of the high ground there lay a wide plateau sloping down very gently towards the south. Towards midday they saw a few isolated pines in the distance. Here the tracks had not been blown away and the animals' traces could be seen clearly, but were for the most part several days old and not worth following. But later, when the shadows were beginning to lengthen, Kinmek raised his nose to the wind, stood stock still, then lay down and pricked his ears. In front of them was a thick clump of large fir trees, and it seemed that this was the spot where they would find their quarry. The captain sent Tojimoto off to the right, and Sinobu to the left. They were to go round the outside of the copse, while Hidaka himself and the dog would go in.

Kinmek hunted like a wolf; one of his ancestors had probably been one. He pressed himself so deeply into the snow that his back almost disappeared from view. Hidaka walked twenty paces behind him watching the snow-laden branches with especial attention because their movements would betray the quarry's path.

But the caribou had got wind of Tojimoto and Sinobu and broke cover. A large buck came crashing towards the captain, who hastily raised his rifle and fired. The animal sank to the ground and almost simultaneously there came a shot from the right. A dull thud indicated that Tojimoto had also made a kill. The rest of the herd turned and charged out of the other side of the wood, where Sinobu was waiting for them. He fired twice.

Tojimoto came up to announce that he had killed a young buck. Sinobu had not been quite so successful. Although he had hit a doe twice, she had got away. A trail of reddish-brown drops ran along the wounded animal's tracks.

"Hit in the liver," Hidaka said. "It could take quite some time."

More than an hour later they caught up with the caribou which had finally collapsed. As the animal was still alive, Sinobu plunged his knife into its neck. They skinned it and cut it up immediately, packed the hunks of meat into the vast caribou skin and dragged the load through the snow behind them.

Night had fallen by the time they reached the bucks Tojimoto and Hidaka had shot. Both carcasses had to be thawed out by the fire, cut up and prepared.

Sinobu climbed up into a large and spreading fir

tree, and the two officers passed the pieces of meat up to him, one by one. Sinobu tied them securely to the branches with strips of skin. Their rich booty would be safe from the hungry forest animals and they could fetch it later.

Hidaka decided to pitch camp beneath the tree. Sinobu went off to collect firewood while the captain and Tojimoto built a sloping roof out of slender tree-trunks and small fir branches. They scuffed the ground free of snow with their snowshoes, spread out the fresh skins on the hard frozen ground and built up the fire.

Later that night Kinmek stood up and began to growl in the direction of the wood, the hairs on his back standing on end. The captain and Tojimoto looked at Sinobu. Kinmek huddled close to his master and began to whine. Now the men, too, could hear the howling of the wolves. From far away the sound came through the still, bitterly cold night, ending on a long, shrill, very high-pitched note—the call of the leader to the wolf pack.

"It's my fault, Taiji-dono," Sinobu cried. "They must have found what was left of my caribou."

The fresh, blood-spattered tracks were the best possible trail hungry wolves could wish for.

"Come on," Hidaka ordered. "We need more wood, and quickly: The pack will be here soon."

The fire was the men's safest shield and would have to be tended constantly. Sinobu was already reluctant to go beyond its light. Hidaka and Tojimoto did not venture very far away either, because it would be impossible for them to defend themselves in the dark against a pack of wolves. The fire-wood lay buried deep in the snow and they only managed to dig out three small dead logs which they dragged back to the camp. When they were about to set off again, Tojimoto thought that the wolves' howls sounded much closer than before.

"It's too risky, Enzo; the beasts are on our tracks already."

"There must be a lot of them if they've managed to finish up the remains so quickly."

Sinobu was trembling uncontrollably. Kinmek crept up against his master and Hidaka could feel the dog's heart racing.

Grey shadows now moved soundlessly out of the forest, the light of the fire reflected in their eyes. More and more emerged and stood as if spellbound by the flickering flames. They wanted their prey. They could smell the meat up in the tree and the remnants of the carcasses on the ground not far from the fire, and they scented the warm blood of the men.

Sinobu, eyes and mouth wide open, was shaking so violently that the captain lost his temper and swore at him angrily. It was the wolves who reacted, with ripples of movement along their ranks. They had never heard a human voice before. Hidaka seized his gun and laid it across his knee, and Tojimoto did the same.

Eventually the wolves, spurred on by hunger, ventured into the firelight and threw themselves at the remains of the two caribou, scarcely a dozen paces from the lean-to shelter. They growled as they seized upon the entrails and tore at the bones.

The three men could hear their hot panting breath and see their teeth flash as they devoured the meat. They knew that when the animals had finished all that was there, they would prowl round the camp until the flames burnt out or until the sun rose.

Soon the carcasses had been stripped of everything edible. Individual wolves, forced out by stronger members of the pack, began to slink around the fire looking for more food. Tojimoto threw a burning log at them. It hit one wolf on the head and gave off a spray of sparks; the wolf vanished, howling. Tojimoto's second and third attempts were equally successful.

"Stop doing that, Yoshi! We haven't got enough wood."

Suddenly Tojimoto realized just how desperate their position was.

"How many rounds of ammunition have you got left?"

Tojimoto counted eleven. Since Sinobu was now incapable of doing anything, Hidaka looked through his pouch.

"He's got seven. Let's hope it'll be enough."

The wolves came nearer, stood in a semi-circle and howled at the three men. Their strong, sharp teeth could be seen quite clearly.

Tojimoto could bear it no longer and shot right into one of the howling mouths. Immediately the whole pack fell upon the wounded animal and tore its twitching body to pieces.

Then Sinobu gave a howl which seemed to echo those of the wolves. With his head thrown back and his mouth open wide, he was trying to outdo the pack. Hidaka hit him full in the face. Quick as a flash, Sinobu slipped past him, leapt right through the fire and threw himself at the pack.

Panic-stricken, Tojimoto emptied his magazine. The captain shot with more deliberation, but already the murderous animals had pulled Sinobu to the ground. Two of the beasts had fastened onto his back, another hung at his throat.

Hidaka shot Sinobu through the head, and the two officers sat and watched their fellow Japanese being torn to pieces before their eyes. Not until the grey of morning came did the creatures slink away.

Hidaka and Tojimoto collected everything together without a word and set off for their base camp. Kinmek stayed close to them, his hair still standing on end.

Towards midday they reached the first hill, and climbed up it to reconnoitre. Even before the captain had raised his field-glasses to his eyes, he could see a grey-white pillar of smoke rising steeply from the tree tops in the distance.

"Smoke, Yoshi, there's smoke over there!"

"Indians or Yankees?"

"More likely Nunamiuts. Alatna's people."

Tojimoto wondered whether they should make contact with them.

"Yes, I think it's best, Yoshi. When we get going again in the spring, we can do with their help."

They plodded down the hill and into the wood again. After about half an hour Kinmek shot forwards and yapped to show he had found tracks. They were covered with snow and invisible to the men, but the dog had scented them out.

"Must be a Nunamiut trail," Hidaka said. "Perhaps Kinmek can still remember it."

The trail and the dog led through the wood and across open country until they reached a wide river. Here they found the fresh tracks of men who had obviously been wearing improvised skis.

"Three men," Hidaka said. "I should think they were here about noon yesterday."

The two men moved upstream and soon reached the place where the tracks led into the wood. Tojimoto went ahead again, followed by Hidaka.

They could smell the smoke now and were picturing to themselves the shock with which the stone-age people would greet their appearance. Hidaka was already turning over suitable greetings in his mind, when Tojimoto suddenly came hurrying back.

"There's a hut there, a proper log-cabin! Those aren't Nunamiuts . . . they're Yankees!"

It was now too late for a rapid retreat. The Japanese had betrayed their presence through the prints of their snowshoes. Whoever came across these tracks would raise the alarm at once, so a surprise attack was now their only course.

"How many rounds of ammunition have you got left, Yoshi?"

"Only four."

"And I've got three, but it'll have to do!"

Keeping well down, they crept through the trees until they reached a small clearing, in the middle of which Hidaka could now see the cabin.

It was an old log-cabin, but had been added to recently, the small window in the extension being covered with some animal skin whilst the older part of the building had a glass window. A pair of long skis were leaning up against the wall beside the door. So there must be at least four people living there: the three who had gone hunting the day before on the handmade skis and a fourth who was the owner of the proper skis against the wall.

"It's our Yankees! See the jacket by the door, Yoshi, with the scout badge on the sleeve?"

They could not be sure that the owner of the skis was alone in the hut. At their last encounter with the enemy, Hidaka had counted at least five scouts, and there had possibly been others he had not seen.

"We'll shoot the first man to come out, and the rest will all come rushing after him to see what's going on."

They waited for a long time. The light began to fail and the shadows lengthened. At last there was a sound from inside the hut. They heard the clang of an oven door and the chimney gave off more smoke. Immediately afterwards, a lamp was lit by the window.

"They've been sleeping and are just getting up," Hidaka whispered.

At that moment the door was pushed open and a bearded man came out, rubbing his eyes. The two men, their guns trained, waited for him to move so that either his chest or back would present a good target.

Suddenly Kinmek barked and raced across the clearing. The two shots came too late and only cracked into the hastily-slammed door.

"*Kono yaro!* Shoot through the window, Yoshi, shoot at the lamp!"

If the Yankees had any sense, the first thing they would think of would be to put out the light so that they would not be silhouetted against it. If the Japanese fired at the lamp now, they had a good chance of hitting a man as well.

Someone was already lifting the lamp. Hidaka's shot splintered the window pane and the light went out.

Immediately the barrel of a gun was pushed through the window, and started to fire. Tojimoto could see the outline of a shoulder, took aim and fired. Curses and a crashing sound showed that he had got his man.

"That was my last bullet, Enzo."

Kinmek was barking and rushing around outside the cabin, and they could no longer hear what was going on inside. But a glowing red light shone through the window.

"The lamp, Enzo! Look, the paraffin must be burning!"

They both leapt to their feet, raced up to the last bush in the clearing, and flung themselves down again in the snow. The man in the cabin had been ready for this advance, and fired twice, quickly.

The American had been too busy to notice what was happening behind him, and only now, with the flames leaping higher, could Hidaka see his skipping shadow as he started trying to put the fire out. But the wood, tinder-dry, had already caught.

"He's got to come out now!" Hidaka cried triumphantly, just as the American rushed out into the open, holding his gun in front of him, and tried to make for cover. Hidaka shot him in the chest with his last bullet.

The wounded man clawed the air and then fell back into the burning cabin.

"Come on, Yoshi, we must try and get some of the stuff out of there!"

Hidaka ran forward, but the flames had reached Bert Hutchinson's powder cask, and with a mighty roar the entire log-cabin blew up. The rafters crashed down in a cloud of sparks, immediately catching fire, and there seemed to be a vast amount of exploding ammunition.

"*Namuami daibutsu!*" the captain shouted. "He is going to hell with ten thousand devils!"

When Tojimoto did not answer, Hidaka looked back. His friend was lying in the snow, curled up in agony.

"What is it, Yoshi?"

The lieutenant lay on his back clutching his right knee with both hands.

Hidaka quickly cut open the fur trouser-leg, slit the hareskin beneath, and saw that Tojimoto's knee-cap was hopelessly smashed.

"Go, Enzo, you must get away at once!"

The other Yankees were sure to have heard the explosion and be on their way back already. The two of them would be at the Yankees' mercy, with no more ammunition and useless rifles.

"Put your arm round my neck. We'll be able to manage like that."

Tojimoto refused. Hidaka would have no chance of escape if he was burdened with his friend. The lieutenant pulled out his knife, and Hidaka knew that, like the proud and honourable Samurai, he wanted to kill himself rather than fall into the hands of the enemy. He quickly snatched the knife from him.

"Oh, Enzo, help me, please give me my knife!"

The wounded had the right to demand this service of a friend; it was in accordance with the rules of *bushido*.

194

A man committing *seppukku* must administer the *coup de grâce* with his own hands.

"Cut open my clothes for me," Tojimoto pleaded, "and turn me to face the east."

But Hidaka put the knife away in his own pocket, picked up his friend and hoisted him over his shoulder. Tojimoto fainted with pain. The dog running along in front of him, Hidaka waded through the deep snow until he reached the river, and laid the unconscious man by the bank. He cut thick branches from the nearest fir tree and tied Tojimoto firmly to them. Dragging the stretcher behind him he managed to make faster progress.

Hidaka hurried through the night with his clothes drenched in sweat, his head throbbing and a searing pain in his chest. At about midnight he realized that he had gone too far to the east and that he would have to leave the river. He untied Tojimoto from the branches. As he lifted him up, the lieutenant regained consciousness and demanded to be allowed to walk unaided. But when he tried to put his weight on his wounded leg, he crumpled to the ground.

"Put your arm round my shoulder, Yoshi, and use just your left foot."

After a while they got the knack of walking three-legged and managed to make slow progress. By daybreak they had reached the edge of the wood, and began to climb uphill. At the top of the slope, Hidaka had to lie down in a snow-drift until he had recovered sufficiently to go on.

"You'll kill yourself, Enzo. You won't be able to make it the rest of the way with me along."

"I'll make you a fire tonight and go and fetch help. By tomorrow night you'll be in the cave. Alatna will nurse you; she is good at that."

"You are forgetting the Yankees, Enzo. They'll catch us up."

195

Hidaka had indeed forgotten all about the enemy. During the last few hours his mind had been blank as he had forced himself to stumble on, following the dog who ran ahead, towards Alatna.

Tojimoto lay on his side in the snow and looked back.

"Enzo, the time has come now. You've barely got half an hour's start."

Hidaka was too tired to start an argument.

"Damn it, Enzo. I need my knife! They've just left the wood and are coming up the hill. My knife! Give it to me now!"

Hidaka pulled himself together, grabbed his field-glasses, and looked down across the snow-drifts. The three scouts could be seen clearly. All were armed with long-barrelled guns and they glided swiftly forwards on their handmade skis.

"Come on, let's have an end to this," the wounded man urged.

Hidaka grabbed him by the shoulders.

"No, you must let yourself be taken prisoner, Yoshi! They must take you alive!"

Tojimoto forced himself out of the captain's grasp.

"Never, never!"

Before Hidaka could stop him he had seized his knife back. He tore open his anorak at the neck and laid bare his throat. Hidaka threw himself on top of him, and held his arms down in the snow.

"I forbid it! As your commanding officer, I order you to stay alive!"

The wounded man gasped for breath under his weight.

"You're the only one who can save me, Yoshi. They cannot kill you, it is against their code. They will have to look after you and take you with them. They will be forced to go back, but I will go on and get through with my report. I promise you, it will get through!"

Yoshi now understood his friend's plan.

"But my name will be dishonoured, Enzo!"

"You're doing it on my orders. You must live for Japan!"

"But if you don't get through, nobody will know!"

"Then sacrifice even your honour for Japan, Yoshi. The gods will know the truth!"

Both of them looked down; they were lying deep in the snow and the enemy had not yet seen them. The three scouts climbed up towards them effortlessly with no sign of tiredness.

"Run, Enzo. I will do what you want."

Hidaka held his friend's face between his hands.

"Farewell, Yoshi."

He leapt to his feet, saluted his wounded comrade and, followed by Kinmek, raced down into the valley ahead. Three times behind him he heard Tojimoto shout: *"Banzai!"*

Quickly he reached the next piece of high ground, threw himself down behind a boulder and looked back through his field-glasses. He pulled the dog close to him and held him tightly.

At that moment the figures of the three Yankees appeared over the top of the snow-drift, the barrels of their guns pointing straight at Tojimoto, who raised his hands hesitantly. In painful suspense, Hidaka watched to see what would happen. The enemy might still shoot the wounded man out of hand, so far away from any eye-witness. They were having an excited discussion, but the tall scout with the thin face appeared to have over-ruled the others. All three Americans bent over Tojimoto and examined his injury, then laid him across two guns tied together to serve as a stretcher, and carried him off.

39

As Captain Hidaka was making for the cave that same night, where he learned from Alatna that, of the entire patrol, he was the only man left, the three Americans were taking Lieutenant Tojimoto back towards the south. They had cleansed his shattered knee with snow and bandaged it with soft skins.

The scouts' decision to turn back had been a very difficult one for them to make. At their next camp they discussed the matter again out of ear-shot of their prisoner. Dick Hamston's view was that it was crazy to keep a vicious enemy soldier alive.

"It doesn't make much sense to me, either," Allan agreed, "but luckily for us we don't have to make the decision. It's against the law to kill a prisoner of war and that's that."

Dick Hamston laughed scornfully.

"And so we have to drag this son of a bitch, by the sweat of our brow, to some well-heated hospital! I wouldn't kill a wounded man either. But letting that other rat get away, that's what really sticks in my gullet."

"The other man must certainly have been Captain Hidaka," Allan decided.

"What makes you so sure?"

"Because I think only Hidaka would have had the infernal cunning to throw us his lieutenant to save himself."

"We should have left the wounded Jap lying there and gone on. That would have been the sensible thing to do!"

"No, Pete. He would have died of exposure or the wolves would have got him. Don't forget the trail of blood in the snow. What is this damned war all about, if we go and behave just as brutally as those yellow bastards?"

"At the moment all I can think of is Mr. Hidaka laughing his stinking head off at us!"

"It makes my gall rise," Allan agreed.

That exhausted the subject and they went on to talk of other things. But nobody spoke to Tojimoto. At the beginning, Allan had exchanged a few words with him and discovered that he spoke English, but the prisoner told him only his name and rank, nothing more.

On the eleventh day of their journey they again reached the little valley where Harry had lost his hand in the Japanese booby-trap. The scouts decided to stop there for a few days to replenish their provisions. It was Allan's turn to stay with the prisoner and tend the fire, while Dick and Pete went off hunting bighorn at daybreak. Tojimoto was resting on a bed of fir branches, gazing up at the sky with half-closed eyes. Small flames flickered in the fire, and the chief scout sat nearby mending his skis.

Allan had no wish to spend the entire day without speaking a word, and decided to break the silence. "How's your knee, lieutenant?"

"It has become stiff . . . thank you." The Japanese let his head sink back again.

"Are you married? Have you got any children?"

"No, Mr. McCluire, only a mother and father, and four brothers who are all soldiers."

"Where's your home, lieutenant?"

"In Japan."

And Allan could get nothing more out of him.

The two scouts came back from their hunting expedition heavily laden.

"How about some really juicy spit-roasted bighorn steaks!" Dick Hamston asked cheerfully.

When the meal was ready he handed the prisoner a piece of leg, dripping with fat.

"Here, fill your belly with that and put on more weight for us to carry, you bastard."

The Japanese first cut his meat into small pieces and then picked them up with two small wooden sticks with which he conveyed the food to his mouth.

"Why make it easy, when there's a more difficult way?"

"That's the only way he can do it—he was taught to eat like that in the cradle."

A little later Allan asked whether the others would be able to manage to take the prisoner to Lake Clifton without him.

"We've seen that coming for some time, Allan."

"Maybe, but can you do it, do you think?"

"Sure, we can. But haven't you had enough yet?"

"No, I won't rest until I get Hidaka!"

Dick and Pete looked at each other.

"Then that's that."

40

Captain Hidaka could not dig a proper grave because the soil was frozen too hard, and the dead had to make do with a cairn of stones.

When he had put the last stone in place, the captain stood back, bowed very low three times and then saluted the burial mound. He stood quite still, his right hand raised to his fur hat. Alatna took this to be the custom in his tribe and did exactly as he did.

Hidaka had to leave the area. The Americans would have another search party sent by air as soon as the scouts had made contact with the outside world. He drew the outline of northern Alaska with its mountain ranges and major rivers on the sandy floor of the cave, to learn from Alatna what lay ahead on their way to the coast.

Yes, there was a great river, she told him. It lay in the direction of the setting sun. But it would take many days' travel to reach its banks. She had never been there herself and knew only that the Nunamiuts called this great river Angalik, a name that was quite unknown to Hidaka. It was the Noatak that he must reach so as to travel down on a raft to the west coast, to Igilchik Island and Boris Nizhinsky. He could only hope that Alatna's Angalik would turn out to be the Noatak.

Alatna prepared a pack that would have been too much for half a dozen men to carry. It included their entire store of frozen fish, all the utensils they had made and their warmest fur coverings. Hidaka explained gently that they would never be able to carry it all.

"I make thing for pulling, you see."

She took a piece of the hide of a caribou they had

recently killed and poured water over it until it was completely soaked through. Then she trod a hole in the snow about six feet long and eighteen inches wide, until it was flat and smooth at the bottom. In this she laid the piece of wet caribou-hide, with the hair uppermost, and braced it against the sides with willow branches. In barely an hour the hide had frozen as hard as a board and had become a serviceable sledge. Alatna filled it with all the things she had assembled. Next morning they set off.

They left the snug cave behind, and the stone burial mound where the bodies of Suda, and Tsunashima, of Lonti, Inaki and Noboru had found their last resting-place. They traversed the whole length of the caribou valley in a westerly direction and then had a very difficult climb to the plateau beyond. There the sledge slid along the frozen snow so smoothly that Kinmek could have pulled it by himself. Towards evening they reached a downwards slope and had to hang on to the sledge from behind to brake its plunge. The landscape before them looked like a petrified sea, one huge wave of snow following the other with monotonous regularity as far as the eye could see.

When darkness fell, they took only a short rest before continuing their journey. The sky was a deep purple, the soft light of the moon gleamed on the snow and the stars shone brilliantly. No sound could be heard but for the creaking of the sledge and their snowshoes.

As they paused again briefly to rest, they saw a curtain of brightest silver appear, covering the entire expanse of the purple sky. It was the Northern Lights; the bright tapestry hung down before them in delicate folds. There was total stillness.

"Arshakpuluk go through the sky," Alatna whispered in awe.

After about half an hour the *aurora borealis* gradually disappeared, dissolving into silky threads which became gradually more and more nebulous until they finally vanished altogether. The two people, the dog and the sledge started off once more.

By late morning they reached a frozen river, and there they built a tent with their skins, lit a small fire inside and stayed until the following day.

Then they set off again, travelling on and on. Hidaka felt that they were making hardly any progress, as each undulation in the ground was succeeded by another. No animal tracks crossed their path, no birds flew through the air, and there was not the slightest breath of wind. It was the stillness of mid-winter. The temperature fell to fifty degrees below zero and their breath formed clouds of tiny crystals. The sun shone for only a few hours in the day and, reflected by the glistening snow, dazzled them painfully. To protect their eyes the two travellers wore snow-glasses, Eskimo-fashion, which Alatna had made very simply out of small pieces of wood, about two inches wide, with small slits through which to see and leather thongs to hold them in position.

Their stock of meat was finished, and only a parcel of fish, frozen rock-hard, was left. It was not enough to maintain the strength of two people and a dog, who were using up more and more energy as each day passed.

When they again reached a river, Hidaka decided to make camp for several days in order to find food. They tried to melt a hole through the ice but found that the river was frozen solid.

Still, Hidaka hoped to come across the run of a herd of caribou somewhere along the river. The only weapons he now possessed were his hand-made spear, his axe and his knife, and to catch any game he would have to creep up to within a few paces of it. However, he could find no tracks along the frozen water, and was about to turn back when he saw a small white cloud rising up from the bank. It could not be smoke because the tiny cloud was curling up from a snow-drift.

Hidaka approached it cautiously and then held his bare hand in the little cloud. It was only vapour, rising a couple of feet in the air before it froze and sank again. A firm crust of ice had formed around the hole, the size of an eye, through which the vapour was rising. The reason could only be that there was a bear hibernating under the snow-drift, and that its breath was producing the mist. Hidaka began to dig into the white hill. The deeper he went, the more carefully he worked. If the bear was awakened too soon, it would be extremely dangerous. Hidaka's axe and knife were certainly not adequate for dealing with the fury of a grizzly disturbed in its winter sleep.

When Hidaka had dug about four feet down, the cracks in the snow widened and the white hill shook. He stepped back and grabbed his axe, but the animal seemed to settle down again. Hidaka stayed quite still for a long time. Then he began burrowing once again, using both hands, and suddenly the bear's great head appeared out of the snow before him.

Hidaka jumped back at once but tripped over his spear and rolled down the hillside. By the time he had found his feet again, the grizzly had risen to its full height. Fortunately it appeared to be dazzled by the bright sunshine.

Hidaka pulled off his parka, so as to be able to move more freely. As he bent to pick up his spear again, the grizzly caught sight of him and went for him. Hidaka took aim and hurled the spear at its heart, but the animal lumbered to one side and only its paw was hit. Fully awakened now by the pain, it charged Hidaka. Desperately the man threw himself to one side.

Still dazzled by the sudden light, the bear took the parka in the snow for its enemy and fell upon it. Making use of this distraction, Hidaka crept up behind it and dealt it a crashing blow on its head with his axe. The huge animal plunged forward onto its side and, shuddering violently, died.

Hidaka had to skin the bear and cut up its flesh quickly before the mountain of meat froze into a solid block. Carrying only the bear's liver, and its paws, he made his way back to the camp. By nightfall, a fire burned merrily in front of their tent, with the liver and the tasty paws roasting on the spit.

Next day they hauled the rest of the prize back to their camp, and cleaned the skin. The meat was packed up into handy parcels and stowed away on the sledge. With their new stock of food they would be able to hold out now for a long time.

However, as the journey wore on, Hidaka began to feel slightly unwell. He thought it must be a passing weakness, and tried to pull himself together, but on the following day he felt worse and had pains at the back of his head. His heart thumped as if it would burst, and he had to lean heavily against the sledge to keep on his feet.

Alatna could feel the sledge becoming heavier and heavier, and realized that Hidaka's strength was ebbing. She pleaded exhaustion herself, to make an excuse to stop earlier, and prepared the most nourishing meal she could, but Hidaka did not recover and the next day he collapsed unconscious.

Alatna did not lose her head. She dragged him onto the sledge and covered him with furs, and, summoning up all her strength, pulled the sledge herself, until she finally reached a broad valley, in the middle of which lay a round lake. On its far side she could see a birch wood, encircled by rocks, which would certainly provide masses of firewood, and probably edible plants as well. She pulled the sledge across the ice, hauled it up the slope, step by step, and looked round for a suitable camping-place among the trees.

Alatna did not think a tent would be good enough for her patient; he would have to have a proper igloo. She cut square blocks out of the solidly frozen snow-drifts and laid the foundations in a perfect circle five paces across. Each additional layer was slightly smaller in diameter, so that the whole structure finally formed a dome. At the top, it was completed with a round block of snow, through which she drove a stick to make a hole for ventilation. She filled the joints with soft snow and smoothed down the outside walls, and to keep the wind out, built a curving tunnel out of the frozen blocks in front of the opening. Finally she made sleeping platforms and a table with tightly packed snow inside the igloo.

Alatna dragged Hidaka off the sledge and through the tunnel. He was still unconscious and lay beneath the furs, breathing fitfully. This was not the first time that Alatna had come across this condition. It always arose after a bear hunt and the Nunamiuts believed that the soul of the dead animal was taking revenge on the hunter. Women and children were seldom afflicted by the sickness.

Alatna kept the most important of the Nunamiuts' healing herbs in a caribou leather bag. This was her duty as the *tonjon*'s daughter. She ground the medicine, put it in the bottom of a cup with some snow and boiled up the brew.

When she put the hot drink to his lips, Hidaka opened his eyes. The daylight filtered through the snowy dome with a pale-blue shimmer.

"You sick, you drink, you soon well!"

He gulped down the brew, shuddering at the bitter taste. Only now did he remember Tojimoto's warning never to eat bear's meat.

"Are you all right, Alatna-kimi, have you no pain?"

No, she was in the best of health, and felt fine.

"You did not eat any of the bear's liver, did you?"

She shook her head.

"Liver of bear belong to hunters, women must not eat it."

As far as Hidaka knew, trichinae were to be found mainly in the liver. Without skilled treatment, almost every case of trichinosis was fatal after four to eight weeks of agony. What was to become of Alatna, who would give birth to his child in the summer? He hoped that she would still be able to find her way back to her own people.

For weeks Hidaka passed his days in semi-darkness. Alatna had to feed him and to force the medicine between his lips drop by drop. The rest of the time she spent mostly out of doors, with her dog, making snares to catch the ptarmigan. The storms had begun again and raged over the land with icy fury. The igloo sank deeper and deeper into the snow.

One day, when Alatna returned from her snares with a silver fox and two hares, Hidaka was sitting up in bed, smiling. The medicinal skill of the Nunamiuts, handed down from one generation to the next from time immemorial, had conquered the deadly trichinosis. But weeks passed before Hidaka could take his first halting steps inside the igloo. He used this time of enforced idleness to increase Alatna's knowledge of his language, while he himself learned more of hers.

Later he started to make plans for the next lap of their journey. They would have to reach the great river before the coming of the thaw, or the tundra would have become a bottomless swamp. One week later they set off once more.

The baby was now heavy within her, but amongst the Nunamiuts it was not customary to give a woman in her condition any special consideration. So Alatna did not understand why Hidaka insisted on pulling the sledge alone with Kinmek, only allowing her to help in pushing it occasionally.

At the end of the week, they reached a river that was broader than any other that Hidaka had yet seen in Alaska. Hoping that it was the Flora, which he knew must flow into the Noatak some fifty to a hundred miles farther west, he decided to stay where he was until the ice broke. However, when they wanted to light a fire they could find no dead wood of the kind they used to rub together to make a spark.

"I'll go down river until I find the right wood," Hidaka said.

"You not go; I make fire with ice."

Hidaka went with her into the middle of the river where the ice lay shining and exposed. There Alatna chose a clear, transparent area with no scratches or bubbles in the ice. She struck her axe into the solid mass and extracted a fragment the size of a man's fist, which she took between her hands and began to rub vigorously on both sides.

"You make small hill with many dry leaves," she said to Hidaka. He understood that it was tinder she wanted and collected dry leaves from the tips of the willows. Then he built a bed for them with brushwood.

Alatna sat down beside the fireplace and continued flattenning the ball of ice. When she had finished her polishing she held a round disc, convex on each side, in her hand. She stood up, looked for the sun and held her shining piece of ice over the pile of dry leaves. The sun's rays were concentrated by the disc of ice onto a point in the dry tinder. Soon the leaves started to crackle, a thread of smoke began to rise and then the first spark glowed. The polished piece of ice had acted as a perfect magnifying glass.

This time Hidaka built a very solid tent with skins and strong branches because they would be there for several weeks before the ice on the river broke.

And finally, one night, the southerly wind did arrive, the air smelt of spring and the snow began to melt. The willows quickly showed signs of life and flocks of wild geese and crane flew across the sky to the north. Only when the snow had completely melted away, and the branches of the trees were in bud, did the great river awaken and burst its bonds. The first crack in the ice was accompanied by a sound like a thunder clap. Then with a noise like a hundred cannon, cracks burst open all over the river. The water shot through the widening gaps, and the great ice-floes piled onto each other, pushed up against the banks, and formed shining mountains of ice. The bursting and breaking lasted two days and nights, and then the battle was over. The river, dotted with shining ice-floes, flowed freely again.

For the next stage of their journey Hidaka selected a large ice floe, three feet thick, that had been left stranded on the bank. He cut two long pieces of wood, one for steering with and the other for poling. They climbed aboard the floe with their dog and all their belongings, pushed off from the bank and let themselves drift downstream.

They moved along effortlessly, having to take care only that their craft did not hit the bank or crash into other floes. One push with the pole was enough to steer them clear. When darkness fell they pulled in to the bank, slept beside a fire, and continued their journey next morning. The floe became smaller day by day, and eventually had to be replaced by another.

In the distance, blue mountains came into view and there were woods on both sides of the river. Large numbers of duck and whistling swan flew overhead, foxes trotted along the bank, and occasionally they saw a black or brown bear.

"Enzo, much great water in front!"

Through his field-glasses Hidaka could see their river widen where it joined a mighty flood. If this was the Noatak, they would be able to reach the west coast and

Boris Nizhinsky in a matter of two or three weeks at the most.

A chain of hills appeared on their left, with fir woods in front and a flat beach leading down to the river, and they pulled in to the bank and carried their things onto the shore. While Alatna set about rubbing up sparks for a fire, Hidaka climbed up to the nearest hill to have a look at the course of the great river which they had reached. At the top he had a shock of disappointment. The river flowed northwards in an almost straight line. With his field-glasses he could make out the shining ribbon and the far off tundra stretching as far as the horizon.

This could only be the Colville River, which later flowed into the Arctic Ocean but which never went anywhere near Igilchik. Hidaka closed his eyes and tried to visualize the map of the area which he had lost. The upper reaches of both rivers, the useless Colville and the Noatak which they needed so desperately, were only about sixty to a hundred miles apart. Even over difficult terrain they ought to be able to cover this distance in about ten days. And then there was always the chance that they might come across a tributary wide enough to take a raft.

He went down the hill again to Alatna and told her of his disappointing discovery. She took it calmly. If this was not the river her husband was looking for, they would find it somewhere else.

They took with them only the few weapons they had, the wooden utensils they had made, the stone lamp, the snares, their sewing materials and Alatna's medicine. Hidaka could carry all this in his skin sack. They climbed over the mountain ridge and walked steadily on through sparse woodlands. The bushes and the agrimony were in full bloom. The short spring had already given way to summer.

They stopped beneath the shelter of a wall of rock.

210

A broad strip of larches and hemlock firs stretched out on both sides and before them lay a lake surrounded by reeds on which hundreds of wild duck were swimming.

Alatna suggested that they stay there for a few days. While she fished and put out her snares for the duck, Hidaka could go off after bigger game. He was glad to give her a few days of rest. He had lost count of time during his long illness, and did not know exactly when his child was due. In the morning he helped her to build a strong shelter in which to camp for several days. He left her the axe and the bone knife, and the dog too, so that she would not be completely alone. Armed only with his Japanese knife and his spear, he set off on his search for game.

Alatna, for her part, prepared to give birth to his child.

41

Allan McCluire had had the great good fortune on his return to the edge of the tundra to come across a herd of caribou which had moved up to the northern foothills of the Brooks Range and were grazing in the forests there. Allan took advantage of the opportunity to stock up with food for the rest of the winter, built himself a hut and stayed with them.

The big storms came, announcing the arrival of the new year. The small caribou herds began to join up with one another, forming bigger and bigger groups. Their wanderlust had returned together with their longing for the lush green feeding-grounds of the unending tundra. Allan decided to accompany the herd. The caribou trail had followed the same, least arduous, route through the wilderness since before the dawn of history.

Allan still had his rifle with eighteen bullets, and one small pistol with a full magazine, in addition to the usual scout's axe, his large hunting-knife and his field-glasses.

He had long ago decided that his enemy was probably making for the Bering Strait. Since leaving the Schwatka Mountains, Captain Hidaka had kept in a steady westward direction, and Allan was convinced that he was trying to reach the Noatak, the only river in that part of the country that flowed to the west coast.

If Allan did not meet up with the Japanese on the caribou trail, he would probably find him on or near the river. And once he had travelled that far there would be no better way back to the outside world for him, either, than the mighty Noatak. As a gamewarden he had heard about the seal island in the mouth of the river, and though he did not know Nizhinsky personally, he knew a great deal about him.

Now, as the south wind rustled through the forest, the caribou set off, Allan following them. He had not fully realized just how much easier this would make his own progress. The many thousands of hooves trampled the slush and cleared the damp ground. Since the animals avoided both mountains and swamps Allan found he had no obstacles to contend with.

The huge herd became bigger day by day. Like tributaries flowing into a river other herds streamed in from both sides. A forest of antlers surged along in front of Allan and in the narrow passes the animals moved along flank to flank. Their horns clattered against each other, and their joints cracked at each step, a strange characteristic of the caribou. Their breath formed a constant cloud floating over their backs. Exhausted, dying and dead animals lined the path, and the wolves were so well fed that they took hardly any notice of the solitary human being.

The caribou did not hurry over their journey. When the snow had finally thawed they would often stay for days on a good feeding-ground, moving on only when everything had been stripped bare. The nights became short and the days warm. Almost without pause the summer followed the short spring.

A few days later his countless companions crossed a slow-moving stream which led in a westerly direction. It was probable that this river flowed into the Noatak and Allan decided to build himself a skin boat.

The caribou he needed for this were quickly bagged, although he did not intend to skin them until the next morning. He set up camp for the night close by the river. Because of the long summer drought, the grass and undergrowth were so dry that there was a real danger of starting a prairie fire, and Allan collected a dozen large stones and laid them round the spot he had selected for his fire.

Next morning he went out to pick up his catch where it lay scattered on the ground and skinned the carcasses. He filled one of the skins with fat and another with the best pieces of meat, and towards midday returned to the fireplace which he piled high with wood in order to smoke the meat over the fire and provide for his coming journey.

It was fortunate for him that he had stood up again to go and fetch some sharpened willow sticks when the stones around the fire exploded with a violent report. Fragments and splinters of stone flew out in all directions and would have killed anyone sitting by the fire.

Allan knew at once that this was Hidaka's doing. He must have seen the fire during the night, and in the morning, while Allan was busy with his caribou, must have replaced the stones around the fire with others from the river's edge. While these had been dried by the sun on the outside, they had lain under water for weeks beforehand and were thoroughly damp inside, so that when heated to a high temperature they would shatter into a thousand pieces. Hidaka's stratagem had failed. So much the worse for him: he had betrayed his presence. Once more the chief scout held one end of a thread in his hand, with the enemy at the other. And, of course, the same held good for Hidaka. Allan would have to be prepared for a further attack at any moment.

A silent duel between the two men had begun; a duel to the death. The captain and the chief scout; each both hunter and hunted.

Allan found his enemy's tracks without any difficulty. They led into a stream and did not continue out on the other bank. As it is easier to wade downstream in swiftly running water, Allan turned upstream, exactly as he calculated his opponent would have done.

214

Since he would also have made sure when he left the water that he would leave no trace, Allan paid close attention to the overhanging branches. When he saw one that would be strong enough to bear the weight of a man, he climbed out of the stream and searched for footprints in the ground around the tree-trunk.

He did not find any tracks on the ground, but he did see some small particles of freshly rubbed-off bark, and immediately after a few tiny damp spots on the dry foliage where drops of water from Hidaka's shoes must have fallen. The man had apparently gone through the thick wood by swinging from one strong branch to the next for quite a long way. Finally Allan found the place in the moss where he jumped down. It looked as if Hidaka had been sure that no one could now be following his trail and he had made no further attempt to hide his tracks.

All the same, the chief scout was cautious. When the tracks led into knee-high grass, he broke a long branch from the nearest tree and held it in front of him through the grass. He had gone scarcely a hundred yards when he felt his pole meet resistance, and leapt back at once as half a dozen tree-trunks came crashing down from above. The trap had been set with admirable cunning, but it must have taken Hidaka so much time to put the fallen tree-trunks in position that he could not be very far ahead now.

Sooner or later he would come back, Allan thought, to see whether his opponent was dead or wounded. It should be possible to lure him into an ambush.

Allan chose a cleft in a rock, just large enough to let a man through for his purpose. He carried all his belongings through the crack and took off his outer garments, which he filled with moss and balls of grass until they had taken on the shape of a man. Leaning this dummy against the rock, he made a head with his fur hat and perched it on top of the stuffed jacket. The

215

scarecrow, sinking forward slightly, looked for all the world like a man who had fallen asleep during his night's watch, and the stick pushed between the stuffed arms could have been a gun.

Allan jammed the real gun firmly between the walls of the crevice, camouflaged it, and with a piece of skin tied on to the trigger a pliable twig which looked as if it grew quite naturally up the fissure. If Hidaka crept inside to overpower his sleeping opponent, he would brush against the twig and fire the gun, which, since it was aimed straight at the twig, could not miss him. Barefoot, Allan now looked for a hiding-place at the edge of the wood and waited for nightfall.

42

Hidaka had underestimated his opponent: the Yankee had twice escaped the traps set for him. When the moon rose he went to look for the enemy's overnight camp. It was nearly midnight by the time he reached the narrow crevice and climbed up the side of the rock to try and see where the American might be sheltering. It took a long time before his eyes could penetrate the darkness deep in the cleft, and then he caught sight of a seated figure apparently asleep. He picked up a heavy, sharp-edged stone and threw it down.

There was a soft thud, and the figure fell into two halves. Hidaka had not expected anything else. He climbed down again, crept cautiously into the crack in the rock, and groped with his finger tips for any obstacle, soon finding the twig and the strip of skin.

With one hand he held the twig in position and with the other he piled up a small heap of stones in front of him. Using it as a shield he pressed himself down on the hard ground and triggered off the gun with a sharp jerk on the piece of skin.

While the shot was still reverberating he jumped up and ran over to the weapon. He found there were no other cartridges in the magazine so the gun was of no use to him. Hurriedly he rammed a twig, the thickness of a man's finger, down the barrel. Then he slipped away into the open again and at the edge of the wood climbed a thickly covered tree to spend the rest of the night in its branches.

When the disappointed American took up his search again in the morning, Hidaka jumped down and ran off through the undergrowth. Allan heard the snapping of branches and hurried after him. Hidaka made sure that his enemy caught a glimpse of him as he ran past a gap in the bushes. At once the Yankee raised his gun and pulled the trigger. The barrel burst, the muzzle opening wide, and if the lock had exploded as well the Yankee would in all probability have been blinded.

The chief scout threw the useless gun into the bushes and quickly followed his opponent, who had gained on him and made off over the pebbly bed of a dried-up stream.

Hidaka's main concern now was to shake off his pursuer. He wriggled through a large barrier of dead branches, emerging into the open once more at the edge of a field of dry grass. In the distance he could see a firwood, and he decided to make for it and climb one of the trees to get a good view of the terrain.

The dry sedge reached up to his chest and rustled at every step. The unusual noise disturbed a black bear with her two cubs; terror-stricken she blundered away. Hidaka took no notice and hurried towards the wood.

Suddenly a deep, steep-sided gorge opened before him, separating him from the wood on the other side. There was no way down its vertical wall, which was quite smooth and offered no footholds. He could never follow the course of the gorge with his field-glasses. Far below, a roaring torrent swept along.

Flocks of curlew rose flapping out of the undergrowth and flew off, hares leapt past, and other animals moved quickly through the sedge. There was smoke in the air. When Hidaka turned round he saw grey clouds at the edge of the barrier of dead wood. The Yankee had set the prairie alight!

There was not a breath of wind, but the fire had no need of it; it greedily devoured the grass of its own accord. Hidaka ran along the edge of the chasm, but the first flames had already reached it. He wheeled around and ran in the opposite direction through the rustling grass, and found his way barred by fire there, too. He was trapped, with the chasm on three sides and the fire on the fourth. He had lost!

Hidaka threw his field-glasses to the ground, and tore off his skin jacket and his shirt. He turned towards the radiant sun sinking in the west. Placing his knife before him in the grass, he knelt down and touched the ground three times with his forehead to show the time-honoured reverence to his far-off emperor and his divine ancestors.

Then a ray of sunshine struck the lenses of his field-glasses and made them sparkle brilliantly. The reflected beam shone into Hidaka's eyes as he lifted his forehead from the ground.

The doomed man paused, then seized the glasses and flung them down on the sharp stones. The frame broke and the lenses rolled out into the grass. He could feel the heat of the fire now; the flames were coming nearer, crackling and licking the ground.

All around him as far as he could reach, Hidaka tore up the grass by its roots until a patch about six feet square was stripped bare. He piled the dry grass into a heap and held one of the lenses over it. The sun was still bright but in a few moments it would be obscured by the smoke. Hidaka forced himself to remain calm. The rays of sunshine concentrated in the lenses were focused on a dry, very thin blade of grass. Round the point of intense light, the blade slowly became brown, then darkened and finally turned black. The spark spread, catching the next blade, and then the others. A jet of flame shot up into the air.

Hidaka spread the burning grass round the edge of his bare patch of earth and stretched out in the middle. The red wall of flames he had started spread out in a semicircle, and rolled away from him in the direction of the Yankee's huge fire. Finally the two walls of flame shot up together in a great glowing red cloud. Sparks fell, singeing Hidaka's hair, and some fell on his skin jacket. He was too busy to take any notice. He was clawing a hollow in the ground and throwing the loose earth over himself.

All night he lay there in a deep sleep. When he rose at daybreak, bitter-tasting smoke still covered the prairie. The dark wood had become a barren wasteland of smoking tree-skeletons.

Late that evening Enzo Hidaka, blackened with wood-ash and covered with blisters, returned to Alatna, and found that his son had already been born. He fell down before him and kissed the tiny hands.

"Nammjo Horen Gekjo," he thanked his gods. "What a day, what a day this has been!"

Alatna washed the ash from his face.

"Baby come and smoke fly through the air. I very frightened but now everything all right."

He saw a new light in her eyes.

"Alatna-kimi, you are my wife, the best wife in all the world."

He took his son in his arms and looked at the small, squashed face by the light of the fire. He had dark eyes, with proper Mongolian folds at the corners, and delicate black down on his tiny head. He looked just like any Japanese baby.

"Soon he will see the cherry blossoms of Japan," his father said, "the gardens of Nikko and the divine snows of Fuji!"

43

Allan McCluire walked along the edge of the gorge, looking for Hidaka's remains. Each step he took raised a cloud of ash from the ground; not a single animal or blade of grass was left in the burnt prairie. From time to time he paused to look into the gorge through his field-glasses. If the Japanese had thrown himself down it, scavenger birds would mark the spot where his shattered body lay.

Allan had almost reached the end of the plateau when he caught sight of a patch of sandy brown earth. It made a striking contrast with the surrounding ash-grey ground, and he quickened his steps.

When he reached it, he found Hidaka's burnt jacket and his broken field-glasses. Allan soon saw that one of the big lenses was missing. It was obvious that Hidaka had started a fire to meet and hold the other and had escaped.

Allan McCluire stood in the middle of the sandy patch on which his opponent had survived the fire for a long time. Against all reason, he felt a sense of relief. The great hunt was not yet over.

Allan went back to his old camp by the river and started to build his coracle-like craft. His only hope now was to catch his enemy on the Noatak.

The framework of the boat consisted of willow branches which he stuck into the ground as if he were about to build an Indian wigwam. Overlapping caribou skins were stretched over them and firmly sewn together with animal sinew. He greased all the joints and seams thickly with fat, lit a small fire and placed the structure over it. The heat ensured that the fresh skins and the greased sinews contracted and made the boat watertight. It was so light that a child could have carried it.

Next morning Allan set off on his journey down river. He fixed a thick leafy bough to the craft to stop it from spinning round in circles, and two hastily bound birchbrooms served as oars. All day the boat drifted downstream past reedy banks, green hills and dark forests. Snow-geese sat brooding in the rushes, and cranes stood in the shallows.

The river became slower and slower, divided into many branches, and flowed away in innumerable rivulets, which were finally swallowed up in a large swamp. Allan had to lift the boat out and carry it through the marsh from one pool to the next.

After some days he reached the foot of a chain of hills and here he left the boat. Much later, on the other side of the hills, he came across many stone circles which had served to hold down the walls of tents. Whoever had made them had been gone a very long time because all the circles were overgrown with grass.

Next day he was astonished to find the remains of a fire only a few days old, and the tracks of a man, a woman and a dog. He could tell that they also had a baby with them, because close by there still stood the four-legged structure from which they must have hung the skin sack holding the baby during their fairly long stay.

Allan climbed the ridge and in the distance saw the blue ribbon of a great river. It meandered towards the west and was lost beyond the horizon. There could be no doubt it was the Noatak.

As the sun was already setting, Allan decided to spend the night on the hillside. He collected dry leaves and lit them with sparks made by hitting a stone with his knife. When night came, he could see the glimmer of another fire in the distance and judged that it must be on the bank of the Noatak.

He could hardly wait for morning. He knew the Eskimos to be the friendliest people in the world, and was looking forward to meeting them. If a stranger had been seen in the area they would certainly know of it and would be ready to help him in his search.

He hurried off towards the Noatak in the grey light of dawn. By midday he could see an earth hut through his field-glasses. Some time later he made out people moving about in front of the hut.

He was still half a mile away when the dog raised the alarm. Although Allan waved and called out friendly greetings, the two figures hastily withdrew into their hut. They had, of course, never seen strangers before and were bound to be frightened by the first one they came across.

The hut appeared to be very old; plants were growing on the roof and there were thick creepers all over the earth walls. Only the window, covered over with skins, seemed to have been put in recently. Allan was certain that he would be able to communicate with the inhabitants. Once he had spent a year on the island of Nunivak and had met the Eskimos and learnt the most important phrases in their language. Of course, it was true that each tribe had its own idiom but all the dialects sprang from a common root.

He stopped and stood at a polite distance from the hut.

"Here is friend," he called out, using the customary greeting. "Friend is come."

He raised his hand, with his palm outwards to show that his intentions were friendly. But the only answer was the barking of the dog and the crying of a baby. Allan repeated the greeting without success, paused, then went up to the low door, bent down and entered with a smile.

Before him sat the little family, a man of about thirty, and his young, very pretty wife, who was cradling a tiny baby in her arms. The man had difficulty in controlling his dog, whose one desire seemed to be to leap at the stranger.

The woman appeared terrified and she shielded her baby protectively with her hands, her whole body trembling. Her husband seemed calmer and he looked searchingly into the stranger's face with his narrow, black eyes.

Allan squatted on the floor, so as not to alarm these small northern people with his enormous height.

"Nutarak hoki kutnit," he said to the young mother, with his pleasant smile. That meant that her child was very fat, and was the greatest compliment one could pay an Eskimo mother.

It had an immediate effect and Alatna's anxious face relaxed. But she did not answer the stranger; her husband did it for her.

"Kavnik kaije garluavna."

This meant the child would become a great hunter. The man's accent was hard and clipped, very different from the soft speech of the Nunivak Eskimos.

"What people are you from?"

"We are Nunamiut," Hidaka told him. "We have never seen a *kabluna* before."

"What is your name?"

"Sissuk," answered Enzo Hidaka. "My wife called Alatna, and my son called Toklat."

The name meant bear, and showed what great deeds were expected of their son one day.

Inside, the hut was tidy and clean. The sleeping platforms were covered with fresh furs and the hearth was surrounded by a circle of new stones.

"I may stay with you?" Allan asked.

"It your house, Kabluna. We glad."

Alatna handed the guest a wooden bowl of fish soup, and Allan began to feel at ease with these friendly people. They talked about the movements of the caribou

224

and of the particularly long winter that year. Then Allan began to speak of his own affairs.

"I look for strange man, he goes to Noatak. You see him, Sissuk, or smell his fire?"

Hidaka shook his head.

"What kind of strange man, Kabluna?"

"Strange man very bad," Allan said. "He come from big island in the warm sea, where are plenty bad men. The man is a devil; he has already killed many good men. But do not worry, I will protect you."

His host's eyes had narrowed to a slit. "We thank you, Kabluna, but we are not frightened."

They were certainly proud words, but all the same the woman seemed to be very nervous. Her lips were pale, and she hid her face from the stranger once more.

Allan stood up and went outside to fetch his pack. As a courteous gesture to the woman of the house, he decided to bring in an armful of fire-wood at the same time. Lifting the logs, he uncovered a long, well-worn steel knife. So the Nunamiuts had had some contact with the outside world after all! He held the knife up to the light, to see if he could tell where it came from. Right by the handle, punched into the steel, was a small circle surrounded by rays—the insignia of the Japanese Army! Sissuk had followed and was watching him.

"Arshakpuluk throw knife down from heaven," the man said in his harsh voice. "Much sharp knife, good, very good!"

"Where you find, Sissuk? Where was the knife? Where did Arshakpuluk throw it down? Show me the place."

"Far away, very far, Kabluna—very long way."

"How far, Sissuk, how many days?"

The other seemed to find difficulty in answering. But then his face brightened. "Sun come again, I lead you

225

to stream where we find knife. When sun very high, we there."

So it was not all that far away, and the man still remembered exactly where he had come across his find.

"Arshakpuluk not throw knife," Allan explained. "Bad man lose it. We find man's tracks, we kill devil or catch him."

Sissuk nodded in agreement.

"I know, Kabluna. Must kill bad man."

44

Hidaka could not account for his leaving the American to sleep in peace. Allan had turned towards the wall and his fur rug had slipped off his shoulder, laying it bare: just a hand's breadth below that, a knife thrust would go straight into the heart. Nothing could have been simpler. But Hidaka was too much of a soldier, and wedded too closely to the age-old traditions of the Samurai, to commit cold-blooded murder, even of a mortal foe.

Alatna was still awake. She lay on her side and watched her husband through half-closed eyes. When nothing happened she pushed aside her furs. The knife was beside her on the table, glinting in the light of the fire. She picked it up and took it over to Hidaka. When he shook his head, she replaced it reluctantly. Then Hidaka rose silently and motioned to her to go outside with him. In the moonlight they stood facing one another, whispering.

"I cannot do it while he is asleep."

"Why not? He is your enemy."

"He must die, Alatna, but not in his sleep, not as our guest."

Alatna could not understand him. The *kabluna* was a very dangerous man, who must be got rid of as quickly as possible.

"I will do it tomorrow, Alatna, on the way to the stream."

When the two men set off early next morning, the young woman wanted to accompany them. She had her baby in his skin sack on her back and a bag of tinder in her hand.

"I will make fire and food," she said.

Hidaka pushed her back roughly. "No, you must stay here. I need new shoes, get to work!"

He turned away from her and went ahead of the *kabluna*. Alatna watched them until they disappeared from view. Then she sent Kinmek into the hut, hung the sack with her son from a beam and locked the door by placing a stone in front of it. She followed her husband and the stranger from far enough away not to be noticed.

It was a dull day, with grey clouds in the sky and the air was warm and humid. Hidaka and Allan walked over the hill and across difficult, marshy terrain. Hidaka had his knife stuck into the front of his leather shirt, where he could draw it out in a split second. He was often on the point of doing so but put it off each time, reasoning that there would be a still better opportunity later. Finally they reached the stream.

"Here you find knife, Sissuk?"

"No, Kabluna, we go further along the stream."

Allan walked ahead now. Hidaka looked at his enemy's back. He grasped the handle of his knife and walked a little faster. Now the Yankee's shoulderblades were an arm's length away. But at that moment they came to some undergrowth, which had to be parted with both hands, and that opportunity was lost too.

The thorny bushes were left behind; now there were no obstacles in their way. Hidaka was breathing fast. Sweat ran down his forehead. Time and again he grasped the knife, keeping his eyes focused on the vulnerable spot between McCluire's shoulderblades.

Then the Yankee stopped and turned round.

"What is the matter, Sissuk?"

Hidaka wiped the sweat from his face.

"I have been ill, Kabluna."

Allan suggested they stop for a rest.

"Here many fish," he pointed to the stream. "I will catch fish for us to eat."

228

Allan lay down with his head and arms over the gurgling water. Most of the trout were near the bank and stayed there by resisting the current with slight movements of their fins.

"Make a fire, Sissuk, I catch fish soon."

Slowly Allan drew his open hand through the water until it lay just behind a trout. Then in a flash, he flicked it out and it came flying through the air, landing wriggling on the bank.

"There the first fish, Sissuk. How is fire?"

"Slow, Kabluna."

When at last the first flames were crackling, there were already half a dozen fish lying on the grass. Allan cut some willow twigs and skewered the trout. They browned quickly, the skin bursting to reveal the delicate flesh.

"Is very good to eat," he said to his companion as they started their meal.

The Nunamiut ate with relish. Allan glanced over at him and saw with a shock that the man was using chopsticks.

Slowly he slid his hand into his pocket, and carefully pulled his pistol out, concealing the weapon with his hand. The man had not noticed anything. "Captain Hidaka!"

Instantly the Japanese froze like a statue. His right hand, still holding the chopsticks, stopped in mid-air.

"Captain Hidaka," Allan said once more, "I must take you prisoner."

Hidaka did not move. Allan pointed the pistol at his chopsticks. "That's what gave you away."

Hidaka opened his hand and let the chopsticks drop.

"I must ask you, captain, to turn round. Put your hands behind your back."

Allan tore off a strip of leather from his moccasins, and tied his opponent's wrists together.

"That's it. Now we can talk."

229

The Japanese stood still with his back to him, Allan had to go round him to face him.

"The long hunt is over, Captain Hidaka. I am very happy at this outcome, because we are both still alive."

The Japanese now looked up.

"It is my fault," he said very quietly. "Shoot me!"

"No. Lieutenant Tojimoto was not shot, either."

"Then I ask for the chance to die by my own hand."

Allan shook his head. "No, I won't allow that. You will think differently about it, yourself, after a little while. Does the young woman belong to you?"

Hidaka nodded, "Alatna is my wife; Toklat, my son."

"So you still have responsibilities in this world. We will take the woman and the child with us to the coast, and leave them at a mission there. After the war, you can come and fetch them, if that's what you want to do."

Hidaka gave no indication of his feelings on the matter.

"I don't like to see you with your hands tied, Captain Hidaka, it is so undignified. Give me your word that you will try neither to escape nor lay hands on yourself."

The Japanese shook his head. "I may not—I cannot."

Allan realized what a difficult position he himself was in. For weeks he would have to drag a bound prisoner along with him, and he certainly could not take the woman and her child, as well, since she would free the prisoner at the first opportunity. He told Hidaka all this quite frankly.

"That means we won't be able to take Alatna with us. I'm afraid you can't even say goodbye to her and the child. The woman will just have to have no idea of what has become of you. I will have to take you to the river another way, build a raft there and set off with you alone. That is bad for me and bad for you, but still

230

worse for the poor woman. She seems to be very fond of you."

The Japanese bowed his head low. He did not want the Yankee to see the tears in his eyes.

"Let's go now, captain. You go in front, but watch for any obstacles, or you'll have a bad fall, with your hands tied."

As the Yankee bent to pick up his pack, Hidaka saw a movement in the bushes behind them and quickly looked away. They followed the stream for about a mile and came to a fir wood which had been badly damaged by a recent storm. The prisoner could not scramble over the fallen tree-trunks with his hands tied and they lost a lot of time in finding a way round them. Whenever McCluire was busy clearing a path through the overhanging branches that barred their way, Hidaka seized the opportunity of looking behind.

Allan pointed out a moose-run which led through the thick undergrowth. Hidaka saw a root sticking out of the ground, and pretended to trip over it. At once McCluire rushed over and tried to help him up.

"It's not good," Hidaka gasped, "it's my hip." Allan threw off his pack and bent over him. He began to turn the Japanese onto his side and in a flash, Alatna was upon him and had driven her bone knife deep into his back.

Allan collapsed and rolled groaning into the undergrowth. Alatna quickly freed Hidaka's hands. He stood up and took her into his arms.

Minutes passed before they realized that their enemy was still alive. Panting, he raised himself up on his hands with the knife still in his back. At each breath, blood poured from his mouth. Alatna pulled Hidaka's knife out of Allan's belt and handed it to her husband. "Now you make him quite dead!"

Hidaka put the knife away, pulled Allan's leather shirt off and examined the wound. It was too high and too far to the right to have penetrated the heart, and so it was not necessarily fatal. Hidaka laid dry moss over the wound, pressed it firmly down in place with a piece of bark and bound it tightly with Allan's cross-belt.

"We'll make a sledge and take him with us."

"He your enemy, Enzo. You must kill him quickly."

"No, you can see he cannot defend himself."

Another of those mysterious customs of his race which she could not understand. Still, she herself was not bound by them.

"I kill him. I Nunamiut."

She tried to seize Hidaka's knife.

"Alatna, you must obey; don't lay a hand on the *kabluna*. Now help me take him away!"

"Not take him away," she persisted. "We go away. He die alone, then everything good."

Hidaka pushed her aside, and lopped a couple of strong branches off the nearest fir tree with Allan's axe, to make a stretcher. Reluctantly, Alatna started to help him. The men from Japan were just as incomprehensible as the *kablunas*. First they tried to destroy each other for months on end, and when they finally had the chance, they let it go by. It seemed that both races were more concerned with taking prisoners than with killing their enemy.

"You want to sell him to your friend on Igilchik Island?" she asked.

"Yes, Alatna-kimi. He will be sold for ten times ten skins of silver fox."

At last Enzo's actions made sense to her, especially as silver fox was considered the finest of furs by the Nunamiuts. Alatna now joined in with a will and gladly helped her husband to lift the large *kabluna* onto the branches.

Allan McCluire was fully conscious and in great pain.

"We will try and pull you through," Hidaka said. "Alatna is a fine nurse!"

45

The raft was ready. Hidaka had taken a full week to make it strong enough to withstand the many rapids they would meet on their way. There was a rudder in the stern and in the middle of the craft a raised platform for the passengers and their belongings. They also had a large basket woven out of branches and twigs and full of sand, in which to build a fire during the voyage. But their stock of food was low. On no account did Hidaka want to break the journey to go hunting, as it would take up too much time without proper firearms. It would be much easier to stock up before they set off in an area which he now knew well, so he built traps among the trees, caught two moose and left it to Alatna to cut up the meat and smoke it.

It was Allan's condition that now delayed their departure. Blood poisoning had set in, as was to be expected. He was delirious and tried constantly to get out of bed, wanting apparently to throw himself in the river. Alatna could not hold him on her own, and they had to tie him down. The wound itself had healed and the scar was now surrounded by a pink swelling. All the same, he could scarcely survive the journey by raft in his present condition. They did not know what currents they would encounter lower down the Noatak. A delirious man would be no help on board when they had to shoot rapids.

But time was passing; night frosts had begun and the leaves were beginning to turn colour. The golden plovers, always the first to go south in the winter, had already left. Hidaka grew more impatient with each passing day. Once the violent autumn storms began, it would be too late to travel down river and they would have to winter where they were.

But his vital report about the caribou valley and its strategic importance to Japan brooked no delay. The information had to be brought to the Japanese High Command as quickly as the raft and the river allowed. It would be irresponsible to hold it up any longer because of a sick American. Hidaka made a difficult but firm decision: he would go to Igilchik alone. Alatna would have to stay and go on nursing the badly wounded prisoner.

It was the only sensible solution to all his problems. Hidaka was already worried about how he could justify taking Alatna with him to Attu, let alone Japan, in the light of military regulations. The difficulties would start when they reached Igilchik, before the flight to Attu. The pilot would no doubt refuse to take a woman and child on board and it was doubtful if Hidaka would be able to talk him into it. If the matter was referred to Yamada, the admiral's sympathy for private feelings and obligations could scarcely be relied upon. To Yamada, Alatna would be just an Eskimo woman to whom one of his officers had given a child while living with her in occupied territory. He could only explain in person how much she had done to save him and to enable him to return from the wilderness.

For these reasons Hidaka had, for some time, been toying with the idea of leaving her on Igilchik until the war was over. There were a few Eskimos living there with their families as assistants to the local representative of the Wild Life Preservation Department. Alatna and Toklat would have been bound to be all right with them. So if a separation was inevitable in any case, Alatna might just as well spend the winter in the warm earth house here and look after the Yankee. He would surely have the decency to take her to a mission on the coast later. If, as was now unlikely, her patient died, Alatna was quite capable of reaching a settlement on the coast by herself. He would, of course, leave her a small, strongly built raft, and enough smoked meat to see her through the first few weeks.

These were sad thoughts, and he kept them to himself for the time being. Then, one day, Allan's fever went down and he raised himself up in his bunk.

"I thought that you were a real Japanese, captain," he said in a clear voice, "but I must have been mistaken."

Hidaka assumed that he was still delirious and took no notice of this comment.

"What do you think I am then?"

"A real human being."

"Aren't Japanese real human beings?"

Allan ignored the question.

"I am a great burden to you, Captain Hidaka. But for me, you would have been on your way days ago. Such tender concern for a beaten enemy is not a normal characteristic of Japanese officers."

The reproach pained Hidaka.

"You should not believe all the wild stories you read in your papers, Mr. McCluire! Japan is a signatory to the Geneva Convention and observes it scrupulously. We are forbidden to leave a wounded man to die."

"That's just on paper, captain. There are eye-witness reports to the contrary. Captain William himself saw how the Japanese behaved in the Philippines . . ."

"These things happen," Hidaka interrupted. "There are people who lose their nerve in the heat of battle. But away from the battle-fronts, where things are quiet, brutality would not be tolerated."

Allan had the impression that Hidaka was firmly convinced of the truth of what he was saying.

"That's all very well, captain, but here you're acting against your own interests. Everything is ready for your departure. Why don't you simply leave me here and set off? No one would see. No one would know!"

Hidaka stood up.

"I would know, Mr. McCluire."

He went outside and looked for Alatna. She was down by the river, inspecting her fish-net. Toklat lay in his cradle tied to a branch, with Kinmek sitting beneath, guarding him.

Hidaka told her what he had been thinking during the past few days. It would be better for her and for him and also for the child if he travelled to Igilchik without them. They could not hope to lead a proper married life together until the war was over, anyway. He would be sent off somewhere to fight, so that they would be parted whatever happened. She would be far better off in Alaska than alone in a completely alien land whose ways she knew nothing about. She would need her husband at her side to become acclimatized to life in Japan. Without him, everything would be too difficult for her. The war would not last much longer: the Japanese Army was victorious wherever it went. He would certainly be able to come and fetch her home the following year. Since that morning the *kabluna* had been a little better; the crisis was clearly past and he would now recover, given good nursing. Alatna could be quite certain that the Yankee would take her to good people where she and Toklat would be looked after until he himself came back to take her to Japan.

The young woman listened patiently to everything and made no attempt to argue with him. Hidaka was touched by her understanding and felt a great weight had been taken off his mind. He began to build a second raft at once.

That evening, on his return to the hut, tired from the hard day's work, he told Allan McCluire of his decision and Alatna's agreement.

"I'm sure it's the best thing to do, captain, particularly for Alatna's sake."

"That depends on you, Mr. McCluire."

"I'll take her and the baby to Talikoot," Allan said

236

at once. "There are a couple of Catholic missionary nuns there who run a small hospital. They'll receive Alatna with open arms, they could do with a good nurse like her. It won't be difficult for you to fetch your wife and child from there when the time comes."

Captain Hidaka carried his things onto the raft. Then he went back to say good-bye to Alatna. She was very calm, and voiced no complaints or reproaches; indeed, she hardly spoke. Toklat slept in his cradle, oblivious to what was going on. Only Kinmek sensed his master's impending departure and whined miserably.

Hidaka asked Alatna to stay near the house. He could not bear the thought of her standing on the bank with the distance between them growing until he lost sight of her small figure completely. He held her in his arms for a long time, without saying a word, then tore himself away and went over to Allan, who sat up as Hidaka approached.

"I don't know what you're trying to do, captain, but—contrary to my patriotic duty—I hope you succeed."

He held out his hand to Hidaka, who grasped it warmly.

"I'll look after Alatna as if she were my own sister."

Hidaka only nodded without speaking.

He saw no sign of his wife and child when he left his prisoner in the hut. Alatna must have been hiding in the wood, alone with her misery, just as a good Japanese wife would have done. He strode quietly down to the river, ready to leave at once. Alatna, the baby in her arms and Kinmek at her feet, was sitting on the raft.

"We come with you," she said.

Hidaka's arms dropped to his sides. "But Alatna-kimi, you can't. You mustn't!"

"We come," she repeated stubbornly.

"You must stay here, Alatna, we have discussed it and it's settled."

She looked at him with her beautiful, slanting black eyes.

"Please, Alatna-kimi, the *kabluna* will die if you come with me. I beg you, go back to him, nurse him till he is well. I promise to come and fetch you next year."

She remained obstinately silent.

"You must go back to the hut. Please do as I tell you!"

His expression was stern and his voice brusque. But Alatna did not move.

"You go alone, I kill Kabluna."

She had to repeat her threat before Hidaka took it in. Then it dawned on him that she really would do exactly what she said.

He jumped ashore, ran up to the earth hut and dragged the Yankee from his bed. Panting, he carried the much heavier man down to the bank, pulled him onto the raft and cast off.

It took Allan a long time to recover from the shock and it was some days before he fully realized that they were all travelling together, after all. Hidaka gave him no explanation.

They drifted along in the middle of the river, water gurgling between the logs and a chilly fresh wind aiding their progress. On both sides of the river there was dark forest. Banks of shingle appeared in the water from time to time. They passed a bull moose with great palmate antlers drinking at the bank. Brant-geese with brown heads and dark backs accompanied them for a while. The whistling swans were flying south once more. Great grey-white gulls hovered over the raft, ready to snap up anything they threw overboard. Alatna sat fishing in the stern, and had already caught a large pike and some salmon on their way back from the sea to the streams where they were born. Toklat's cradle hung between two poles that Hidaka had put up immediately after they had set off. The chief scout lay on the platform covered with thick skins, his head propped up on his old knapsack. Kinmek kept him company and a fire burned beside him in the sand box, its smoke spiralling upwards.

Captain Hidaka stood beside Alatna and held the tiller. So far he had had no trouble; there had been neither rocks nor rapids to negotiate. The Noatak was a calm, leisurely river and he could always see in good time before it branched, and act accordingly.

Nevertheless, he did not want to risk travelling by night. The sky was overcast and there were no stars or moonlight to give warning of approaching sandbanks. He steered his craft towards a flat, wooded island and made fast with two poles. Alatna went ashore at once to collect firewood. Hidaka picked his son up and carried him to the fire-place.

"Tell me, Captain," Allan called from his bed. "What do you propose to do with me?"

Hidaka sat down beside him and asked how he was feeling.

"Not too bad, thanks, but where exactly are we going? You won't take me with you all the way, or I'd discover all your secrets."

"What secrets?"

"Well, surely you must have some idea of how you are going to get away from the coast. Arrangements must have been made about where and when you'll be picked up."

Hidaka had already worked out what to say if this subject came up.

"No, McCluire, I'm not being picked up anywhere. I have no hope of getting back to Japan, or even to Attu. The distances over water are too great."

"So what are you going to do?"

239

A little helplessly, Hidaka shrugged his shoulders.

"Frankly, I have no idea yet."

"But, of course you have, Hidaka! You're planning to submerge yourself amongst the Eskimos with Alatna and Toklat, until the war is over, disguised as a nice little Nunamiut family. But it won't work, Hidaka, believe me! You were able to pull the wool over my eyes, I admit, but the first Eskimo you meet will see through you at once. A stranger who looks like an Eskimo but isn't one, and isn't an Indian either, why, news like that would travel like wild-fire through all the settlements along the coast and in no time the nearest police station would hear about it. I shouldn't be telling you this, but you would certainly have done better to stay in the hinterland!"

"And never hear when the war is over? No, that's out of the question!"

Hidaka's reply was not out of character: a man such as he would not be able to bear being left in the dark for long.

"First of all, McCluire, I will have to put you somewhere where you will be well looked after."

"What's wrong with the deep waters of the Noatak, with a stone tied round my neck to make sure I stay there?"

Hidaka did not appreciate this remark at all.

"I have already told you: I don't like easy solutions like that. There is bound to be a police post somewhere along the river, surely, near which I can drop you at night?"

"I wouldn't tell you even if I knew."

"Of course not," Hidaka said with a broad smile, because he could be certain now that there was no such post. As a civil servant, Allan would certainly have known if there was one.

"Listen, Captain, I have a better idea for you. After all, I owe you a debt of gratitude. In the mouth of the

Noatak there is a seal island called Igilchik. The current will take us right up to it. Have you ever heard of it?"

"What did you say the island was called?" Hidaka asked, trying hard to conceal his excitement.

"Igilchik."

"Can't say I have. It must be very small indeed, this island, because I still have a pretty clear picture of the map of this part of Alaska in my head."

"It isn't very big," Allan agreed, "but it is very important to us, because it is inhabited by a vast number of seals. That is why the Wild Life Preservation Department has an outpost there with a white manager in charge. My colleague's name is Nizhinsky, a White Russian. I have never met him, but I've heard he's a very good man. He has to keep a close watch over the seals, because of their valuable furs; otherwise the poachers would come and eventually exterminate them. Nizhinsky has a few Eskimos working for him whose families live there, too. Altogether, they have quite a comfortable set-up there."

Allan made no mention of the gamewarden's transmitter, which they would be able to use to bring up a patrol boat to take Hidaka off as a prisoner of war. He would be well looked after behind barbed wire and would be reunited with Tojimoto. Allan would then have done his duty by handing over the enemy infiltrator to the authorities, as he had been ordered. As for Alatna and the child, no one could deny Allan the right to look after them until Hidaka was released.

"I can see it would suit you very well if we made for this island," Hidaka said cunningly, "but it would be entirely against my own interest!"

"Oh, no, not at all," Allan was eager to explain. "I wouldn't have suggested it otherwise. My colleague Nizhinsky is completely cut off from the world except for one visit a year by a supply ship. It won't get to Ig-

241

ilchik again till next August and by then anything might have happened."

Hidaka pretended he would have to think over Allan's suggestion carefully first. But it was, of course, an ideal solution, particularly to the problem of what to do with Allan. From Igilchik they could take him straight to Attu, perhaps even to Japan. His return home with such an interesting prisoner from the heart of Alaska would create a sensation. The Japanese propaganda machine would have a field day and would be able to enhance Japan's prestige still further throughout the world.

"Yes, I think you are right, McCluire, many things will have sorted themselves out by next year. We'll make for your island."

"You couldn't do better," Allan said.

That was very true, Hidaka thought to himself, and nodded.

The river soon became so wide that it resembled an elongated lake. On both sides the terrain was completely flat and devoid of trees. They had reached the tundra again and here the short summer was already over. Only a few more weeks now, and all the animals would have left, and the swamps would be crusted over with ice again.

Alatna lived as contentedly on the raft as she had done in the cave, and looked after her patient with the same quiet confidence as she did her child. She came from a nomadic people and a travelling life was what she was used to. She took it for granted that it was her duty to keep the fire going on board and to collect fresh wood each time they stopped for the night. Now that the forests had disappeared behind them this became more and more difficult. Hidaka had constructed a shelter on board with the fire-box in the middle and three bunks round the sides. It had become too cold and wet to stay in the open any longer. The gusts of wind were growing stronger and the lower part of the raft was often awash.

"Can you smell the sea air now, Hidaka?"

"Very distinctly. How far out does the island lie?"

Allan was not sure. "It can't be far. Nizhinsky's reports sometimes mentioned caribou swimming across."

Alatna had never seen the open sea and was very much afraid when the river banks opened out and the land disappeared from view. However, a dark line appeared almost at once on the horizon before them.

"That's Igilchik, Alatna. We're almost there."

The raft pitched and tossed on the choppy sea, still propelled by the current of the Noatak. Further on, they watched the grey-green river water mingle with the deep blue tidal water of the Bering Strait. The long island rose before them, a dark shoreline dotted with something darker, surrounding a low, flat-topped hill, yellowish in colour, which ran down the centre.

"There's something I want to make absolutely clear, Captain, before we get there. It was you who wounded me. It was you who stabbed me in the back while we were grappling with one another. It was a perfectly legitimate fight between the two of us."

Hidaka did not understand what Allan was trying to say.

"We're approaching civilization again, Captain Hidaka, and we'll be subject to its laws. Strictly speaking, according to those laws, Alatna's a citizen of the United States. By aiding a Japanese against the American Army—that's me—she becomes a traitor. And that normally means the rope or the electric chair or some other abomination."

Hidaka was appalled.

"But she doesn't understand ... she has no idea of any of these things!"

"Of course not, Hidaka, and all extenuating circumstances would be taken into consideration. Perhaps she would be let off altogether in the end. But the great cumbersome machine of justice would have to roll into action first, crushing everything that got in its way. That's why I think it would be better if we two just . . ." he hesitated.

"Yes, very much, McCluire, it's very good of you to tell me. Thank you!"

They could now hear the rough barking of many tens of thousands of seals from the shore. The animals had caught sight of the strange monster bobbing towards them on the waves. They formed a living fringe around the flat coast as far as the eye could see, lay flank to flank between the rocks and swam cheek by jowl in the breakers. Huge numbers of them were crammed together on the beach, and every open space, every rock, was covered.

"They eat us," Alatna said in a terrified voice.

"They are the most peaceful creatures in the world," Hidaka assured her. "They wouldn't even harm Toklat."

Now the corrugated iron huts of the gamewarden and his Eskimo assistants came into view; four or five flat buildings supported by wire guy-ropes to prevent them being blown away in the Arctic storms. A thin radio mast with a red light glowing on top rose from their midst.

"Do you see that, McCluire? Your colleague has a transmitter at his disposal!"

"Yes, I know."

"Do you mean that you were aware of this before, McCluire?"

Allan admitted it frankly.

"But you won't have a bad time of it as a prisoner of war, Captain Hidaka, my report will see to that. And Alatna can stay here with the Eskimos until you come back for her."

"A clever trick," Hidaka said with a friendly smile.

244

"What would you have done in my place, my dear Captain?"

"Exactly the same, McCluire, exactly the same!"

And he had in fact done just that. There was a big surprise in store for the Yankee.

Hidaka grasped the tiller more firmly. The raft had been spotted and three figures ran out from the corrugated iron huts and waved, pointing to a place on the shore to indicate an approach through the boulders.

"Hold tight! We are going to run aground!"

Alatna had her baby on her back and clung to the platform. Allan McCluire held on to a post and the frightened dog took refuge inside the shelter.

The breakers were roaring onto the beach, and Hidaka struggled with all his strength to hold the tiller. The raft was lifted up, seeming to be thrown into the air, and then its bows slid steeply down a deep trough of water, shot through a mass of white spray, reared up again, plunged past a hundred seal heads and crashed onto the shore. The next wave picked the raft up again and deposited it far up on the beach.

Hidaka sprang down, made the raft fast with the poles and breathed a deep sigh of relief. He had carried out his orders and had reached Igilchik.

The swarming hordes of seals receded round them and a mighty swelling roar expressed their disapproval of the intrusion. The excited animals left a wide passage open for the three men who now came down the slope. The King of Igilchik strode regally through his subjects' guard of honour, two Eskimos walking behind him like attendant lords.

The gamewarden of Igilchik was a powerfully built man, needing a shave, and wearing oilskins and thigh-length rubber boots. Before he had reached Hidaka, his hand was stretched out in greeting.

"What brings you to my island, stranger? Did the current carry you on?"

He spoke fairly good English in a loud, hoarse voice. Hidaka seized his hand.

"There is a sick American with us. We hope you can help him."

"Of course, of course!"

He motioned to his companions to fetch the white man from the raft.

"Where do you come from? What brings you here?"

Hidaka stepped aside to make way for Allan McCluire, whom the two Eskimos had lifted and were carrying up the beach.

"Where we come from is a long story," he answered evasively.

"All right, all right, you can tell me all about it later. You have your wife and child with you, I see."

Alatna was hesitant about leaving the raft.

"My wife is frightened of the seals."

"No need to be frightened. They won't do her any harm."

Hidaka went up to Alatna and helped her down.

"Please go on up with the others, I'll join you in a moment."

He turned back to the gamewarden of Igilchik.

"Roughly how many seals are there, Mr. . . ?"

"My name is Nizhinsky, Boris Nizhinsky," the other said. "I am here to protect these peaceful animals."

"How many are there?" Hidaka insisted.

"You seem to be interested."

"That's why I asked."

"Very well, then, all in all there are . . . 319,156."

Hidaka beamed with pleasure and relief. "You are very precise, Mr. Nizhinsky."

"I made a very careful note of the exact figure."

Then Hidaka stepped back a pace, raised his hand to his fur hat and bowed.

"Captain Enzo Hidaka of the Imperial Japanese Army!" he announced.

246

Nizhinsky embraced him warmly.

"At last! I have been waiting for you for over a year."

Hidaka withdrew as soon as he could from the other's bear hug.

"My courageous companions have all been killed," he reported, "except for Lieutenant Tojimoto, who only allowed himself to be captured on my orders and very much against his will."

Nizhinsky expressed his deep regret, adding that a war like this must always involve heavy and painful losses.

"What is our general position now?" Hidaka asked, but Nizhinsky was evasive.

"There's plenty of time for that later, Hidaka-san, but things are not going too badly. Now let's go up to my house."

It wasn't a bad life being gamewarden of Igilchik, Hidaka discovered when he went inside the house. A large oil stove filled the sitting-room with a comforting warmth. There were upholstered armchairs and a large sofa, bright pictures on the walls, book cases, soft carpets on the floor and curtained windows, cupboards and lockers, and stuffed birds on every available space. In the corner stood a Russian samovar.

Alatna stared at all these strange things with astonishment and awe. Nizhinsky had to invite her to take a seat several times before she ventured to sit down nervously on the edge of the sofa. She took Toklat down from her back and held him protectively, pulling the dog to her, as well, lest he come to any harm in these frightening surroundings. A camp bed had already been put up for McCluire by the stove. He had propped himself up and was looking even more astonished, if that were possible, than Alatna. It was Captain Hidaka who was being treated as the most important person there, and scarcely any notice was being taken of the

American. A complete and friendly understanding seemed to have been established between the game-warden and the Japanese captain.

An Eskimo woman entered bearing mugs of steaming coffee. Nizhinsky passed round the mugs himself, serving Hidaka first, even though Allan had told him the stranger's identity immediately.

"I thought all Russians drank tea?" Hidaka said, pointing at the samovar.

"Oh, that. No, I've gradually lost the habit. Please help yourselves, ladies and gentlemen, there are cakes here as well. We'll have our celebration banquet later."

"As you see, captain," McCluire called out from his corner, "we really spoil our prisoners of war. My colleague can hardly find time to spare me a glance."

Captain Hidaka went over to him.

"There is a reason for that, McCluire. The man you call your colleague happens to be on the Japanese side. This island and its radio station are what I have been making for all along. As soon as possible we shall be picked up by a Japanese aircraft—if the weather is good, in a day or so. You will do me the honour of accompanying me. It is just as possible to survive the war not too uncomfortably behind Japanese barbed wire. I will personally see to it that you are sent to our show camp, Karuizawa."

Allan McCluire needed time to adjust to the news. After a short pause, he said: "I congratulate you, Hidaka, you managed the whole thing brilliantly. I am most impressed."

He sat forward in bed to look at Nizhinsky who had his back turned and was searching for something in his desk.

"You dirty swine!" Allan shouted. "You filthy bastard! You traitor!"

Their host was unperturbed.

"That's right, my friend. You get it off your chest if it makes you feel better."

"Will there be any trouble," Hidaka broke in, looking anxious, "about Alatna . . . about my wife and son flying out with us?"

Nizhinsky reassured him.

"None at all, Hidaka-san. I make the decisions here and only the really big chief can give me orders. For all I care, you can take your dog with you, too!"

Hidaka translated his answer for Alatna, who had in any case never seriously doubted that she would be allowed to stay with her husband.

"Ah, here it is, Hidaka-san," Nizhinsky said, holding up a piece of paper at his desk, "a message for you from Admiral Yamada; very good news, in fact, already deciphered. It's been around here for months, in case you did manage to get through."

"Wasn't that a bit careless, Nizhinsky?"

"Certainly not. Nobody comes poking their noses in here and anyway, my Eskimos can't read."

Hidaka stood under the lamp in order to see better. He had to re-read the message several times before he took in what it said.

"Major! I've been promoted Major in the Imperial Guard!"

He swallowed with emotion: this was a signal and unhoped for honour. He turned and bowed deeply three times in the direction of the Imperial Palace in Tokyo. Because the stove happened to be in front of him as he did so, it looked as if he were making obeisances to it, and Alatna, imagining this was normal practice among her husband's people rose from the sofa and solemnly followed his example.

"Do you want me to do it, too?" Allan called out. "Maybe prisoners of war are expected to go in for that kind of thing, as well!"

"In the case of foreigners," Hidaka told him earnestly, "it is demanded only in the presence of His Divine Majesty himself."

"Well, that's a relief. I'm not likely to get that far!"

Nizhinsky suggested that they draw up a brief report to the admiral straight away. He wanted to code it at once and radio it through to Attu, together with a request for a flying-boat as soon as the weather was suitable.

"It can refuel here," he said. "We've got enough stocks."

Although Hidaka made his report as brief as possible, it covered a full page, because he wanted the news of the possibility of flying into the caribou valley to reach the Japanese High Command at once, in case his own aircraft should crash on the way to Attu. He gave the precise location of the valley, the width and length of the natural runway and the number of large caves, all of which he had conscientiously enumerated and measured while he was there.

"It's half a book," Nizhinsky grumbled. "It'll take a while before I'm through with it."

"I'll be glad to help you," Hidaka said.

"Unfortunately, you can't, my dear major. We are using a new code now and you wouldn't be able to make head or tail of it. There's only one man on Attu who knows it. But I'll be as quick as I can."

All the same, it took him nearly an hour. Allan had turned his face to the wall and refused to speak to Hidaka. That suited Hidaka well because Alatna had so many questions which needed long and involved answers. Each object in the room was completely strange to her. She had never seen a picture before, or a transparent window, or an iron fireplace. When the Igilchik Eskimo woman poured some liquid onto the fire without putting it out, Alatna was dumbfounded at the wonders of this strange new world.

At last Nizhinsky returned, looking very pleased with himself.

"Your radio report has gone out now, Major Hidaka. But they won't be reading it on Attu. It's gone to Washington."

He propped his chin in his hands, his elbows on the desk, and enjoyed Hidaka's bewilderment.

"Yes, sir, I said Washington. To be precise, it's gone direct to the Pentagon. Your detailed description of that marvellous natural airfield in the heart of Alaska is bound to interest the generals concerned. Your fine caribou valley seems to me to open valuable prospects for our aviation industry, civilian as well as military."

Hidaka started to walk slowly towards him.

"Stay where you are, major! I'm armed."

Nizhinsky took an army revolver out of the drawer and laid it on the table.

"So, that's it. You're a double agent!" Hidaka hissed. "The rich Yankees could afford to pay you more than we could."

The burly man behind the desk did not let this pass.

"You do your friend Nizhinsky an injustice, and me as well, Major, although I did not particularly enjoy impersonating him. The bearded Boris has been behind bars at Alcatraz for the last six months now. He didn't put a foot wrong in carrying out his duties as a Japanese secret agent; he was caught because we managed to capture intact a copy of the Japanese naval code. This gave us the very welcome opportunity of decoding a number of interesting messages including the radioed exchanges between you and Admiral Yamada. Nizhinsky's name cropped up in these and it was easy enough for us to track down a man with such an unusual name and to pick him up. Boris was reluctant to talk at first, but he lost his nerve when we showed him a man going to the electric chair at Alcatraz. He saved his skin by talking, and we got a full confession out of him which included the code-number by which you would identify him on your arrival on Igilchik. I was given the job—and until today it was a very dull one—of waiting for you. Now that you have arrived, I have great pleasure in welcoming you."

He laughed with pleasure at his own little speech.

"But I slipped up with the coffee. I should have poured myself a glass of tea from the samovar."

Hidaka took this unexpected development with admirable composure, in view of the fact that his whole world had suddenly fallen apart. The damned Yankees had out-witted him after all and he had walked into a perfect trap. They had captured a major of the Imperial Guard without his offering the slightest resistance, an unprecedented stain on the honour of the Japanese Army.

The chief scout had managed to pull himself to his feet.

"Don't take it too hard, captain. No man could have put up a better fight than you did."

Their host objected.

"We must observe the proprieties, whatever the circumstances," he said. "This gentleman is now a major."

He took a bottle from the cupboard and filled some glasses.

"Your health, Major Hidaka! This is a splendid vodka, left over from our friend Boris's most generous supplies."

He offered the glasses round and pressed one upon Hidaka, who seemed scarcely to notice as he took it in his hand. Only Alatna declined; the very smell repelled her.

"Well, Major Hidaka," Allan McCluire said as he raised his glass, "here's to your captivity. May it be neither too disagreeable nor too long."

Their host agreed.

"Yes, my dear fellow, the major deserves every consideration. Particularly now."

"That's nice of you," Allan said, "but why particularly now?"

For a moment there was complete silence. And then the answer came.

"Because Attu was re-captured by the Americans a few months ago."

46

Twenty years later Hidaka's vision of the caribou valley had come true, although, of course, the airport now served civilian aircraft.

A four-seater government Cessna stood on the runway. Its pilot, Allan McCluire, waited in the bar. A jet coming in from Tokyo had just touched down; the steps were wheeled up, the door pushed back and the first passengers emerged.

Hendrik, the Superintendent of Caribou Valley Airport, greeted one of the Japanese passengers with particular courtesy, evidently on special instructions. The visitor was a small man in a black coat and hat. His hair was greying but he walked like a young man—he could have been anything between forty and sixty.

Hendrik invited him to a meal, but was politely refused. After vainly trying to change the visitor's mind, the superintendent took his leave. He found Allan McCluire in the airport lounge.

"Strange fellow," Hendrik said. "Refuses to eat. Had too much on the 'plane, he says. Look at him now, Allan! He's over at that old pile of stones, and is bowing right down in front of it. What next!"

A few minutes later the Japanese entered the lounge. Allan McCluire went up to him. "Major Hidaka?"

"Allan McCluire!"

The two men shook hands warmly, if a little self-consciously. "I've booked a quiet table, Hidaka, come on."

There was only a short time in which to cover twenty years. Allan's first question was about Alatna, and Hidaka at once brought out photographs of his family and laid them on the table. The untamed young woman from Alaska had become a Japanese lady, and part of Tokyo society. Hidaka was obviously very proud of her. Toklat was studying medicine. He had two enchanting sisters with their mother's features and warm smile. Enzo Hidaka had every reason to be contented.

Nor had McCluire any reason for complaint. Quite without ambition, he had risen rapidly in the Service on the strength of ability alone and was now Director of the whole Alaskan Wild Life Preservation Department. As such, he had been successful in having large tracts of his country set aside as game reserves.

Allan asked if Hidaka still had time to go hunting.

"There's not much left to hunt on our islands," Hidaka said. "You are much luckier, Allan. I've admired your trophies in the New York Natural History Museum and envied you."

Allan leant forward. "A snow white moose has been spotted not far from here, Hidaka. No museum in the world has anything like it."

The loudspeaker above them crackled and then broadcast a flight announcement.

"Passengers for New York, please prepare to embark."

Hidaka picked up his black brief-case.

"Let's go and hunt the white moose together now, Hidaka. Try and get some time off."

Hidaka pointed to his brief-case. "This is our new trade agreement with Washington. More important, I am afraid, than hunting any moose."

The loudspeaker chimed in, underlining his last words. "Will His Excellency please board the aircraft now. Last call for Mr. Hidaka."

Allan McCluire accompanied his guest onto the tarmac. "Do you know when your talks will be over?"

Hidaka paused at the foot of the steps. "In about two weeks, but by then I expect it'll be too late."

Allan saw the glint in the slanting eyes. "I shall expect you in two weeks' time, Hidaka. We'll get the white moose together or not at all."

With obvious delight, Hidaka nodded.

"In years to come, when people visit the museum and read the names of the two men who killed that rare animal," Allan said as they shook hands, "none of them will have the slightest idea that twenty years before they caught him they were doing their damnedest to kill each other."

Hidaka was more deeply moved than his expression betrayed. "Luckily, they failed."

Hidaka stood bowing low as the cabin door was pulled across in front of him. Only as it closed did Allan realize that he had been copying his friend's example.

Followed by a flurrying whirlwind of snow, and rapidly gaining speed, the sleek aircraft swept through the Caribou Valley, rose, and soared away over the white-topped mountains.